Tangled Paths

Robert Bull

authorHOUSE™

1663 LIBERTY DRIVE, SUITE 200
BLOOMINGTON, INDIANA 47403
(800) 839-8640
WWW.AUTHORHOUSE.COM

First published by AuthorHouse 12/02/05

ISBN: 1-4208-7894-8 (sc)

Printed in the United States of America
Bloomington, Indiana

This book is printed on acid-free paper.

Dedication

To recognize all the family and friends who have supported me and helped me to complete this first book, would take too many pages and I undoubtedly would miss many important people. However, without the love, friendship, support and guidance of three specific people, I would never have been able to write this particular story.

It was my two brothers-in-law, Art and Jim, who first took me into the mountains and fields of eastern Pennsylvania to hunt deer, rabbits, squirrels and pheasants. Their encouragement in climbing that first mountain when I literally felt I couldn't make it, will stay with me forever. Their love for the woods and instructions on hunting and shooting meant so much to me as a young teenager.

Many years later, God brought another person into my life. It was my good friend Rich who introduced me to God's country – Potter County. It was Rich who pushed that first buck past me as I huddled against the cold breeze on a quiet mountaintop; and it was with

Rich that I jumped my first flock of wild turkeys. So many of my wonderful experiences at the cabin, in the mountains, and on the streams have come with Rich by my side.

God has created so many wonders amidst the mountains, fields and streams for us to experience. Art, Jim and Rich have provided the opportunities for me to see, smell, hear and sense so many of them. Thank you!

Prologue

Vasser, New York
Friday October 15, 1971 9:15 AM

Jason pounded on the flimsy aluminum door for the second time. The cold, drenching rain threatened to drown his joy and excitement over the new life he was about to start. For the first time in over five years Jason actually felt good about himself and what lie ahead. He vowed that the water soaking his thin army-issued jacket and running into his worn out combat boots would not push him back into the dark hole from which he had pulled himself.

"Hey Oscar!" Jason yelled. "Open the door. I'm getting soaked out here".

Only the sound of children's cartoons answered him as he pulled open the screen door and tried the knob on the paint-chipped wooden door.

"Oscar! You know you shouldn't leave your door unlocked. How many times have I told you —"

"Jeez Oscar! What's that smell? Some giant rat crawl in your window and die? Where are you?"

As Jason stepped inside the door, which opened into the living room, he almost tripped and fell over the floor lamp lying at his feet. The wooden chair that was once next to the lamp was also on its side with one of its legs splintered.

"Where are you Oscar, this place is a mess. Since when do you watch cartoons?"

Jason glanced into the bedroom, which had obviously been used, as evidenced by the mussed-up bed and open dresser drawers. The pillows from the bed lie crumpled on the floor, as did the lamp that once sat on the cheap nightstand. Jason's mood, which had already been dampened by the cold October downpour, now began to turn sour as he approached the open door to the bathroom.

"Oscar? You in there?"

Jason stared at the dark red shower curtain that obstructed his view of the old porcelain tub, which he knew Oscar used on a daily basis. A man with only one leg and one arm could not take advantage of a hot shower without risking permanent damage to the rest of his body. The slow dripping from the faucet into the water that was hidden behind the curtain told him that the tub was not empty. As he reached for the curtain he could not tell what was louder: the beating of his heart in his chest or the smacking of the dripping water.

"Oscar?" Jason whispered as he slowly pulled open the curtain.

The breath, which he hadn't realized he had been holding within, exploded from his mouth as he gazed at the empty tub. Empty, except for about 6 inches of murky brown water in the bottom of the tub.

"Oscar! Come on, you're making me nuts."

Jason stormed out of the untidy bathroom and stomped into the kitchen. There, he froze as he gazed upon the lifeless body of his only friend. Oscar's head, or what was left of it, rested upon his muscular right arm. The lifeless right arm was spread across the table as if reaching for a cup of coffee. A dark liquid, which once carried life through Oscar's body, covered the once white metal table. Tears that he had locked inside him for so many years slid slowly down Jason's cheeks and rested in his matted black beard. The pancakes and sausage he had eaten earlier at the shelter pushed at his throat and threatened to spew out onto the dirty tiled floor, but he refused to be sick. Both anger and sadness swept over him. Anger at what someone had done to his friend who had never attempted to hurt anyone. Anger that someone had robbed both him and Oscar of a new life. Sadness at the loss of a life. Sadness that he was once again alone. Eventually it was the anger that overcame his soul. Anger and hate.

Jason stumbled back into the living room and quickly tore open the closet door. He wasn't sure what he was looking for, but he knew it had to be a large container. Nothing. He ran into the bedroom. The dressers contained only clothes. The closet also did not hold what he was looking for.

He sat down on the soft bed where his friend would sleep no more. He wiped his blurry eyes and stared at the small window that tried unsuccessfully to keep out the pouring rain. Cold winds were already blowing off the lakes. Soon the rain would turn to snow and ice. Jason shivered at the thought.

As the water seeped slowly around the windowsills, Jason thought back to the night before. The night he signed his best and only friend's death warrant. Anger, hatred, guilt .... and revenge pushed at his thoughts. He no longer wanted to live in this world. He had seen too much pain and suffering. Oscar was his last and only hope. He would take that step into the unknown. It didn't matter what was on the other side of life. It couldn't be worse than life itself. But first, he would find the person who had robbed him and Oscar of hope and joy and peace. He knew who that person was. He knew where to find him. He didn't know how he would kill him, but he would. Then, both of them would take a long, lonely trip. If there was a God, maybe, just maybe, they would head down different paths.

Jason stood slowly and walked through the living room to the front door. He debated calling 911. It didn't matter anymore. His friend was dead. The cops would never find Oscar's killer. It would be just another robbery-homicide. Another unsolved case. Someone would notice the smell eventually. A mailman. A neighbor. A bill collector. Jason gazed once more around the disheveled room. He opened the screen door and stepped out into the rain. The water quickly soaked through his coat to his thin T-shirt. He didn't notice. He was going home.

Chapter 1

Clint pushed the sliding door out of his way and twisted his broad shoulders sideways to step onto the deck. As he closed the door, he turned to marvel at the view of the valley stretching out before him. Although his property sloped down only a few dozen acres, he could literally see for miles. The colorful fall foliage never ceased to bring a quiet peacefulness to his often-troubled soul. He set his 220 pound, 6' 2" body down on the wooden glider hanging from the ceiling and closed his eyes. The smell of the colorful oak, maple and pine trees, mixed with the scent of freshly cut grass served to relax him even further. A gentle breeze from the west seemed to whisper a sweet melody in his ear.

It wasn't that sweet melody that caused him to suddenly open his eyes and focus all his senses on what was approaching along the side of his house. A low growl, barely audible, brought him to his feet. He silently stepped back against the closed deck doors and bent down on his hands and knees. Slowly he crept

1

toward the corner of the house. The growling, although softer, grew closer. As he quietly sat down with his back against the log frame of his house, he checked his back pocket to make sure it was not empty. Checking the direction of the wind, he was thankful that it would not give away his position.

Suddenly a black snout appeared about two feet above the floor. Without waiting for the animal to expose more of its body, Clint reached out with his massive left hand and clamped it down over the animal's now fully exposed jaw. He lunged with his right arm under the animal's body, lifted it into the air and flipped it on its back. As the animal's legs kicked at the open air, it let out a loud yelp of surprise. Clint's body was off balance and it caused him to roll onto his back. The black furry animal, quicker than its adversary, broke Clint's grasp and pounced on the large man's chest. Clint raised his left arm just in time to stop the animal's open mouth and bared teeth from clamping down on his neck. The animal closed his sharp teeth around the thick arm, squeezed his mouth shut and shook, but did not break the skin. With his left arm still in the jaws of the attacker, Clint reached up with his right hand and grabbed the animal around the throat. The two of them struggled and rolled around for several seconds, each expelling their own sounds of exertion. Finally, the animal, which weighed over half as much as the man, shook his mouth free and lunged at Clint's head. His teeth closed on the bill of Clint's baseball cap and with one snap of his head, tossed it over the side of the porch, to float unobstructed down to the ground.

"Shack!! Now look at what you did!" Clint yelled. "You threw my brand new Philly's cap off the deck!"

With that, the would-be attacker sat on his haunches and stared dully at his owner. Slowly Shack turned his head to gaze at the discarded piece of cloth. He didn't understand what the difference was between this piece of cloth and the bigger piece around his owner's growing midsection, but apparently it served some unique purpose. The big Labrador turned his head back to face Clint and looked at the bare spot on the top of his body. Perhaps it was necessary to cover that spot so it didn't get any bigger.

"Go get it Shack."

Shack snorted once and slowly moved his large body to the end of the deck and down the steps. When he reached the odd looking piece of cloth, he pawed it once to make sure it wouldn't get away. Then he picked it up in his mouth and trotted back up the steps to sit at his owner's feet. He patiently waited for Clint to remove the now dirty and wet garment from his mouth.

"Oh man, look at this thing. It's got more slobbers on it than a baby's bib."

Despite the bantering, Clint loved the big black lab. He removed the two extra large dog bones from his back pocket and tossed them in the air. Shack jumped once and grabbed them both before they could hit the deck. With three loud crunches they were broken up and swallowed.

"Well, whadaya wanna do tonight Shack? We could go see Paula, or I could leave you home and go have a couple of beers at the Old Timer's Inn. Or, we could take a walk up into Porcupine Hollow. I heard a couple of coyotes howling up that way last night."

Shack shook his head rapidly, slinging the last bits of crumbs and slobber across the deck. This was all part of the ritual they went through at least several times a month when his owner came out on the deck. Shack would try to sneak up on the big man and try to attack him before he knew what hit him. For some reason, the man always knew he was coming and made the first move. Even if he tried to disguise himself by making that growling sound like his master's stomach sometimes did, it never worked. Then the man would seem to ask him some questions. He knew who Paula was. She was a nice human too, but she looked a little different. Sometimes she wore pretty pieces of cloth that didn't cover all of her legs. That looked a little funny, but he had seen many different kinds of funny looking humans. Shack also new what the Old Timer's Inn was. It was a big place with a whole lot of animals stuck in the walls. He didn't get to go there anymore. His master took him there one time, but the woman everyone called Sadie seemed to get really mad when Shack started talking to one of the little bears standing in the corner and nipping at its leg. They were only playing and the bear didn't seem very interested because it didn't even move. His owner took him out to the truck and that was the last time Shack was ever in the strange building. Shack also knew what a coyote was. He saw them occasionally when he and his owner went on long hikes into the woods. Although he figured his owner was asking him which one he would like to see, Shack knew it didn't matter what he wanted. He wanted to see Paula because she petted him a lot and gave him neat food like ice cream and chocolate cake. But his owner always did what he wanted anyway, so Shack just walked over to the edge of the deck, laid down and stuck his head out between the two wooden posts. He would have to be careful not to get his head stuck between them. He did that once and it hurt when he pulled his head out. His owner got a big laugh out of that.

Clint watched the big dog walk to the end of the deck and lay down. Then he resumed his position on the hanging glider. He really wanted to see Paula. It had been two weeks since they had been together. She had been away with a group of her 'disadvantaged' kids at some retreat. Paula taught these kids at the local middle school. They actually came from various school districts, since Paula's class was the only one of its kind in the area. The kids had many types of disadvantages. Some had physical handicaps, some emotional and some just had a hard time learning in the public school system. Clint owed a lot to Paula. When he came to Elk Run five years ago, he had no direction in his life and his mind was reeling from the many mistakes he had made. He was into his 40's now and Paula had helped him understand a lot about giving to others and the peace that came from helping those less fortunate. He really wanted to see her, to hold her in his arms and feel her body against his. He wanted to feel her moist lips against his and spend the cool evening next to her in the warmth of her bed.

But he knew that wouldn't happen. As much as Paula seemed to like him, maybe even love him, she was not into the physical relationship much and the intimacy that he needed and wanted right now. Maybe someday. For now, he guessed he would just go to the Old Timer's. Besides, a few cold beers and some bantering with the other locals always made for an enjoyable evening.

Chapter 2

Vasser, New York
Tuesday September 25, 1979 9:15 PM

The dark night surrounded Jason as he huddled inside his large cardboard box home. The sides were taped shut with duct tape he had gotten from the mission over on the corner of 15th and Spruce Streets. Strategically placed 'vents' allowed just enough air into the enclosed space to circulate the odors escaping from his infrequently bathed body. The cold from the sidewalk underneath him seeped through his thin flooring and the two well worn blankets that made up his bed. The alcove that surrounded him on three sides helped block out most of the driving wind and rain and snow, but the one remaining opening left plenty of opportunity for the forces of nature (and man and beast) to assault him.

This had been his home for almost twelve years, since the day he decided that his country had no place for a veteran of Vietnam. His almost constant shakes, fears and anger that resulted from flashbacks and nightmares scared his family and friends. The few employers who were willing to give a menial job to someone with only a high school education, soon found reason to fire him when his nervous jumping and darting eyes began to terrify his co-workers and customers. Of course, his almost constant fighting with those who just didn't understand "how he could kill innocent women and children" didn't help any. It didn't matter that his good old Uncle Sam had forced him to go. It didn't matter that he was not smart enough to go to college to get a deferment. It didn't matter that he didn't WANT to go to jail or Canada or anywhere else to avoid the draft. It didn't even matter that he had never set his rifle sites upon any individual who was not attempting to end his life. No, he was a "baby killer". He was "the enemy". He was a person who could crawl undetected through mud, rain and dense forest toward an unsuspecting human being and, in one swift and silent motion, slice the delicate skin of his neck and cause the life to drain out of him onto his black "pajamas". He was a person who could sit in the darkness for hours, as silent and still as the trees surrounding him, not even noticing the leeches, spiders, snakes and other nocturnal creatures crawling around and over him. He was a person who could wait and watch, with eyes barely blinking, for the dark clad figure to innocently stumble into the waiting ambush. He was a person who could fire that first shot and put a bullet through the poor young man's head, silencing him forever. This was the person who Jason Shark had become. He was all those things and it was all those things that had caused his nightmares and fears and confusion and anger when he returned home. He did all those things because that is what his government had trained him to do; told him to do; expected him to do. And it would be all those things that would allow him to avenge the life of his last friend and companion.

Through a somewhat larger opening, Jason stared at the circle of light cast by the street lamp a hundred yards away. Ruby and his pack of roughnecks were huddled against the cement wall of an old building that had once been grand and glamorous. Time, weather and other changes within the city now made it just one more abandoned building that had been claimed by rats (some four legged and some two legged). The large red ring on his right hand for which his followers christened him, sparkled in the lamplight. Jason couldn't hear what they were saying, but he knew it had to have something to do with how to spend more of the money. Money that should have been Oscar's. Money that Oscar was going to use to start a new life and to help Jason begin a new life as well. A life with meaning and purpose. A life with a future.

* * *

Vasser, New York
Wednesday October 13, 1971 2:00 PM

Jason entered the old diner on Cherry Street a few minutes past 2:00. Oscar was already seated in a booth by the window. Jason walked past the owner, who was ringing up a customer, and slid into the seat opposite Oscar. Elmer, the owner, glanced once at Jason to make sure he was properly attired and resumed talking to the departing customers. Elmer was one of the few "good guys" around the city. He didn't mind the homeless entering his establishment, as long as they were wearing somewhat clean clothes, including shoes and shirts, and as long as it wasn't during his busy times. "Elmer's", which was the not-so-creative name of the diner, as well as the owner, was never really busy any more. However, the homeless that frequented the diner respected Elmer's wishes and normally rearranged their busy schedules to delay their breakfast, lunch and dinner hours to avoid the sparse crowds. Besides, Elmer's had special discounts for the homeless. Jason, when his funds did allow him to schedule a visit to Elmer's, would stop by the mission just 3 blocks away and try to pick up some cleaner clothes, use the bathroom and wash up as good as he could.

"Hey Oscar, how are you doing?"

Oscar raised his eyes to look at Jason, but did not say a word. His left leg bounced nervously under the table. A somewhat strange smirk creased his lips. He started to open his mouth but then stopped, apparently not sure exactly what to say. Oscar extended a two-page letter across the table and placed it in front of Jason. Although many people became uneasy around a man who had a stump for his left arm and right leg, Jason never blinked an eye. He had seen much worse in his days. Oscar was also a veteran of "Nam". Somehow though, Oscar, despite returning home with fewer body parts, had kept more of his mind intact than Jason. He had fewer nightmares and, although he never talked about his time in the foreign country, he didn't seem to mind the banter, accusations, insults and other painful words thrown his way. Perhaps it was because Oscar had some college education and had actually volunteered to go fight for freedom and democracy in a foreign land. Perhaps it was also because Uncle Sam had realized he owed a debt to Oscar for his loss of limbs. Uncle Sam figured those two limbs were worth approximately $900 a month. It didn't get Oscar a home in the country, but it did get him a bigger house than Jason had and it did have wooden floors, walls and doors and glass windows that at least kept out most of the wind, rain and intruders.

Jason looked at the papers Oscar had pushed toward him and noticed they were some type of legal documents. The top of the paper said "Mathews, Paunches and Truckman, Attorneys at Law" and had some fancy logo.

"What's this Oscar? Are they taking your disability pay away? Those sons bitches! I told you our country was going to hell. Man, you almost gave your life — "

"No, Jason. Read" Oscar was actually smiling.

Jason returned his eyes to the document and read. It was dated two months before:

Dear Mr. Orion,

It is with much regret that I must inform you of the untimely death of your mother, Mrs. Agnes Orion. She suffered a massive heart attack yesterday, August 5, 1971. Although I am extremely sorry for the pain this must cause you, please take comfort in the fact that she suffered very little and passed on to her life with Jesus very quickly. Her maid, Annabelle, upon arriving to begin cleaning, found her in her bed in the morning. The coroner said your mother died in her sleep.

I personally knew your mother, as well as your dear-departed father, for many years. I know Agnes never did fully understand why you never allowed her to help you after your return from the war. However, she respected you for your wishes and prayed for your well-being every day. When your father passed away five years ago in the automobile accident, he left her with a great deal of financial security. She had deeply hoped that you would allow her to pass much of her inheritance on to you. Your refusal of this support hurt her at first, but, as she talked this out with me, Pastor John and her other friends, she realized that you were only thinking of her and of your deep desire to face life on your own.

However, now that this dear lady has gone on to join your father in eternal peace, she has once again offered her hand to you. As executor of her estate, I have read her Will and am in the process of disbursing her assets. Based on her wishes, the house and all her furnishings will be sold at auction. After payment of administrative fees to the executor and the auctioneer fees, ten percent of the remaining funds are to go to her church. Annabelle, who began working for your mother four years ago, will receive a sizeable amount to help her with her children's education. The remaining funds from the sale, as well as the insurance policy that she took out with most of your father's insurance money, and the proceeds from the stocks and bonds that your father had left to her (which she never sold), will go to you.

I have enclosed a notarized copy of her Will. If you wish to contest anything in the Will, I have also enclosed the necessary documents for you to pursue this course of action.

Again, let me express my condolences to you. Unless there are some unexpected disputes with the Will, the estate should be able to be liquidated and closed by the end of September.

Sincerely,
Markus A. Truckman, Attorney at Law

Jason lifted his head and his eyes met Oscar's. There were tears in Oscar's eyes.

"Your mother died two months ago?"

"Yeah"

"You never said anything. Did you go to the funeral?"

"No."

Oscar turned his face toward the dirty window and stared out at the world passing before him. Jason knew when to let Oscar alone and not interrupt his thoughts. This was one of the things he liked about Oscar. The two of them could sit in silence and not feel it necessary to speak meaningless thoughts or words. Most of the friends that Jason had in the past always felt they had to be talking or doing something. Many times, it resulted in the wrongs things being said. Many more times, it had resulted in pranks or other actions that served no purpose other than to gain pleasure at someone else's expense. After a few minutes, Oscar turned to face Jason, his eyes clear and full of excitement.

"No, I didn't go see my mother. A week before she died, I called her. We had a wonderful long talk.

She told me how I had hurt her when I didn't take my father's insurance money. I explained to her that I wanted her to have the money. That I wanted her to have a better life. I was doing okay and I didn't really need it. She said Pastor John and Annabelle told her the same thing. We laughed and talked and cried for over two hours. Of course, the VA office may have a problem when they get that bill, but that's another story. Before we hung up she said, 'Oscar, I don't know how much longer the Lord has planned for me on this earth, but when my time comes to go Home, don't come to the funeral. There is nothing left here for you. Your father has passed. You have no more family and friends here. You have a new home. There is no need for you to stand over my body and grieve. Instead, rejoice in knowing that now my spirit and your father's will be together, and we will both be watching over you from above. I know that you love me."

"It was like she had a premonition."

Again there were tears in his eyes, but his voice was calm and at peace.

Oscar answered the next question Jason had in his mind, but did not know how to ask, by pulling a second letter out of his coat pocket and handing it to Jason. Patrons began to enter the diner as the dinner hour for many of the local employed population drew near. Jason noticed Elmer checking his watch and knew his welcome would run out soon. He pushed the first letter back to Oscar and picked up the second. It was from the same legal firm and was dated three days ago. It was much shorter, and much more shocking.

Dear Oscar,

Your mother's estate has been liquidated and settled as of September 30, 1971. After payment of fees and distribution to your mother's church and Annabelle, there remains a balance from the sale of $ 51,626.78. At your request and pursuant to the legal authority that you assigned to me, I have also sold all of the stocks and bonds that your mother had left to you. Again, less fees and taxes, the balance of these funds totals $ 125,888.93. The payment on the insurance policy that your mother had taken out after your father's death has also been received. Per your request, these proceeds have been used to cover all funeral expenses. After these expenses and administrative fees, the balance remaining from this policy is $ 155,600.10.

I have enclosed a certified check to you in the amount of $ 333, 115.81.

I know that no amount of money can replace the love of one's family and friends. Take heart, though, in the love that guided your mother and father to prepare as best they could to keep their son as safe and well as possible.

If my firm or I can ever assist you in any way, please don't hesitate to get in touch.

Sincerely,
Markus A. Truckman, friend

Jason, his mouth agape, lifted his head to view the person sitting across from him. Was this still his friend, or was he now a stranger. He thought back to the day they met two years ago.

* * *

Jason had been living on the streets for a couple of years. It had taken a while to learn the rules of the street. Each homeless person had his or her own "space". Most of them respected this, but in the end, it was still a matter of the stronger versus the weaker. Jason had learned quickly that he had to be one of the stronger ones to keep whatever little possessions he was able to find. A few coins found on the street. Some change from returning recyclable cans. A couple of dollars from panhandling on the corner next to the big office buildings or the little convenience stores. Some new clothes and warm food from the missions. Discarded items from people who had no more use for old but perfectly usable items such as a transistor radio, a can opener or a pocketknife. Large appliance boxes made good "homes". Discarded blankets and clothes could make a somewhat warm bed.

Jason had settled into a routine of sorts and was surviving. But something was still missing. Then one day an awkward man literally stumbled into his newly acquired empty dryer box, crushed it to pieces and fell on top of him. Jason jumped up and threw the heavy man off of him. With both fists flying, Jason pummeled the man's head mercilessly. After several sound shots to the stranger's head, Jason realized that the man was not fighting back and was simply shouting; "Stop! Stop! Please". Jason stood up and gazed at the man lying prone on the crushed cardboard. A stump ending where the man's left elbow should have been and another one where his right knee should have been caught his attention.

"What the hell ya doing?" Jason shouted, rage slowly but not totally leaving him. "You ruined my home!"

"I...I'm sorry" whispered the man bleeding from his nose and several cuts above his eyes. "I....tripped on the curb and my crutch broke."

Jason now noticed the splintered piece of wood lying worthless in the street. In the darkness he also noticed the broken curb, which probably caused the man's fall.

"Damn government! Jason explained. "Can't keep the sidewalks fit for people with two good legs. How they expect someone on crutches to walk? Get up. Go home. Don't let me see you down here again or I'll really beat the crap outta you."

"I will. I'm sorry."

Jason watched the man struggle to get up. One eye was closed, partially from swelling and partially from the blood now running from his forehead down to his swollen lips. He was a large man. Just under 6 feet tall, his stomach was round and flabby. His double chin dissolved into his thick neck, which sat on top of his wide shoulders. His thin hair extended down to his eyes in the front and over his ears on the sides. The man turned on his left side and tried with his right hand to move the hair out of his eyes. Off balance and weak from the beating, he rolled onto his stomach and moaned. Still he struggled to get up. Jason now realized the one-armed, one-legged man was not going to get home by himself. He had no crutch and was in pain from the punches Jason had thrown.

"Damn it man! Where ya live?"

"About 6 blocks. On Fisher near Spruce. I'm sorry about wrecking your box. If you…."

"My *box*? That's not just a box, that's my *home*. That's where I live. That's where I keep all I own. You didn't wreck a box, you ruined my home. You're an intruder. I have every right to kill you for intruding into my home. Oh what's the use! Come on!"

Jason leaned down and put the man's good arm over his shoulder. He lifted the man up and propped him against the building.

"Don't move."

"Don't think I will" replied the man. The pain and shock of the encounter was slowly wearing away.

"Wise ass!"

Jason stooped over the destroyed cardboard and threw it all out into the street. Quickly he put the few items he had into a heavy black trash bag and slung it over his right shoulder.

"Come on, put your arm around me. I'll help you home and then come back and get myself a new 'box'!"

"My name's Oscar."

"Jason!"

"I really am sorry about your…home. I don't have a big place, but I'd like you to stay there tonight….if you want. I only have one bedroom, so you would have to sleep on the couch. You could look for a new home tomorrow when it is light out."

Jason stopped and looked at the man who was now leaning on him. It had been a long time since anyone had relied on him for anything, physically or emotionally. There was something good about being needed.

"You ain't afraid I'm gonna rip you off?"

"Huh!", Oscar laughed. "Wait until you see my place. You'll realize I don't have much to steal. But, no, I'm not afraid you'll rip me off. I don't think you're the type."

"And what makes you such an expert on people. You a psychologist or something?"

"No, I just think I can spot another vet from Nam when I see one."

Again they stopped. Jason looked at Oscar. He didn't have to ask how Oscar knew. He knew no one could answer that question, but most vets had that sense. Some said it was something about the eyes. Some said it was an "aura", whatever that is. Whatever it was, it was true.

They entered Oscar's home a half hour later. Jason found some supplies in the bathroom and cleaned up the cuts. They drank a couple of beers and talked until late into the morning. Jason didn't even have to decide if he would stay. After a while he fell asleep on the couch. Oscar retired to the bedroom. Jason did not take up residence with Oscar. He wasn't ready for that. They reached somewhat of a business arrangement. Jason would do odd jobs and Oscar would pay him. Jason didn't do a lot of work and Oscar didn't pay a lot of money, but over time, their business arrangement progressed into a friendship – something Jason had missed since returning from the war.

* * *

"Jason."

Jason shook off his thoughts of their meeting and anxiously looked at Oscar. What was Oscar going to do with over $ 300,000?

"Jason, I have it."

"You have what?"

"The money."

"Yeah, I know, it says you got a check for…."

"No, not the check. The money. The cash. Three hundred thirty three thousand, one hundred fifteen dollars and eighty-one cents!"

"What!!! My God man, keep your voice down! You have all that money in cash here in Elmer's diner?"

"No, not HERE. At my house."

"Why in the world do you have that much money in cash? It should be in a bank."

"I know, but I wanted to see it in cash. Have you ever seen that much money in cash? I haven't."

"I've never seen a man-eating shark in person either, but that doesn't mean I wanna go look for one."

"Jason. I'm going to put it back in the bank eventually, but I have something to ask you."

Jason stared silently. His stomach churned and his head felt light. No matter what the question was, it was going to change his life. Oscar was either going to take the money and move to some deserted island by himself where he could live in luxury forever, or somehow include him in this new-found wealth. Either way, it was going to be too much for him to comprehend.

"Jason, we have grown pretty close as friends. Heck, I'd let you marry my daughter, if I had one. You have also helped me live a much better life than I did before I met you. I want to get out of that hell-hole that I live in, but I want you to come with me."

"Ahhh, you're not asking me to marry you, are you Oscar?"

A quick slap of his right hand grazed the top of Jason's head, but the smile on his face betrayed the easiness with which the two were able to rib each other.

"You know, I would want a large family."

"Shut up Jason, and listen. I'd like to find a bigger home. Preferably out in the country. Two or three bedrooms, yard, peace and quiet. No police and ambulance sirens at all hours of the night. No rats and cockroaches stealing my food. You know what I mean?"

"Yeah I've been dreaming of that too, since we partnered up. My box isn't all it's cracked up to be.

"Here's the deal. I buy the house. You live there as long as you want. No strings — "

"I ain't a freeloader" Jason responded.

This was the main reason Jason had never moved in with Oscar. Although they had grown to be like brothers, Jason refused to be a freeloader. It was one thing to get paid for working and an occasional "sleep over" or meal at Oscar's house was okay. But, to live there and not contribute? That was unacceptable.

"You sure can be a jerk, you know it Jason? Just listen. How do you expect me, with one leg and one arm, to take care of a house with two or three bedrooms? How am I going to cut the grass and do all the chores? You get free room and board, but you buy your own beer since you are such a lush. I pay the utilities and supply you with a place to stay. What do you think?"

"Oh, so you want me to be your maid and handyman."

"Jerk."

"Do I have to wear a short black dress when I cook?"

"Superjerk."

Their smiles sealed the deal. The future looked very good indeed.

Chapter 3

Clint parked his dusty green Explorer in the lot beside the Old Timer's Inn. The fall turkey season in northern Pennsylvania would not start for another couple of weeks, so there were only a few other vehicles in the lot. Once the hunting season got into full swing, this watering hole, as well as many others in this mountainous part of the state, would be packed with outdoorsmen (and women), each vying to tell the bigger, better and more exciting story of the day's hunt. Eventually the conversations would lead to hunts from the past. It was one of the things Clint and most other people who frequented these places enjoyed most. Of course, the cold beer and sports on the large screen TV played a significant part of the lure as well.

Clint pushed open the door and strolled up to the bar which extended in a U shape from the side wall. A large open doorway behind the bar allowed a glimpse into the spacious kitchen where the "monster" burgers and heaps of fries were made. These were the "chef's" specialty, but you could also order roast beef sandwiches, steaks, chicken and other assorted items. Homemade pies were also a treat, if you left room for them.

A group of six "non-locals" were perched around two tables that had been moved together in front of the big TV screen. They were watching some kind of special sports broadcast on ESPN. Based on the number of empty bottles and pitchers on the table and the volume of their bantering with each other, they had been here a while.

"Hey Sadie," Clint shouted as he planted his heavy body on the wooden stool in front of the bar. "You're as beautiful as ever. Give me one of them Old Mills on tap."

"Watch yourself Clinton. You start hitting on me and I'll have to have Ralph give you a good swift beatn'."

Sadie and Ralph had taken over the establishment from the prior owners about twenty years ago. They were life-long residents of Elk Run and lived in several rooms above the tavern. In their early fifties now, Clint had no doubt that Sadie and Ralph were deeply in love with each other. Sadie usually tended to the bar and Ralph did most of the cooking, except for the homemade pies, which were Sadie's specialty. Sadie was the only person who could get away with calling him "Clinton". Anyone else would have received a strong rebuke and realized quickly he (or she) had made a mistake.

"Who's hittin' on you honey!" Ralph bellowed as he came charging through the open doorway from the kitchen. Most people, upon seeing the six foot, four inch giant come charging out the doorway, would have shriveled in silence.

"I am," Clint returned. "What are you going to do about it?"

"Well you little whipper snapper. I'm gonna send you home crying to your mamma."

The smile on Ralph's face gave away his true intentions. Clint grabbed the man's huge hand in his and shook it firmly. Clint and Ralph had become close friends since Clint arrived in Elk Run. Clint had "loaned" Ralph and Sadie money many times. Sometimes it was to purchase things for the Inn (like the large TV screen or the new fryer when the old one almost started a fire) and sometimes it was for personal needs (like the time Sadie had to have some surgery and their insurance wouldn't cover all of the costs). Ralph repaid Clint in various ways. He was an excellent carpenter and Ralph, or a group of locals who he supervised, did much of the renovations to Clint's property. Ralph's brother owned a small lumberyard nearby and Ralph was always able to get a special discount on whatever he needed. With Ralph's help, Clint had been able to turn his 200-acre property, which he bought for a little over $ 300,000, into something that was now worth twice that. The main house had been totally renovated with Ralph's help, and the once run-down barn had been turned into a comfortable two-story bunkhouse with 4 rooms on each floor that easily housed 24 people. A kitchen, bathroom and shower on each floor, as well as a common social room that had been added on the side, allowed several different groups of individuals to live in the same building and yet still have a degree of privacy.

Clint still had plans to renovate the two small cabins that sat on his property and the horse barn that had not been used in decades. The maintenance building that housed his Explorer, his Chevy pickup truck (that had a detachable snow plow he used in the winter months), snow mobile and other miscellaneous tools and "toys", also needed work. But, he had plenty of time to do that. Clint wasn't planning on abandoning Elk Run any time soon and Ralph didn't seem to be ageing at all.

"How you doing Ralph? I see you still let the riff-raff in here," Clint said pointing the full glass of beer that Sadie had placed in front of him at a disheveled looking old man sitting several chairs away at the bar.

"Up yourshs!" the old man responded as he turned his glazed eyes toward Clint.

"Heck, Clint, Stubs is like a fixture here. I don't think he could find his way home if he didn't stop in here first. He has to come in here to get his bearings straight."

"Well, in that case, then give him another one on me. Don't want him getting lost. Stubs, I'm taking you home though. I don't want you driving on the roads and hitting any deer."

"Yea, well, I'm sure you're only thinkin' bout the wells being of the deers. Thanks for the drink."

A loud yell from the table near the TV caused Clint to turn to see what was going on. A white-uniformed football player in a red helmet was barreling over one would-be tackler after another on his way across the goal line for a touchdown. All the fans at the tables appeared to be in their twenties. They were probably staying at one of the local cabins. Many owners allowed friends and family members to come up before hunting season to check on the cabin and make final preparations before the main season began. Grass needed cut, propane tanks needed filled, trees that came down in storms needed cut and removed, wood needed chopped and stacked, fireplaces needed cleaned and checked, and many other preparations needed to be made.

"Hey Jack, fill me up," one of the men at the table shouted above the cheering.

"Pass me your glass Bob," the man named Jack instructed.

Clint watched Jack fill the empty glass and pass it back. As Bob lifted the full glass to his mouth, he spilled half of it onto his pants.

"Ah shit!" the man with now wet pants exclaimed.

As Clint shook his head and turned his attention back to the bar, a waitress came out of the back-room kitchen carrying a tray of six plates loaded with one-pound burgers and heaps of greasy fries. Clint had never seen her before. She was beautiful. Her jet-black wavy hair was cut short around her ears. A small pudgy nose and dark eyes that were full of life accented her oval face. Her loosely fitting blue denim shirt was a sharp contrast to her tight fitting jeans. The open buttons of her shirt gave just a hint of the not so small breasts underneath. Clint watched her head toward the loud voices competing with the announcer on TV. A smack on the side of his head brought his attention back to the woman standing in front of him.

"Sadie, what did you hit me for?"

"I know what was going through that no-good mind of yours. What would Paula say if she caught you starin' like that?"

"Oh, you know Paula and I are just friends. We......"

"Give me a break, Clinton. You and Paula been seein' each other for over two years. Just because you ain't hitched, don't mean you ain't a couple."

"A couple?" Clint tried to explain as his face began to turn a light shade of red. "Why, we... ah... we're just good friends. Besides, I was just wondering who the new waitress was. I've never seen her before. Who is she?"

"That's Jake and Sarah Simson's daughter. She just moved back here last month from New York."

"She's quite a dame, isn't she Clint?" Ralph added as he returned from his duties in the kitchen.

Sadie gave Ralph a backhand to his massive chest. He apparently didn't notice, as he continued.

"She left here about six years ago to go to some fancy college in the city. Said she wanted to get away."

"Huh, they all says that," Stubs contributed.

Ralph continued, annoyed at the interruption.

"Met up with some young accountant or something. Got married. Last year, he divorced her and moved to California. Megan there finally realized that she missed the open spaces and mountains and moved back with Jake and Sarah. She works part-time at the animal place up in Ridge Heights – "

"It's called a Vetrinary Clinkit – " Stubs tried to correct Ralph.

"Drink your beer Stubs."

"– and works here part-time during the week," Ralph finished.

"Me too?" Clint sheepishly asked Sadie holding up his empty glass.

Sadie took the empty glass and refilled it. Ralph returned to the kitchen to refine his burger-flipping skills; Stubs contemplated the surface of the bar; and Clint turned back to admire the new person who had entered his train of thought.

"Hey honey," the one named Bob spoke to Megan. "You got a fine looking dairy-air." With that, he smacked his hand on Megan's backside and wrapped his arm around her waist. The table shook and the half empty pitcher of beer spilled into the plates of french fries. Megan dropped her empty tray and found herself sitting on the man's lap, unable to remove herself from the man's groping hands.

Clint slid off the bar stool and moved behind the man assaulting Megan. Clint's hand clamped down on the man's neck and squeezed. Pain shot down the man's spine, causing him to release his grip on Megan. In one swift movement, Clint turned the man toward the wall and firmly planted the man's face against the day's list of specials. Another man at the table moved to stand up and help his friend. Clint swatted him once in the face with the back of his left hand. As he tumbled to the floor, the man Clint held against the wall began to squirm and cry out. Two of the remaining four got to their feet and came at Clint. The other two stared in awe at the man holding their friend pinned against the wall with one hand.

"That's enough!" Ralph bellowed as he charged from behind the bar. He was also pretty fast for a big man who was already a member of AARP. The two friends who had started to approach Clint looked at Ralph and then back at Clint. They decided that their friend was in this alone and sat back down.

"Megan? You okay?" Ralph asked.

"Yes. The jerk hanging on the wall started it. This man was just helping me." Megan explained pointing toward Clint.

"Clint, let junior go."

Clint did as he was told and the man dropped to the floor on all fours. Clint's heart was pounding so hard he thought it would burst through his chest. He took a few deep breaths to regain control. It had been many years since he had felt like this. The power. The excitement. The force. The pleasure. But that was the past. That part of his life was gone. It felt good to help this beautiful young woman. He didn't know why. He had never seen this lovely person before tonight, but for some reason, it was important that she liked him.

He turned and looked at her. Her eyes still sparkled. But now, there was something else. Compassion? Kindness? Confusion? Fear?

"Thank you. My name is Megan Simson." She offered her outstretched hand to Clint.

"Clint Jameson," he spoke softly as he took her hand in his. Her small, strong hand disappeared inside his.

"We'll do introductions later," Sadie said as she came around the bar. "You gentlemen better get in your trucks and go home. If you ever want to come back in here again, you better learn your manners better. Take that one with you and get out."

"But, we're not done eatin' yet," one of the more timid ones said as he looked back and forth between Sadie, Ralph and Clint.

"I'll give you a doggy bag. You owe $ 45. Pay Ralph while I get you some boxes."

The four who could still stand without wobbling took out their wallets. Three of them placed twenties on the table.

"That's a nice tip you gave the lady you just sexually assaulted. You don't want any change, do you?" Ralph asked firmly.

"No!" the four answered in unison.

Sadie came out with four Styrofoam boxes and threw their uneaten burgers and fries in on a heap. Beer and grease saturated the entire mess.

The man on the floor finally pulled himself up and looked at Clint. Standing, he was just an inch shorter than Clint, but about a hundred pounds lighter. As he followed the other five out of the building, his eyes stayed riveted on Clint. Not out of fear, but out of hatred. Clint had seen it before. He had faced it before. It looked like he would face it again.

Ralph followed them to their vehicles to make sure that no one bothered Clint's truck or anything else before they left. When he returned, he called the local police department and explained what had happened. No, there would be no charges pressed. Just keep a look out for the vehicles to make sure they didn't get foolish and return. They probably wouldn't. They would go back to their cabin, assuming they could find it, and fall asleep with their clothes on. When they woke up, they would probably find the boxes of food and beer and grease in the back of one of their trucks, soaked into their nice, expensive seat cushions. Two of them would still have some ringing in their ears. Hopefully, it would be a reminder of what NOT to do.

When Ralph returned from making the phone call, he found Clint and Megan sitting at the bar, apparently getting to know each other better. Stubs was resting his head on the hard surface of the bar, snoring softly. He sat down beside Clint and motioned for Sadie to bring three more beers.

"Don't think they'll be back anymore tonight. I told Rooster down at the station to keep a lookout for them. You shouldn't have got involved with them trouble makers, Clint. That's my job."

"Well, you were busy and I thought Megan needed a hand before things turned ugly."

"Thank you again, Clint. I don't know why some guys have to be such assholes."

Clint looked quizzically at Megan. Hearing a woman use such language didn't shock him. In these parts of the woods, the women could be as crass as the men. But it wasn't something he was accustomed to. Paula never used any foul language. Perhaps that was because she was a school teacher and couldn't afford to let some inappropriate words slip out of her mouth.

"Sorry, that wasn't very lady-like. Guess I picked up a few bad habits in the city. Especially having to deal with my jerk of an ex-husband, Danny."

"That's okay," Ralph said. "Sadie uses worse language than that before she gets out of bed in the morning, and she's more of a lady than I can usually handle."

"What happened in the city?" Clint asked. He hoped he wasn't getting too personal, but he wanted to steer the conversation in a different direction. He also wanted to get to know more about this woman.

"Danny got tired of my nagging him to move out to the country. I hated the city. Cars were everywhere, people were yelling, honking their horns, pushing, shoving. There wasn't any room to breathe. I tried to get him to move up to the Watkins Glen area, but no dice. Finally he got a big promotion. Said he had to move to Los Angeles, was I coming or not. I said no, he filed for divorce and the rest is history. Now I have a great job at the clinic and some day I'll be able to move into a place of my own."

"Yeah, I know how you feel. I spent most of my adult life in one city or another. Seemed like there was some low-life on every corner. Finally I had to get away. Came up here about five years ago, and don't think I'll ever leave."

"Hey, you're the one who owns the Bull's-eye Ranch up near Porcupine Hollow, aren't you?"

"Yeah, that's me."

"Mom and Dad have told be a lot about you. Well, not actually about YOU, but about what you've done to help the people of Elk Run. Helped Miss Oakmont with her school for disadvantaged kids. Donated books to the library. Financed that clinic to teach people how to defend themselves. You've done quite a bit in only five years."

Clint downed the remains of his beer and pushed the empty glass away from him. He'd better stop now; the conversation was starting to make him feel uncomfortable. Too much beer and he'd say things he didn't want to.

"Another one Clinton?" Sadie asked.

"No thanks. I gotta get back to Shack and take Mr. Stubs home."

"I'm sorry. I didn't mean to pry," Megan apologized. "You are a very interesting man. But I wouldn't call that beautiful home of yours a Shack."

Clint turned his head back toward Megan. Again, he was captivated by her sparkling eyes.

"Huh? Oh, Shack. No, that's my dog."

"You have a dog named Shack? How did he get a name like that?"

"Well, a friend of mine had a litter of black lab puppies. Told me I could pick any one I wanted. He figured I was alone too much and needed a companion. I wasn't sure I wanted to be a dog sitter, but I went to have a look. This one pup was about twice the size of the others, but he let his siblings walk all over him. When they sucked, he waited till the rest were finished and then tentatively nuzzled against the mom. I was hooked. My friend pointed out that he would grow to be as big as a 'shack'. So, that became his name."

Megan smiled and Clint felt a warm sensation press upon his chest.

"Well, anyway, he certainly did become big as a shack. I better be going. Are you sure you'll be okay going home?"

"Oh yea! If I run into any trouble, I'll just introduce those guys to my 12-gauge Mossberg."

Clint eyed Megan from her neck down to her toes.

"You have it hidden well."

"Silly," Megan laughed, "it's in my truck hanging over my seat. Never know when you'll jump a flock of turkeys or grouse."

"Hey, that gives me an idea. You working tomorrow?"

"Not till three."

"Want to come out to the ranch and try to find some grouse?"

"That's a new one. Will you show me your Shack too?"

Clint's neck turned red again. "Be there by eight. Know how to get there?"

"Oh, I'm sure I can find it," Megan smiled.

"Stubs!" Clint yelled. "Let's go. Train's a leavin'."

"Wooh! Wooh!" Stubs shrieked as he stumbled into Clint's arms.

Clint guided Stubs toward the door. Before leaving, he turned one last time to wave goodbye. He didn't even notice that Sadie and Ralph had retired to the kitchen. His eyes were riveted on Megan's beautiful smile . . . and those eyes.

* * *

Shack waited for about an hour after his master had gotten into the truck and driven away. Shack figured that the man was going to the place with the animals stuck in the wall. Poor animals, it was too bad they didn't have a place to run around like he did. How boring.

Finally, realizing that his master was not going to change his mind and return, he walked down to the lake. What should he do first? He decided on a swim. Shack stared at the large lake and wondered if he could jump from one side to the other. He was a pretty good jumper. He sprinted toward an opening in the brush along the edge of the lake and leaped as far out into the water as he could. With a loud splash, he landed about five yards from shore. Wow, the other side of the lake was pretty far away. He swam back to shore and moved further back up the bank toward the house. This time he ran even faster and sprang up into the air as far as he could. Still he was way short of the opposite bank. Several times he moved further away from the lake and took a running shot at crossing the lake. Finally, he realized that by the time he reached the edge of the lake, he was too tired to jump very far. He was never going to make it. He decided to just swim to the other bank. By the time Shack reached the bank and slipped and slid up onto the soft grass, he was exhausted. He decided to just lie in the bushes and see what other animals would come out to the lake for a drink.

After awhile, his breathing returned to normal and he just rested his nose on his paws. He gazed up at the bright white lights far up in the sky, but this began to hurt his eyes. Soon, two mother deer came down toward the lake, their fawns trailing a slight distance behind them. The mother deer glanced around several times, making sure there was no sign of danger. When they were sure it was safe, they turned and snorted for the young ones to follow.

Shack watched them drink a couple hundred yards away. He loved to see his other friends. Once, he tried to join them and play with them, but they ran away. This made him sad for a while, but then Shack figured it wasn't personal. He knew there were other dogs that often chased the deer until they fell from exhaustion. Then the dogs would eat the deer. How disgusting.

Another hour passed and the deer moved slowly back into the trees to find their beds for the night. It was time for Shack to return to his bed on the porch and await the return of his master.

Shack had no sooner flopped his tired body down on the thick blanket near the front of the house, than he heard a vehicle come up the drive. A low growl rolled uncontrollably out of his throat. When his master wasn't home, it was his job to protect the property. He wasn't going to let any stranger get into the house where his master lived. Besides, Shack's supply of dog food was inside and if anyone stole it, he may have to resort to chasing deer. That could be hard work and it was disgusting too.

The vehicle pulled right up to the front of the house. The bright spotlights that came on by magic every night around the same time, even when his master wasn't home to turn them on, lit up the driveway as if it was daytime. Shack recognized the red Subaru immediately. Paula had come to see him. Well, probably not him, but since his master wasn't home, she would have to talk to him instead.

Shack jumped up as fast as he could and trotted toward the pretty woman. Her hair was the color of the straw he often ran through in the neighbor's field, but it was much softer. Her eyes were the same color as the soft summer sky when there were no clouds in sight.

"Arf! Arf! Arf!" Shack greeted Paula.

"Shack! Oh you beautiful dog you. How are you? Oh come here boy."

Shack didn't understand everything she had said, but he knew what "come here" meant, and he knew she was talking to him.

Paula watched the big dog wiggling his whole hind end as she sat down on the wooden rocker on the porch facing the driveway. She reached out with her two hands and roughly rubbed behind his head. She knew he must have been in the lake because his thick fur was still somewhat wet underneath. She gently scratched behind his ears as he laid his head upon her lap.

Shack didn't know what heaven was, but he figured it must feel like this. Paula's long fingers kept scratching behind his ears and it was all he could do to keep his eyes open. Her legs were soft like the pillow that he once had on his blanket. He didn't have the pillow anymore. He kind of tore it all up one night when he got bored and didn't know what else to do. His master had never given him another one.

Just as he was about to fall into a deep sleep, he caught sight of Paula's hand reaching toward a cardboard box she had set beside the chair. His head jerked up and he watched with anticipation as she reached into the box. Could it be? A cake? A chocolate cake? He sat up as straight as he could and stared at the box, willing it to be a chocolate cake. His tongue slipped out between his teeth and hung down the left side of his mouth. The smell from the now open box confirmed his expectations. Thin white lines of spittle slowly slid down the sides of his mouth. He hated when that happened. It was so un-cool. Quickly he licked his jowls, hoping Paula had not noticed.

"I brought this cake for Clint, but I guess he isn't here. Hate to see it go to waste. Would you like a piece?"

Shack stood up on all four legs and nervously pranced around in front of Paula. Of course he wanted a piece. Heck, he wanted the whole thing, but he knew that was too much to hope for. His big tail began to swish back and forth, pounding on the wooden banister dividing the porch from the flowers on the ground in front of it.

Paula took out a plastic knife that she had hidden in her coat pocket and gracefully cut a large piece of the cake.

"Now sit down and relax Shack."

Shack did as he was told but did not take his eyes off of the large piece of cake she held in her delicate hands.

She placed the cake on the floor of the porch and stood up. She was almost as tall as his master, but not as heavy. Shack looked at the cake and then back at Paula, his eyes pleading to be told he could have the cake. He barked once as if to say "enough already, tell me I can have it."

"Go ahead Shack, you can have it."

As Shack devoured the rich chocolate cake, Paula entered the large home. She loved what Clint had done to the place. The living area contained a large, cozy, mountain-stone fireplace where they had spent many hours cuddling on long, cold winter nights. The full kitchen with the center island contained all the appliances one would need to prepare a full-course meal. The dining area, with a large oak table and matching hutch, was big enough to host a family of eight. The sliding glass doors opened onto the deck that extended along the back and one side of the house. The bright spotlights at the back of the house shown part of the way down to the lake, but she could envision the entire panorama as if it was daylight.

As she walked toward the refrigerator to store what remained of the cake one of her students had baked for her, she stopped and glanced down the hallway toward the bedrooms. At the end of the hall was the master bedroom. It was more of a suite than a bedroom. It contained a king-size bed with a cherry headboard, to which she had only been invited a couple of times. Of course, she also had not pushed to enter its boundaries much herself. A matching sofa and chair, huge walk-in closets that stretched the entire length of one wall, a large bookshelf and two bathrooms completed the ensemble. Two other average-size bedrooms and another full bathroom opened on either side of the hall.

"Oh Clint, I wish you were here. I really wanted to be with you tonight. Suppose you're at the Old Timer's. I knew I should have gone there instead."

Paula placed the remains of the cake in the refrigerator and pulled a pen and paper off of the counter.

Dear Clint,

Sorry I missed you. One of the girls in my class baked me a great chocolate cake. At least I think it was great, based on Shack's reactions to it. I put what was left in the frig. I missed you these last two weeks and am sorry I didn't call you. Sure seem to be sorry a lot. I am tired from the trip back, so won't wait for you (hope you had a good time at the Old Timer's). If it's okay, I'll stop over tomorrow.

Love you,
Kisses and hugs, P.

Paula left the note on the kitchen table where she was sure Clint would see it. She returned to the front porch and shut the door tightly behind her. Most people left their doors open in this part of the world. It was normally a safe place. A good place. A place where you felt good about raising children. Children. Would she ever have her own? She had hit the big 40 last year. It wasn't too late but, for someone who wasn't even engaged to be married yet, it might never happen. Her school kids were precious. But it wasn't the same.

She shook the depressing thoughts from her head and glanced down at Shack. He was meticulously licking every last crumb from the floor. She wasn't sure if he was doing it to be tidy, to make sure he ate it all, or if he thought that by hiding the evidence, Clint would give him another piece.

"Good night Shack."

Shack reluctantly rose to say good-bye to Paula. He placed his wet nose on her right thigh, just above the knee, and sighed once. He was sorry to see her go. He liked Paula and wanted her to rub behind his ears some more. But, there were more crumbs to lick up and he didn't want some other animal sneaking up behind him and stealing them.

Paula scratched behind Shack's ears one last time and got in the car. Shack watched her leave the driveway. Maybe she would come back tomorrow morning and they could have cake together for breakfast. For now, however, he had some more crumbs to find.

Chapter 4

The loud roar of the engine and the splashing of the water against the side of the thin wall of his home brought Jason awake with a start. Tires screeched and doors that had been yanked open, slammed shut. The sound echoed down the deserted street. Jason pulled himself into a sitting position to watch the latest antics of Ruby and his pack of wolves. In addition to Ruby and the four goons that normally never left his side, there were two slim young girls. Both had short skirts that barely covered their butts. Strings of gems around their thin necks and tiny wrists sparkled in the sparse light overhead. Anger began to heat up the frigid air inside the crowded box. Over the last several years Ruby had been spending money as if it flowed from the sewers underneath the run-down building he called his "Post". A brand new Chevy Suburban with every feature imaginable. New fancy clothes. Different girls wearing different jewelry every week. Even the punks that hung-out with Ruby had finer clothes than many of

43

the honest working people Jason often watched entering and leaving the large financial buildings uptown. Ruby's fingers, which once held just one lone red ruby, now sported an assortment of gold rings containing different-colored stones. On nights like tonight, when they were conducting business, all five compatriots donned expensive black leather jackets and pants. The center of the back of each jacket contained a hand-sewn big red gem, which marked the members of the "Rubies". Their supply of booze and drugs never seemed to run out.

Jason knew where the money had come from. The motley gang had never been more than a bunch of small-time losers. They sold some drugs and guns to high school kids who didn't know any better. Occasionally they would heist a car if it was left running with the keys in the ignition and then sell it for a few grand. If they got really adventuresome, they would rob a few hundred dollars from an all-night convenience store. They always went after the sure thing, which normally meant small-time payoffs. No, Jason knew where the big bucks were coming from. He had practically given it to them, and sacrificed his best friend's life in doing so.

* * *

Vasser, New York
Thursday October 14, 1971 9:30 PM

Jason had just left the "Pint House" and was staggering down the lonely, dark alley toward his soon to be forgotten home. He didn't often drink himself into a tizzy, but there was cause to celebrate. This was to be his last night on the street. Tomorrow he would pass what little fortune he had onto some less fortunate street people and then he and Oscar would start searching for their new home. Jason didn't like crashing at Oscar's place, but it seemed that now was the time to move in. He and Oscar would be partners. It wouldn't take long to find a place that suited them. They weren't looking for some castle. Just a modest home outside the city with a couple of bedrooms, two bathrooms and a little yard where they could have cook-outs and sit and relax listening to the ball games on a small radio. It would have to be along or close to a bus route, since Jason didn't have a car and he certainly wouldn't let Oscar buy him one.

He would spend one last night on the street, making sure he locked every last memory away before embarking on his new life with Oscar. No matter what happened with him and Oscar, he vowed never to return to the streets. Oscar had helped him get over the pain and guilt and ridicule he once felt when people put him down for fighting in Vietnam. He came to understand that things were not his fault. The government may have screwed up and some of the officers that tried to do what they felt was right may have screwed up, but Jason hadn't screwed up. He had done his best. He did what his country had asked of him. Now, he was ready to take that menial job and earn what little pay he could get. Oscar would cover the expenses for a while and by the time the money began to run out, Jason could start to help pay the bills. No, he would never return to the streets again. He began to hum some song that had been playing on the jukebox as he concentrated on placing one foot in front of the other until he reached his box just a few blocks up the street.

By the time he focused on the two dark legs that had loomed up in front of him, it was too late for him to react. Two strong arms struck his chest and he crashed backwards onto the hard sidewalk. He couldn't tell if the pain bouncing around in his head was from the blow it took from the concrete or from the dozen pints he had downed within the last couple of hours.

"Hey Ruby, it's that homeless guy from up the street" an unfamiliar voice spoke.

"Oh, Moose, look what you did." Jason vaguely recognized Ruby's voice. "You know you shouldn't pick on poor, defenseless bums. Here, let me help you up mister."

Jason sensed a movement to his right where his empty hand lay in the cold gutter.

"Aaahhhhhh!" Jason yelled as a hard-soled boot stepped squarely on the back of his hand.

"Oh, I'm sorry" Ruby's voice returned.

Jason used all his dwindling strength to sit up on the curb. His legs extended into the street and he held his swelling hand in his lap.

"Ruby?" a third voice chimed in, " Don't you know this is a bona fide Vietnam veteran baby killer? Why, I bet his hands are registered lethal weapons."

"Well, we can fix that," Ruby answered.

Jason watched helplessly as the one who first struck him in the chest held his only good hand on the hard pavement and Ruby brought his heavy boot down on his extended fingers.

"Aaaaaaaaahhhhhh!" Jason screamed. "You bastards!"

Five voices laughed together at Jason's weak rebuke.

"You're a loser!"

"Drunken faggot!"

"Baby Killer!"

"Smelly goat!"

"Worthless piece of –"

"I AM NOT!" Jason yelled with all his might. "I'm going to be rich! I'm going to leave this stink hole with Oscar. We've got more money than you'll ever see in your short lifetime. You're the losers. Bunch of no good, petty –"

At that, a fist struck Jason on the side of his head as he was pushing himself up off of the curb. He fell back down on his side. The whole ground was moving around him. He felt like he was going to fall over, even though he was already lying with his face on the cold surface.

"Grab his arms and sit him up against the wall!" Ruby commanded.

Jason felt his body being lifted and his back was pushed against the jagged brick surface of the building. His head hurt and his hands hurt. Why did his hands hurt so bad?

"Who's this Oscar guy?" Ruby asked.

Jason knew who Oscar was, but for some reason he felt he shouldn't tell the voice yelling in his face. Why did they want to know who Oscar was? A fist struck him in the stomach and the beer that was churning in his stomach exploded up his throat and out his mouth. He felt better . . . for a while.

"Son of a bitch!" a new voice yelled. Another fist came swinging up under his chin and knocked his head back against the unyielding building.

"I'll bet Oscar's that cripple lives over near Spruce."

Jason faintly heard voices somewhere around him, but he couldn't make out what they were saying. He was so tired. His eyes shut and blackness covered him. The hands that had held him against the building let go of him and Jason slid to the ground. He must be home. One more night on the street. Oscar wasn't a cripple; he was a man. Tomorrow, his life would begin . . .

Chapter 5

Ruby led the way into the "Post" and sat his tired body onto the chair behind the big oak desk he referred to as his office. The other four members of his "club" followed after him and took their usual places on the assorted chairs and sofas spread out around the open room that once served as a lobby for a not-so-prestigious loan company. Ruby often joked about how his small "company" was carrying on the high finances of the now bankrupt previous tenants. Ruby had found this quiet place a few years ago when he decided he needed a place in the city to run his ever-growing business. The building had been empty for almost a dozen years. Occasionally a police cruiser could be seen passing by a couple of blocks away, but unless provoked, Ruby knew they wouldn't bother him. Not only would they lose Ruby's monthly payment of "protection money", but it would jeopardize their take from many other "fine upstanding citizens" who expected certain "security" in return for payments. Ruby tried to make sure that all his business transactions were conducted a safe distance from his office. The developers, although they occasionally talked about rebuilding this part of the city, also kept their distance from this particular building. Perhaps that was because one of the most respected city councilmen didn't want the other members of the council to find out about his close relationship with one of the current residents.

"Moose!" Ruby commanded, "go and check out the other doors and windows. Make sure they're secure and the alarms are set."

"Ah man, why can't someone else do that? I'm beat. I always gotta check out the building. It's a big building."

"Shut up and do as I say. Besides, if you run into anyone, I have the upper-most confidence that you can dispel the threat with as little harm to our establishment as necessary."

Moose smiled at the big words Ruby used. Ruby often used big words. That was because Ruby was smart. He had a high school education, which was more than Moose or his other three friends could say. Moose wasn't quite sure what Ruby had meant, but he figured Ruby was paying him a compliment. He raised his shoulders to his full six-foot height and proudly sauntered back toward the rear of the building.

"Hear that?" Moose bellowed, "Anyone who's back there is gonna get dispelled all over this establishment."

"Dumb shit," a short, stocky youth observed. "He don't even knows what you said."

"Either do you, Speedy," a high-pitched voice chimed in. "You ain't any more educated than any of us, so stop pickin' on my brother."

"Screech, your brother's dumber in all of us put together. Good thing he's strong as an ox and big as a moose, cause he sure couldn't think his way out of a paper bag."

"He is not!" Screech defended his older brother. "He's just as dumb as you and me!"

Ruby, Speedy and Whispers, who was lounging comfortably on the new sofa just recently added to their furnishings, broke into roars of laughter at Screech's failed attempt at defending Moose.

"All right, that's enough," Ruby said, noticing that Screech was starting to get really upset at the laughter directed his way. "Let's go over our strategic plans for the rest of this week. Screech, you're reconnoitering the 24-hour place over on 9th Street tomorrow, right?"

With a final penetrating stare at Speedy, Screech turned his attention to Ruby. Ruby sure was the smartest of them all. He probably could have gone to college if he wanted to. Ruby was always talking about making "strategic plans" and "reconnoitering" places and doing all sorts of things that most of the others didn't even understand. But Ruby would always explain things over and over until they got it. That's why he was the brains of the outfit.

"Yeah, Ruby. I'm goin' over there around two in the morning and stakin' the place out. I got my notebook and pencil to write down everything I seen so we can determine any patters."

"Patterns! Dumb head," Speedy corrected, "We're looking for PATTERNS, not PATTERS. Do you even know HOW to write?"

"Of course I know how to write. I made it to the tenth grade, didn't I?"

"Knock it off Speedy," Ruby interrupted. "That's right Screech. You keep track of everything that happens from two to four in the morning and then we'll rendezvous back here at 4:30 and review your notes. If we find a safe way to grab a few bucks and maybe some supplies, we'll hit the place next week. Speedy, how you comin' with that new supply of weed for the kids?"

"Big John says it'll be here day after tomorrow, but he wants five Gs tomorrow to hold it for us."

"He's never stuck us before with bad shit. Any reason to think he's gonna screw around with us?"

"Nah, he knows we are into some big gun things and doesn't want to make any waves."

"Whispers," Ruby directed his attention to the quiet one still lying on the sofa. "You got a home for those four crates of AK-47s of ours?"

"Sure thing. Rudolph wants delivery at the end of the week. Says he'll have the two grand for us by then."

"What's Rudolph gonna do with two crates of AK-47s?" Moose asked as he rejoined the group. "He ain't gonna start a war in *Vasser* is he?"

"No," Whispers answered. "He says he got some big connections gonna double his money and send them out west or something."

"The further away the better," Screech added. "I don't like selling all those guns to local peoples. Scares me."

"Why we dealing with this small shit anyway, Ruby?" Speedy asked. "Thought we made a bundle on that old cripple some years back. How come we just don't take all that money, move into some better place and start playing with the big boys."

"Hey!" Ruby yelled as he stood up, knocking over the chair that he was sitting on. "I told you, we'll use that money when and as I say. You wanna move in with the big boys, go ahead. You think they'll take care of you brain-dead idiots like I do? You think they'll buy you fancy clothes, get you all the sweet two-legged honeys you want, hand you brand new 44's and provide for your safety like I do? You wanna have cops and feds breathing down your necks? What, you're not happy here? Then leave!"

Ruby stood just a couple inches under six feet. His wavy, reddish-brown hair flowed over his ears and down to the base of his neck. His thin, yet muscular arms, gripped the edge of his desk as his chest expanded with each breath. The vein in his neck pulsated as the blood returned to his pounding heart.

The four sat quietly with their heads down. Even Whispers rose from his prone position at the outburst. Ruby had taken good care of them. So what if Ruby didn't share all the profits with them. They lived well, dressed well (when they wanted to), ate well, partied well. Their home, which was just five small rooms off of the lobby they called the office, had all the comforts they needed. They even had two side entrances that they could use to escort their female friends to their private rooms, without exposing them to their office area. Best of all, they felt safe. The security system that Ruby had installed a couple of years ago was better than most banks. Four large generators which Ruby had also purchased a couple of years ago, provided enough power to run their refrigerator and other electrical needs. Gasoline was never a problem because the garage down the street was always willing to trade ten or twenty gallons for some weed and an occasional handgun. Several steel gun cabinets held their revolving supply of weapons, drugs and "petty cash". The only thing that was lacking was plumbing. Using the port-o-potties at a nearby construction site covered that or, when they needed to get fancied up, they could use the showers at the local YMCA. The barter system worked well at several places.

"Speedy, you're an asshole," Screech observed.

"Ruby, I don't wanna go join the big boys. I like runnin' with you. I trust you. You take good care of us."

"Yeah," Moose and Whispers echoed.

"I don't really even mind checking the security every night. Makes me feel like a Security Personnel," Moose added.

Speedy gazed back at Ruby.

Although several inches shorter than Ruby, Speedy's strong arms and thick chest were intimidating to most people who crossed his path. His dark eyes, square jaw and broken nose added to his fierce features. But Ruby knew what was in the man's heart. Ruby knew Speedy would often back down from confrontations if he felt he couldn't come out on top.

"You know I didn't mean anything by that," Speedy finally responded. "Just seems like we scratch and claw for a few measly thousand each week, when we have all that money from the cripple sittin' doin' no good. Don't even know how much we got."

"I told you," Ruby spoke, anger boiling near the surface. "We can't spend all that money so quickly or the cops will get suspicious. That money's been invested and is earning us plenty. Whata we need that we don't got? You don't like how I'm investing our funds? You want to be the Controller?" Ruby was now standing in front of Speedy, glaring at the one who had been running with him the longest. If any of them was a threat to tear things apart and upset Ruby's control, it was Speedy. Even though he hadn't finished high school either, Speedy had more street sense than the others. He had been on his own the longest, and Ruby had to be careful or things would get out of hand. He had to put Speedy in his place. Without warning, Ruby picked the stocky person off the chair on which he was sitting and threw him back onto the sofa that Whispers had vacated. Ruby pulled the 44 out of the back of his pants and aimed it at Speedy who was pushing himself to his feet.

"Decide now Speedy! You with us or you want out? I don't have time to get your approval on everything I do. You unhappy? Say so and I'll give you a pass to greener pastures."

Speedy nervously eyed the large weapon extended from Ruby's hand. He had pushed Ruby too far and he knew it.

"No man, no. I'm with you. You know that. Take it easy. I didn't mean nothing. Don't man. Don't. I'm sorry. Okay? . . . . . . Okay?"

Ruby lowered the weapon and he heard three sighs of relief from the others in the room. Speedy ran his trembling hands through his dark, greasy hair. Ruby had succeeded in putting things back in order, but he couldn't afford to be looking over his shoulder at Speedy. He had to restore some of Speedy's pride.

"Tomorrow I have to run across town to collect on a little deal I'm making," Ruby informed the group as they all relaxed. Whispers resumed his prone position on the sofa. "If all goes according to plan, when I get back, we're gonna party hearty."

A chorus of "all rights", "yahoos" and "yeah mans" erupted from the once tense partners in crime.

"Let's get some sleep. We all have big days tomorrow."

As they got up and headed to their own little rooms, none of them even thought twice about questioning Ruby about his special deal.

Chapter 6

Elk Run, Pennsylvania
Tuesday September 25, 1979 11:30 PM

Clint opened the passenger door to his Explorer and helped Stubs inside. The fresh night air seemed to give him new life.

"I cen get myshelf into your blasted truck by myshelf, youngen."

"I know you can, Stubs. I just want to make sure you close the door after you. Don't want you to fall out and make a mess on the road."

"Humph! You better...."

Clint slammed the door, which put an end to Stubs' babbling, and moved around to get in the driver's seat.

"I coulda walked you know. I done it plenty of times before your came along."

"I know, but you ARE my neighbor. It's the least I could do."

Clint pulled out of the parking lot and headed north on Route 6. Stubs struggled to stay in an upright position as the vehicle rounded the many curves in the road.

"Jeez a willy, Clint. Take it easy. My head can't keep up with the rest of my body with you speedin' around these curves."

"I'm only going forty. Put your seat belt on."

Stubs reached down behind his side to find the buckle and promptly smacked his head on the window. That brought another string of garbled complaints that Clint didn't even bother to try to figure out. After a few failed attempts to snag the elusive strap, Stubs gave up and concentrated on staring at the approaching shadows. After a few minutes, Clint turned off the macadam road onto a dirt one that led to Stubs' home. A couple hundred yards down the road, Clint pulled to a stop in front of a small house with a light burning above the door.

"Someone left the light on for you. You got some young babe waitin' up for you?" Clint knew Stubs lived alone.

"Iffin I did, I wouldn't invite you in. You'd likely put the moves on her like you did that pretty little lassie down at Sadie's. But since I don't, how 'bout comin' in for a beer. I need somethin' to calm my nerves after that drivin' you just did."

"I don't think so, Stubs, I –"

"Oh, come on. You got another date or you just goin' home to look at girly magazines."

"All right," Clint laughed. "You win. Here, let me help…"

It was too late. Stubs had opened the door and proceeded to fall head first into his weed-infested flower garden.

"You all right? Jeez you're more stubborn than a mule with sore feet. Let me help you up."

"I can get myshelf up by myshelf." Stubs spat dirt from his mouth as he wiped more off his previously not-so-clean face. "Come on in."

Stubs weaved his way to the front door. After successfully pulling open the screen door, he pushed open the inside door without unlocking it. He flipped a light switch nearby and Clint entered behind him. As Clint shut the door, Stubs continued his maneuvering past strategically placed furniture until he entered a small room Clint assumed was a bathroom. This was confirmed shortly as he heard Stubs answering the call of nature. He apparently had waited a long time before answering. Clint sat down on the well-worn sofa in front of the wood-burning stove. Two end tables with short, fat lamps sat on either side of the sofa. The place was small. In addition to the sofa and stove, the living area included a recliner and a bookshelf loaded with all sorts of outdoors magazines. There was a small radio, but no television. The kitchen and dining area contained a small metal table and four chairs that had seen better days. The refrigerator was new, but the gas stove was old. The counter top next to the stove held a two-slice toaster, boxes of cereal, and assorted packaged chocolate cup cakes. Light bulbs, boxes of matches, a fly swatter and various other essential items completed the counter-top arrangement. Despite the age of the furnishings, the house was tidy. No dishes were left waiting in the sink and the carpeting was recently vacuumed. Even the magazines and tabletops were dustless. Stubs finally finished his business and returned to the living area.

"Feel much better now. How 'bout a beer."

"Sure you have any extra?" Clint kidded.

"Humph!" Stubs moved to the refrigerator and took out two cold cans. He opened one and had it half empty before he crossed the twenty or so feet to where Clint was sitting. Clint took the offered can and popped the top.

"Thanks for bringing me home. Don't get much company 'round here. How come you never stop over anymore?"

"I'm sorry 'bout that, Stubs. I should stop by more often." Clint eyed the over-used furnishings. "You know, I have been meaning to talk to you. I could use a little help over at my place. You know, cutting the grass and such. My snowmobile isn't working again, either. You're pretty handy with machines, aren't you?"

"You betcha." Stubs' eyes perked up at the thought of someone needing his services.

"I could pay you –"

"No way. I'll help ya, but you ain't gonna pay me."

Clint knew Stubs wouldn't take any money, but he would find a way to replace at least some of the furnishings.

"How long you been living here Stubs?"

"All my adult life. Mary, my wife, and I built this place the year after we got hitched. Got out of high school, got married, built this house and lived here ever since."

"Mary's been gone some time now, what happened?"

"She got eaten."

"Eaten? By what, a bear?"

"Nope, got eaten alive by that cancer thing. Weren't married but for five years. Ever see someone get eaten alive from the inside out?"

"No," Clint answered sheepishly. He was sorry he had touched on this subject.

"Terrible! Hope you never have to see it either. Hear they got all sorts of new medicine nowadays. Wish they had back then. I need another beer. You?"

"No, thanks Stubs."

Stubs went to retrieve another can.

"You got any other relatives around here?"

"Nah, had a brother up in *Vasser*. Haven't heard from him forever. Think he had a kid or something. Never heard from any of 'em for a long time."

Stubs was starting to take on a depressing tone, and Clint didn't want to dwell on the subject of *Vasser*. He hadn't realized that Clint and Stubs shared a common point of reference. Clint changed the subject.

"Shack been over to visit you lately?"

Stubs' eyes perked up again.

"That old dumb mutt? He meanders over here ever once in a while. Full of briars. Sits on my front porch waitin' for me to come out and pull them off. Then he plops that ton of weight on my feet and won't get off till I brush him with my old horse brush. He sure does have a sweet tooth, too. He'd eat me outta house and home if I let him."

That explained the boxes of cup cakes. Stubs didn't impress Clint as someone who spent much time eating sweets.

"Well, if you come over to the house more often and help out, you could help get him into shape. He's getting entirely too fat."

"Get in shape for what? He enterin' the Olympics?"

Clint laughed and stood up with his empty can.

"Speaking of Shack, I better get home and see what trouble he's gottin' into. Thanks for the beer." Clint crushed the can in his hand and tossed it on top of the others that almost filled the ten-gallon plastic garbage can.

"You know Stubs, you should cut back on your drinking."

"Why? Now you plannin' on enterin' me in the Olympics?"

"Take it easy Stubs," Clint laughed as he headed for the door.

"Don't be a stranger."

Clint got in his truck and headed back the dirt road. Through his rear-view mirror, he watched the lights go out in the small house. *I wonder who his brother is?*

Chapter 7

Shack heard the sound of the truck as it came down the drive. He wanted to get up from the cool leaves that surrounded the big oak tree, but his belly hurt too much. He was afraid that as soon as he got to the porch to greet his owner, he would have to return to the depths of the woods to use God's bathroom. It seemed that every time he ate some of that sweet chocolate stuff, this happened. He would just have to rest here for awhile and let this evil pain inside him go away. His owner would figure he was out chasing some other animals. It was not unusual for Shack to be gone until late in the morning.

Clint pulled his Explorer into the maintenance shed next to the pickup truck. Sometime tomorrow he would have to muddy up the engine to the snowmobile and ask Stubs to come over and fix it. Of course, that would have to wait until after his excursion with Megan. He didn't know if he had done the right thing by asking her to hunt with him. He was just so hooked by her, that he couldn't let the opportunity pass. But what about Paula? They had certainly been dating for some time now. They had even gone to bed together several times. It wasn't that he hadn't tried to push their relationship to another level. He really did like her a lot. He wasn't sure it was the "love thing" that made two people get married and live together forever after, but he was willing to make more of a commitment. Paula, however, always seemed to put her kids first. Outings between Clint and Paula always got scheduled after she had all her plans with her kids figured out for the next ten years. At least that's the way it felt. Clint admired her for her commitment to the kids. She was doing a wonderful job. Many kids, who would have been driven out of the schools by their unsympathetic peers in a public environment, actually learned and changed their behavior as a result of Paula's teaching, field trips and week-long retreats. She was an amazing woman. Clint even helped on occasion. But Clint's interests lay in the outdoors: hunting, fishing and wandering through the woods. Paula seemed to like that too, but those interests took a distant second to her first love: the kids. Even sex was not the same for the two of them. Paula enjoyed it, but could take it or leave it. Clint loved it and wished Paula would pursue it more aggressively.

"Shack!" Clint yelled once. When there was no reply, he figured the animal was out chasing his tail or some other animal's. He was too big and slow to catch anything. He figured the dog wouldn't know what to do if he ever did catch another creature of the woods. So far, Shack hadn't tried to make friends with any skunks. That was one of Clint's fears. What a stink that would be.

As he hung his jacket on a peg by the door, he spotted the piece of paper and pencil lying on the table. After reading the short note, he cringed at the thought of Paula in his home feeding cake to Shack, while he was at the bar feeding lines to Megan. Even worse, Paula wanted to come over tomorrow. He checked the Grandfather clock standing against the wall. It was too late to call Paula tonight and she was not an early riser. If all went well, he and Megan would be done hunting, and she would be gone before Paula decided to drop in.

He strolled to the master bedroom and stripped to his underwear. That was another difference between he and Paula. Even in the winter months, Clint slept in just his skivvies, while Paula dressed as if she were on the Alaskan Peninsula. He wondered what Megan slept in. *Enough!*

Clint did his business in the comfort of the master bathroom and climbed under the warm comforter and sheets on his bed. Suddenly the bed seemed awfully big.

Chapter 8

Clint woke at six like he usually did each day. It didn't seem to matter what time he got in bed. His internal clock always got him out of bed at the same time. He threw on sweatpants, wool socks and a pullover sweater and went to the kitchen to start a quick breakfast. He tossed a few leftover sausages, chopped onions and fried potatoes into a pan and turned the burner on low. After mixing them all up a bit, he put a lid on and went to the door to see if Shack was around.

Shack had come back to his bed on the side porch around three in the morning. His belly had stopped aching and making funny noises, and he was downright tired. He vowed never to eat chocolate cake again. After three hours of sound sleep, Shack sensed his owner moving in the house. He was probably fixing breakfast. Wonder what it would be: Pancakes? Eggs? Tuna fish? That was his favorite breakfast: tuna fish with mustard, and a chocolate cupcake. He patiently

67

sat in front of the door to make sure his master wouldn't miss him if he came looking. Soon the door opened.

Clint stared at the large animal sitting in the middle of his porch.

"You're a mess!"

Shack tilted his head sideways in an effort to understand the strange words. He didn't think it was an invitation to come inside.

"You need a bath."

"Hmph." Shack stretched his head to see what was cooking on the stove. He knew what "bath" meant, but he was more interested in the smell coming from behind the big man blocking his entrance into the house. Finally he looked back at his owner and barked twice.

"You sound just like Stubs. Come on you dirty mutt. Come in."

Shack wondered where his friend Stubs was. His owner had mentioned his name. He must be around somewhere, but he wasn't going to wait around. Stubs could find his own food. Shack trotted toward the kitchen table before his owner changed his mind and made him take a bath first. He almost knocked his owner over as he rambled by.

Clint smiled and closed the door. "Make sure no one steals our breakfast Shack. I'm going to take a shower."

"Grrrrrrrr." Shack let his owner know that he would watch the simmering food closely. Not even Stubs would get to it. Shack turned to search the counter and the table and then looked longingly at the closed refrigerator. He wondered what had happened to the rest of the chocolate cake. He hoped his master hadn't eaten it all.

Clint used the shower in the master bedroom and, when he finished, he donned camouflaged pants and shirt, over an insulated top. It was going to be a little cool in the mountains today. After putting on his thermo socks and waterproof boots, he strolled back to the kitchen. The aroma from the simmering onions and sausage had caused Shack to drool all over his massive chest. The dog was still sitting in front of the stove and turned his pleading eyes back toward Clint.

"Hold your horses, Shack."

Clint cracked open a half-dozen eggs and dropped them into a mixing bowl. After whipping them together, he poured them into the pan with the sausages, onions and potatoes.

"Now, let me get a couple of plates and we'll eat."

At the sound of the word "eat", Shack began walking back and forth in front of the kitchen sink. He could hardly contain himself. He hadn't realized how hungry he was. After what seemed like an eternity, his owner finally filled a bowl with water and filled a plate with half of the wonderfully smelling concoction. He would worry about the cake later. This stuff was going to be good.

Clint set his plate with his share of the morning meal on the kitchen table and got himself a glass of milk from the refrigerator. As he opened the door to the refrigerator he caught Shack peaking at the shelves to see if he spotted the remaining sweets.

"Oh, I see we have some leftover cake from Paula."

Shack stopped chomping on a sausage, half of it protruding from his furry face. Should he drop the sausage and go beg for the cake or finish what he had started. Clint slammed the refrigerator door. Oh well, that decision was made for him. Shack went back to trying to maneuver the slippery piece of meat back into his mouth. Finally he let the sausage fall to the floor and concentrated on the egg, potato and onion mixture. He didn't think the hot dog-like piece of meat would go anywhere.

"A new friend is coming over in awhile to go hunting. Her name is Megan. You'll like her."

Shack stopped eating again. He hated these interruptions, but he wondered who Megan was. He cocked his head sideways hoping his master would explain more.

"She's a waitress down at Sadie's. She also works at the vet's office."

"Grrrrrrrrrr." Shack didn't particularly like the vet's office. Every time they went to visit that place someone would stick something sharp into his backside. The last time, he was sore for two days. This Megan person must be one of those big, mean people. Oh sure, they smiled a lot and talked real nice, but eventually all they wanted to do was stick that sharp thing in him. Nope, he wasn't going to like Megan at all.

Clint smiled. He could imagine what was going on in that small brain of Shack's. Clint finished his breakfast and put the plate in the sink.

"Hurry up and finish Shack. I'm going to get my gear."

Clint went down to the "lodge room" as he liked to refer to it. The room ran the entire length of the house. Four steel fireproof gun cabinets lined up next to each other separated his work area from the lounging area. One of the cabinets held his rifles, shotguns and pistol. He wasn't into antique or expensive guns. The closest thing to an antique he had was the Marshwood double-barrel 12 gauge shotgun that was once his father's. He preferred the simpler, practical weapons used for hunting or target shooting. He also preferred rifles and shotguns to pistols. His lone pistol, a 9 mm Beretta, was mostly used for shooting paper targets. The 22 Marlin bolt-action rifle was occasionally used for hunting groundhogs and squirrels. His favorite, a 308 Winchester lever-action rifle had brought down many deer. Two Mossberg shotguns, a 10-gauge and 12-gauge, were used for turkeys, rabbits and grouse.

The boarders who rented out the bunkroom used the other three cabinets. Clint's main source of income came during the hunting seasons. Beginning with the fall turkey season and ending with the spring gobbler season, he rented out the rooms to individuals or groups who were looking for a place to hunt turkey or deer. Between October and April, he kept the place pretty full and took in a sizeable income. He had worked out a system of assigning quadrants of his property to one or two individuals. This helped ensure a reasonable degree of success for the hunters, minimized the risk of accidents caused by having too many hunters in the same area, and also helped avoid depleting the amount of game on his property. Each year he assigned different quadrants to be hunted. He used the late spring and summer months to scout his entire property to see where the game was, or wasn't. Most of the hunters only hunted hard for a day or two and then spent the rest of the time drinking and telling stories. That was the reason for the three extra gun cabinets. There were several rules that hunters using his land had to follow. One was that there were to be no firearms in the bunkrooms. He registered each person's gun and required that it be kept in the cabinet when not being used or cleaned. Each person got a key to the cabinet and the workroom was available for everyone's use to clean their weapons. He even supplied a wide assortment of cleaning supplies. Reloading equipment for a dozen of the more common cartridges was also available and Charley, a local gunsmith, was available (for a small fee) to reload cartridges if necessary. Most of the people who frequented Clint's hunting club had been coming here for several years and many of them would call Charley before the seasons began to place their order. That should be starting soon.

The lounging area held several large sofas, lazy boy chairs, tables with stacks of magazines and books, and a large 38" television. Although there was a living area on both floors of the bunkhouse, this room served larger groups who wanted to get together. The walls were adorned with a wide assortment of deer, turkey, grouse, and fish, all bagged on Clint's property. This served as a major marketing tool. Occasionally, when someone bagged a trophy animal on Clint's property, Clint would offer to refund the person's fee (usually several hundred dollars) if he would give the animal to Clint to add to the collection. A plaque mounted under the animal proudly announced the person's name, the date the animal was bagged and the quadrant in which it was obtained. Many hunters liked the idea of their successes being shown to all the other people who came through Clint's club. A wet bar in the corner could be used to store hard liquor that the patrons wanted to bring along, but Clint provided unlimited beer and soda. It helped to keep the deer and turkey population up. Most hunters spent so much time drinking and talking about the hunt that they never woke up in time to actually find the real thing. It also helped support the local distributor. The local grocery store also benefited from Clint's club. Most of the people who came to this part of the state drove for hours to get here. It was much easier to call Mable down at the grocery store and tell her what snacks and food they needed, than it was to buy, pack and transport all that food along. Mable and her crew would have the refrigerators and cupboards stacked when they got here. Most of the patrons simply left the unused items for the local "food pantry" that provided food for those less privileged. Clint also provided a full dinner on Tuesdays and Thursdays as part of the package price. He paid several locals to prepare, serve and clean-up the meals.

Clint removed his Mossberg 12 gauge shotgun from the cabinet, along with a box of shells. He removed his vest from a rack on the wall, stuck a half dozen shells in one pocket and returned up the steps. As he opened the door to the kitchen he heard the sound of a vehicle coming down his drive, and Shack started barking.

"Now be quiet, Shack, it's only Megan"

"Arf Arf," Shack answered and then proceeded to run down the hall and into the bathroom. Clint saw his big head sticking out of the bathroom door gazing anxiously out at his master.

"Scaredy cat. If you want to stay in here on such a beautiful day, that's fine with me, but Megan and I are going to go find some grouse."

"Arf Arf," Shack explained. He was not going to get any sharp object plunged into him right after he ate breakfast.

Clint ignored him and headed for the front door. Megan was just getting out of her truck as Clint stepped outside. She was dressed in brownish-green camouflaged pants and a vest. The tan long-sleeved cotton shirt did not hide the fact that she was definitely a woman. Clint had a hard time focusing on her bright smile and cheerful eyes.

"Hey guy. You ready to blast a few birds."

"Boy, that is some way for an animal lover to talk. You'll really confuse poor Shack."

"Where is that big dog of yours? I thought he'd be out here peeing on my tires."

"He's hiding in the bathroom. I think he believes you're going to give him a shot or something."

"Oh, that's too bad. I guess I'll have to eat both these cupcakes myself."

"Arf, Arf, Arf." Shack had apparently snuck out to the kitchen and, with the mention of cupcakes, wanted to get a closer look at this rump sticker. Maybe she wasn't as bad as he had thought.

"Well, you just became his best friend."

Clint opened the door and Shack tore off the porch straight toward the woman with the jet-black hair. He stopped and sat with his front paws on Megan's feet. She wasn't going to get away until she gave him a cupcake.

"Boy, you must be starved."

"Arf." Shack agreed.

Megan opened one of the packs and dropped one of the cupcakes in Shack's open mouth. Shack ran around to the other side of the truck to eat the chocolate treat and keep a good distance between him and the perhaps-not-so-evil woman. After three chomps and a swallow, the desert was gone.

"You need to use the facilities before we head out?"

"No, I'm fine, but I would like the grand tour when we get back. Your place looks lovely."

"Thanks, it's comfortable. I'd be happy to show you around. Let's find some birds first. Shack, you coming?"

Shack looked at his owner and then turned his head to study the pretty woman with the hair that was the same color as his. He figured it was safe as long as they didn't try to get him into a vehicle and drive him somewhere. Shack caught up to them as they turned off the dirt driveway and headed north up a slight incline. Shack had been on many hunts with his owner before. He knew that as long as he stayed behind the people with the guns, he would be safe, and he wouldn't get yelled at for scaring any game. Sometimes other friends of his owner's would come over to hunt, and they would bring their own dogs. Those dogs were usually kind of "uppity" and even got to run out in front of the hunters. That seemed stupid to Shack. He preferred to stay behind and hunt on his own. The air was cool, and it looked like it was going to be a pleasant day. Maybe he'd even get some more cupcakes.

"How long you been hunting?" Clint asked after they had topped the slight incline and started down the other side. The brush was thinning out and several blow-downs with some cover on them held some potential for the fast flying birds. Clint and Megan veered off from each other.

"I haven't hunted much in the last five years or so. Tough to find four-legged game in New York, although there were some two-legged bucks I would have liked to plug between the eyes."

Suddenly a blur flew up from under one of the trees that both Megan and Clint had been keeping their eyes on. Shack yelped at the startling noise the bird made. Clint and Megan both brought their guns up to their shoulders. The bird had flown off toward Megan's side so Clint held his finger outside the trigger guard.

Boom!

Megan's shot was dead on target, and Clint watched the bird tumble to the ground.

"Nice shot!" Clint commented.

"Lucky," Megan answered. "These things are so darn fast. All I do is aim and shoot."

"Well, you aim good." Clint admired Megan from behind as she approached the still bird. She picked it up and slid it in her back pouch. Shack had come up to make sure the bird that scared him so bad was dead. He watched Megan stuff the dead animal in her backpack, and then turned to look at his owner on the other side of the tree.

"Hmph!" Shack snorted. His master could shoot like that too. That wasn't any big deal.

"Let's head up to that ridge over there," Clint suggested. "I want to show you something."

Clint, Megan and Shack slowly walked down into a valley, which was listed as "Porcupine Hollow" on most topographical maps, and then up the other side. Occasionally, Clint and Megan discussed mundane topics: college, books, movies, and prior hunting trips, nothing too personal. Most of the time, they just walked, lost in their own thoughts.

As they neared the top of the ridge, two grouse sprang up from some dense brush. They flew in opposite directions and Shack darted behind a large boulder as the big guns boomed three times. Megan's bird once again flopped to the ground. Clint's two shots missed their target, and the fast moving bird lived to see another day.

Shack came out from behind the boulder and trotted up to Megan, who was stuffing the bird in her pouch. Shack turned his sad eyes toward his master. Poor guy. This woman was showing him up big time.

"Oh, don't give me that look you dumb mutt. My bird flew through the dense trees and I couldn't get a clean shot."

Shack turned back to gaze at Megan as if to say "he usually isn't this bad."

Megan laughed and bent down to rub behind Shack's ears.

"Good boy. Maybe you and I need to go off on our own and let the big guy go get in some target practice."

Shack closed his eyes and started to drift off as her gentle rubbing began to put him to sleep. He jumped with a start at the sound of cellophane tearing. Oh boy, another treat.

Shack took his time finding all the crumbs that had fallen into the crisp leaves. Sometimes leaves could be such a pain.

Clint and Megan finished their hike to the top of the ridge. When they stopped, Clint pointed back the direction they had come. What Megan saw was breathtaking. Clint's massive house stood surrounded by large oak and pine trees. Just below the back of the house, she could make out a small pond. To the right of the pond and directly south from where they were standing was a line of trees and then a small, open, grassy area, which sparkled from the remains of the morning dew. Below them and to the west was a large, dense area. It was hard to imagine any animal (two or four-legged) being able to maneuver through that piece of woods. As she shifted her gaze, she noticed a small cabin just north of the dense part of the woods. Smoke drifted lazily out of its chimney. She could see the main road running west and east parallel to the ridge on which they were standing. A dirt road cut off of the main road and headed south toward the occupied cabin. She turned her gaze toward the east and noticed another small cabin about 300 yards away, sitting a short distance down the northern side of the ridge. The cabin was obviously unoccupied and the dirt path, which ran up to it from the main road, was once a well-used road. She turned back to face Clint.

"Let's sit and rest awhile. This old man needs a break."

"I doubt that."

The two of them sat on a large flat rock and looked down the northern side of the ridge. Their legs touched as they stretched out on the soft ground.

"That cabin down there," Clint explained, "is Stubs'. My property stops about two hundred yards short of his cabin and then runs down to the main road. That beautiful building over there is mine. Some day I aim to fix it up. Don't know why. Maybe I'll rent it out. About a mile over there to the east is the main road you came up to get to my house. That's the eastern edge of my property. Property line runs along the main road, just past the pond that Shack thinks is his swimming pool. The southern edge of my land runs along the far edge of that grassy opening. People use that area for picnics. I put in a couple of charcoal grills for them to make hot dogs and such."

Megan followed Clint's arm as he pointed out the boundaries of his land. He had such strong arms. She had admired his strong body the first night they had met. Although he was developing a slight pouch over his belt buckle, she knew he possessed a great deal of strength. He was somewhat of a contradiction. Strong body. Outdoorsman. Able to pick up a man with one arm and plant his face in a wall. She had seen the almost uncontrolled anger on his face that night at Sadie's when he had come to her defense. She was so embarrassed by that night, even though she knew it wasn't a result of anything she had done. Yet, this man sitting beside her, cradling the large gun in his left arm, whose strong, massive thigh was gently touching her leg, was also kind and gentle. She saw the kindness in his eyes when he looked at her and talked with his four-legged companion. She saw how he had taken care of Stubs the other night at the tavern. Her parents had told her many stories of how he had helped so many people in the community. Clint Jameson was a strange, but wonderful person. She decided right then that she wanted to get to know more about him and spend more time with him. She had been alone for a couple of years since the divorce. She loved the mountains and fresh air, but she yearned for a male companion to share her feelings, her thoughts, and more.

"Who ARE you, Clint Jameson?" she ventured.

Clint turned toward the beautiful voice and gazed into her eyes. Something stirred inside him. He had kept so much of himself inside. He wanted to share things with this woman that he had never shared with anyone else since coming to Elk Run. Not even Paula knew who he was. He decided it was time to bring his past to the present.

"Well, I used to be a cop. Actually, a detective."

Megan didn't blink. It didn't really surprise her. That explained his ability to deal with the threat in the bar. But there was more. She waited.

"After high school, I applied for and got a job in the Philadelphia police department. I'm not sure whether it was my grades or my all-state football ranking that got me in. I came up through the normal channels: walked the beat, then got to ride the beat on a beautiful horse called Dancer. He was a great horse. Full of energy. Could hardly stand still. Always seemed to be looking for action. Then one day we found ourselves in the middle of a riot in south Philly. Some punk with a shotgun put two shots into Dancer's face. We both went down, and I chased the sonofabitch for twenty blocks. I eventually caught him and beat the tar out of him. Turned out he was a major drug pusher. He got off with a slap on the wrist for giving up the major source. That took a lot of drugs off the street, but it didn't help Dancer. He was blind in both eyes so he had to be put to sleep. I got my first citation for that, but things were never the same."

Clint was standing now and slowly pacing back and forth in front of Megan's feet. He seemed lost in another time, another place. Although the sun was near the top of the clear blue sky, for some reason, Megan felt colder. She leaned her gun against the rock and wrapped her arms around herself.

"I always seemed to have this sixth sense of who the scumbags were. I could pick out a purse-snatcher before the crime went down. But I would wait until it happened and then I'd collar the guy with all the force I could muster. I eventually moved up to a radio car. My partner, Luke, and I took dozens of "shots fired" calls. The adrenaline would soar as we raced to the scene. We broke down doors, hurtled fences, smashed faces. No one got away. Commendations piled up. Then, all of a sudden, Luke was gone. He wasn't even on duty. He stopped at an all-nighter to get a pack of cigarettes. He picked the wrong store. Two punks had apparently beaten the small Asian clerk and were on their way out when they spotted Luke coming in. They hid behind some racks. Luke never knew what hit him. When he saw the bleeding clerk on the floor behind the register, he pulled his gun and swung around. Two shots from a 12 gauge from less than five yards away made it a closed-casket funeral. At least that was what the detectives and forensic people figured happened. The only witness said she saw two young men running away from the store after the shots were fired. Grey sweatshirts covered their heads. No surveillance cameras in the store. From that moment on, every dirty, longhaired, greasy-looking male in a grey sweatshirt became a suspect to me. I tormented the streets looking for Luke's killers, even though I had nothing to do with the case. I worked my normal area during the day and played detective on my own at night. Commendations turned to reprimands. Disciplinary actions replaced citations. City attorneys spent hours and hours trying to defend "police brutality" charges against me. Finally, I passed the detective's exam and realized it was time to get out. I took a job in *Vasser* as a Detective. Luke's murder was never solved."

Clint had stopped his pacing and was pushing with both hands against a giant oak tree that was leaning down the hill toward Stubs' cabin. Sweat was running down the sides of his face. Megan wouldn't have been surprised to see the giant tree come uprooted and crash to the silent forest floor, echoing the pain and anger and suffering that had been bottled up inside Clint for so long. But, when Megan moved her eyes back to this tormented man, his shoulders were shaking. The sweat had turned to tears.

Megan stood, somewhat weakly, and moved over to Clint. She placed her slender arms around his shoulders and gently tried to turn him toward her. She was scared of what he could do when his rage overtook him, but she also felt the need to comfort him. To somehow tell him that it was okay. Clint finally yielded to the pressure of the woman's firm hands and turned to face her. His eyes pleaded for forgiveness and understanding. Megan moved her body against his and wrapped her arms around him. She rested her small head against his large chest. When his quiet sobbing stopped, Megan stepped back and looked up into his face. Her smile told him that it was okay. Clint took his rough hand and gently lifted Megan's chin toward his. He bent down to kiss the smile on her lips.

"Yelp! Arf. Arf. Arf . . . " a string of barking and sounds of pain came from the once silent valley in the direction where Shack had been finishing his snack.

Clint pushed past Megan, grabbed his shotgun that was leaning against a tree, and charged toward the cries from Shack.

"Clint!" Megan yelled. She was afraid there was a bear or coyote or some other dangerous animal waiting for him as he blindly ran toward the sound. She picked up her gun and went after him.

Clint had not gone more than ten yards back down the side of the mountain when he saw Shack. He was lying on his belly. His tail was still. Both front paws were clawing at his nose, which was planted in the ground.

Clint's worse thoughts were that Shack had stuck his nose in a trap. Not many people used them this far up in the mountains anymore, but he had occasionally come upon ones that had been left years before and had never been sprung. Most were rusted and didn't work anymore, but . . .

Shack raised his head at the sound of the large creature running down the mountain toward him. He was in no mood to fight off another animal or to run. That darn porcupine was downright mean to stick him with his quills. All Shack wanted to do was play or at least talk a while. Then, all of sudden, the porcupine jerked and before he could move, Shack had a dozen pointy quills sticking in his whiskers.

When Shack realized it was his owner, he was both glad and embarrassed. How was he going to explain this? Well, he was a dog, wasn't he? He wasn't expected to explain things. Things just happened, didn't they? Like the time he ran head first into the big glass door in his owner's dining room. It looked like it was just open air and he wanted to get outside onto the porch fast when he heard the turkeys gobbling down by the lake. How was he to know the clear glass was there? Usually he could tell the difference between glass and air. Glass usually had some smudgy stuff or marks on it. That's what his master gets for making it so clean. Shack had ended up with a bad headache and his master had to replace the glass. At least this time, his master wouldn't have to replace the porcupine. After Shack yelped, the porcupine wobbled quickly down through the woods. Shack hoped he would never see it again.

Clint stopped short when he saw the pointy quills sticking out of Shack's nose. He tried to hold back his laughter, but couldn't. Megan came to a sliding stop beside him and grabbed onto his waist to stop from sliding down the hill. When Megan saw what the problem was, she also broke into laughter.

Shack calmly sat on his haunches and stared at the two laughing fools. He couldn't understand what was so funny. How would they like it if they had a porcupine stick needles in their nose? Oh no, would this mean the pretty lady was going to have to stick him in the hind end as well? Wouldn't that just beat all!

Chapter 9

Clint finished wrapping the skinned birds and placed them in the chest freezer. After cleaning up the mess he had made and washing his hands, he pulled six cans of beer out of the refrigerator and tossed them into a small cooler. Filling the cooler with ice, he went out the basement door into the bright afternoon sunshine. Since Megan had bagged the game, she had felt it was only fair that Clint do the cleaning. They had agreed to plan a cookout after she had brought home at least a couple more birds for the three of them (Clint, Megan and Shack, of course). Clint hadn't even bothered to suggest that maybe he would bag the next two. Megan had definitely proved her hunting skills this day.

Clint climbed the wooden steps to the deck. Shack was sulking in the corner. Clint pulled a can of iced beer out of the cooler and plopped his weary body down on the glider.

Shack refused to move from his spot on the deck. Despite Megan's gentleness, each time she pulled one of the sharp objects out of his snout with her tweezers, pain shot through his body. Then, she poured some smelly clear liquid on a cloth and doused his nose with it. This caused even more stinging. By the time she was done, he couldn't eat the chocolate cupcake she offered him. He turned his head slightly to see if it was still lying next to him. Maybe later he would feel more like eating it. For now, he just wanted to sleep and dream of playing with other animals, but not any of the ones with sharp needles sticking out of their bodies.

Clint watched as Shack rolled onto his side without even touching the cupcake. The poor dog really must be hurting. Clint had his own problems. Paula had called while Megan and Clint were eating a light lunch of ham sandwiches and chips. Clint had told her about the morning hunting excursion and Shack's encounter with a porcupine. Although Paula had laughed at the thought of Shack with quills sticking out of his nose, Clint could tell she was having a difficult time hearing about his trek in the woods with Megan. Despite her reluctance to come over later in the afternoon, she finally agreed. She would be here soon. Clint wasn't sure what was in store for them. He gulped down the cold liquid and reached in the cooler for another one. As he popped the tab on the cold can, he tried to figure out what to say to Paula. He felt very deeply for her, but the few hours he had spent with Megan yesterday at Sadie's and then again this morning in the woods, had given him feelings that he hadn't experienced with Paula for some time. Paula was beautiful and smart and very loving, at least when it came to the kids in her school. For a while, after they had been seeing each other for about six months, Paula had become very affectionate toward Clint as well. But then things seemed to get comfortable. They would watch movies or take walks in the woods. Paula didn't want anything to do with guns or hunting, but she loved the outdoors. Maybe that was it. He was comfortable with Paula, but he felt alive with Megan. Of course, he had only known her for two days. Maybe that excitement would die out also. He knew a lot more about Paula, and he liked everything about her. He wasn't getting any younger. Maybe the fact that he was comfortable with Paula meant more than he was giving it credit for. The more he thought about Paula, the more he wanted to take her in his arms, hold her, touch her –

The sound of the vehicle coming down his driveway brought him out of his dreamlike trance.

Shack's head popped up and he turned to look toward the front of the house. It was Paula. Shack could tell by the color and form of the car. He jumped up and started to run toward the automobile, forgetting about his aching nose. Unfortunately, the slippery wooden boards caused his feet to loose traction, and for a while, Shack was spinning his feet and not going anywhere. His hind leg knocked the cupcake off the deck, and it drifted to the ground below. His nose smacked against the deck, and he yelped in pain. Finally, Shack got control of his feet, and he shot toward the slamming car door.

"Shack, baby! How are you, you poor thing?" Paula cried from the front of the house.

"Back here, Paula," Clint yelled. He finished the second can of beer and started on the third. He was feeling much more relaxed now. He couldn't wait to see Paula. Her soft footsteps mixed with the excited padding of Shack's feet as they both came to the back of the house. As Paula rounded the corner and came toward him, his heart started beating faster and a warm feeling spread over him. She was so beautiful. She wore a thick, brown, wool sweater over her pressed blue jeans. Her large breasts swelled under her sweater as she walked toward him.

Clint stood up and took a step toward her. A tear appeared at the corner of her right eye as they wrapped their arms around each other and embraced tightly. After a few moments, they separated. Clint took her hand in his and led her back to the swing. As they sat down, Clint pulled another beer from the cooler and handed it to Paula.

"I missed you so much, Paula," Clint stated.

"Guess not too much," Paula responded.

Clint stared at her as she took the can in her hand and dropped her head.

"I'm sorry, that was uncalled for."

"You were gone for two weeks and didn't call me once," Clint stated. "Didn't you get my messages at the hotel?"

"Yes, I did. I'm sorry. I was just so busy. One of the speakers didn't show up and I had to prepare something myself. Then, Amy, you know, the blind girl, sixteen? She fell down some steps outside of the hotel and had to be taken to the hospital. I was swamped."

Clint concentrated on his can of beer.

"I love you Clint. I know I don't show it much, but I do love you. I wanted you to be with me every day the last two weeks. I went to bed dreaming of you and I woke up thinking about you. But then I would get started working on the conference, holding hands, breaking up fights, and trying to make all those kids feel good about themselves. I guess by the time I got back to my room, I was just too drained. That sounds so terrible. Maybe I'm just not capable of loving anyone."

Clint finished his third can of beer and tossed it into the cooler. He hesitated, and then grabbed another full one. He opened it as he stood up and walked to the banister. Turning, he reached his long arm out and gently lifted Paula's chin up so her eyes met his.

"No, that's not it. You are capable of great love. You show it every day. Just not to one person. You share it with everyone. You have endless love; you're not selfish with it. You give it to everyone. No one person gets it all. I'm the selfish one. I do want it all, or at least more than you can give any one person. I don't want to share your love. I want it all for myself. Now, that sounds terrible!"

Shack sat quietly in the corner of the deck and watched the strange exchange of words between the two people. Not once did they mention his name, so whatever they were saying couldn't be too important. Then his owner grabbed Paula's chin. That was what Megan had done to him, just before she pulled the painful sticks out of his nose. Shack cocked his head sidewise to try to see better. Did Paula have pointed needles in her nose also? He hadn't seen any when he met her getting out of her car. Hey, where was that cupcake that Megan left for him? He anxiously looked around the deck, walking in circles. Finally, he spotted it lying on the ground below him. Darn, now it had all that crunchy dirt on it. Shack decided he better go get it before someone else ate it. Casting one final glance at Paula and his master, he decided not to disturb them. He trotted down the side of the house, went out into the yard and circled around to the back to retrieve his snack. His nose was feeling much better. Maybe Megan wasn't so bad after all.

Paula stood up and moved against Clint. She wrapped her arms around him and rested her head on his shoulder. She felt Clint's hard chest against her soft breasts. She felt his heartbeat mingled with hers. Finally she looked up at him and smiled.

"Make love to me?" she whispered.

Clint glanced at the half full can in his right hand. What he wanted at that moment would not come from inside the aluminum can. Slowly, he set the can down on the edge of the banister and leaned his face down toward Paula's. Their lips separated and their tongues sought out each other's. Clint's hands slid under Paula's sweater and felt the warmth of her soft back. Paula's hands sought out the back of Clint's firm thighs. Their breathing became heavier. Clint's hands moved under the front of Paula's sweater and gently pushed her bra up over her breasts. He held them in his large hands and could barely contain his growing urges as he slowly rubbed them.

"Come on," Clint barely spoke.

Clint took her hand in his and led her through the sliding doors and back to his bedroom.

Shack lifted his head and gazed up at the deck above him. His owner and Paula were walking through the sliding glass doors. He wondered where they were going. Hopefully they weren't going to eat all of the leftover cake Paula had brought last night.

* * *

Paula lay naked under the cool sheets. Her head rested on Clint's right shoulder. Her right arm stretched across his chest and her right leg crossed over both of his strong and sweaty legs. Clint's breathing was slow and deep. She stared at the top of the dresser near the window. There was a picture of her sitting on a blanket by the lake. The summer breeze was rustling her hair. She was smiling at the camera. Shack's head was nestled on her lap. Three plates of leftover fried chicken lay scattered on the white blanket spread beneath her. She remembered that day from the previous summer as if it was yesterday. It was a perfect day. A hike in the woods. Failed attempts to catch fish in the lake. A quiet, romantic picnic on the soft, cool grass near the water. An evening sitting on the deck watching the sun settle behind the mountains. And then a night of wonderful lovemaking. She cherished the memories of that day and yearned for more.

Clint took a deep breath and gently stroked her back with his hand.

"Do you love me Clint?" she whispered softly, anxiously awaiting his response. She felt his body tense and his breathing stopped. After what seemed like an eternity, his body relaxed and he exhaled a deep breath.

"Yes, darling, I do love you. I want us to be together forever."

Paula rolled over on top of him. She kissed his belly and his chest. As she moved up his body, she kissed his neck and their lips met. A long, wet and deep kiss caused something to stir in both of them. As she pulled her knees underneath her and sat across his thighs, the sheet and blanket slid off of her. Clint ran his hands up her soft belly and found her large soft breasts. A moan escaped from her throat as he gently lifted her up and slid inside her.

Shack was lying on the deck outside the closed window. He couldn't make out the strange sounds coming from within the walls, but somehow he knew they were not about to make supper very soon. He barked once in annoyance and trotted to the edge of the steps leading down from the deck. With one last glance back toward the window, he descended the steps to go for a swim.

Chapter 10

Vasser, New York
Wednesday September 26, 1979, 9:43 PM

Ruby pulled the big black Suburban to a stop along the sidewalk. He put the keys in his pocket and stared at the dark building two blocks away on the opposite side of the street. No one was on the street. He was about fifteen minutes early for the meeting with Andy Redmond. Andy had fallen into Ruby's web a little over three years ago when a chance meeting between Andy and one of Ruby's "working girls" turned into pay dirt. Andy was looking for a quick night of wonderful bliss. Little did he know what was in store for him when he invited the lovely Candy into his Mercedes and drove off to Candy's two-room apartment. After a successful consummation of their deal, Andy opted to use Candy's bathroom to clean up before going home. As was her normal routine, Candy used this opportunity to check the man's wallet for any interesting information. A picture of a lovely woman and two elementary aged children suggested a close family relationship. Several credit cards, a license to trade on the New York stock exchange floor, membership cards in several exclusive country clubs, and an employee ID card for a Fortune 500 company suggested that Andy was a man of extensive wealth. Candy quickly copied down the address and phone number from an "Emergency Contact" card onto a memo pad she kept in the drawer of her nightstand. When Andy returned from the bathroom, he got dressed and left. His life was about to change.

Ruby watched as the familiar silver Mercedes pulled to a stop in front of the dark abandoned building. Andy got out of the car carrying a brown paper bag and walked alone into the building. The man was about 5' 5" tall and wore an expensive gray suit. Despite having lost weight over the last couple of years, he was still overweight. The bald spot on the top of his head had expanded, and what hair remained had turned a salty-gray color.

After waiting another ten minutes to make sure Andy had come alone, Ruby got out of his vehicle and walked toward the building. He checked to make sure the 44 Special was still tucked in the waistband in the small of his back. Andy was a spineless human being, but everyone had a breaking point. Ruby had to be cautious. As he approached the door, the light from the street lamp outside illuminated the man standing in the middle of the room holding the paper bag.

Ruby opened the door and stepped inside.

"Greetings Andy."

The man standing in front of him was silent. In past meetings of this nature, the man had visibly shaken as Ruby approached. Beads of sweat would collect on his forehead. His green eyes would dart around nervously. This time he was stone still. Something was different.

"You...worthless...no-good scumbag."

At that, the man dropped the bag on the floor and pointed a large pistol at Ruby. It was too dark for Ruby to see what kind of gun it was, but it didn't matter. At this close range, any caliber weapon would end Ruby's life.

"Hey man, what are you doin'? Are you nuts?"

"Am I nuts?" Andy shouted. "You have stolen over $500,000 from me over the last three years and you have the nerve to call me nuts? What did I ever do to you? I had one weak moment and sought some intimate sexual contact with another woman when my wife was going through some depression, and you have ruined my LIFE! No more! You will NOT live one more day to ruin another person's life."

Now Andy began to shake. The gun, heavy in his hand, began to move in small circles. Tears began to stream down his cheeks.

"I had a wonderful family. A successful business. A comfortable life. My kids' education was paid for no matter where they wanted to go to school. Now, because of you, I can't even look at my wife and kids. My wife is practically suicidal. My kids are barely passing in school. You've ruined it ALL! But no more. My life is over. So is yours. I know you don't think I'm smart, but I am. I AM!"

Andy began to walk back and forth. The gun remained pointed in Ruby's direction, but Andy's hand was growing weaker from its weight. His whole arm was shaking now. Ruby needed a little more time.

"Okay. Okay. You're right man. I got too greedy. I should of thought more of your family. I'm sorry. Tell you what. You keep that hundred grand. We're done. I promise you'll never hear from me again. I'll – "

"SHUT UP! It's too late. You've already taken everything. I'm not dumb. I'll never be rid of you until I kill you. So that's what I'm going to do. I'm sure you have a gun too somewhere on you. After I kill you, I'll use your gun to kill myself. The cops will figure it out. You were blackmailing me. I shot you, you shot me. I even put a letter in my safe deposit box with your name and description. My wife will get the insurance and their lives will get back to normal. See, I'm not dumb . . . One lousy night with Carmel or Candy or whatever her name was . . ."

Ruby inched closer. He couldn't reach for his gun for fear it would push Andy to pull the trigger. Ruby didn't think Andy could do it. He had to get Andy to doubt himself.

"You dumb shit," Ruby tried. "How you gonna shoot yourself with my gun. Put it to your head? There'll be powder residue on your hands. The insurance company will determine it was a suicide and then your stupid wife and kids won't get any of your insurance."

Andy stopped at the remark. He hadn't figured on that. He couldn't leave his family with nothing. He looked down, uncertain now of how smart he was. He had never been involved in anything like this in his life. How had he gotten into this mess?

Ruby moved swiftly toward Andy, keeping to his side, away from the waving gun. A shot rang out and it tour through the sleeve in Ruby's jacket. Ruby grabbed the hot weapon and twisted it from Andy's hand. Ruby used it as a club and pounded Andy's head with it. Rage overcame Ruby and he continued to beat Andy until he crumpled to the floor.

A few moments later, when Ruby's breathing came back to normal, he stared at the lifeless body lying on the cold floor. Andy's skull had been smashed in and blood and gray matter lie all around him.

"Shit!"

This was the second murder Ruby had committed. One had been a physical cripple and one had been a mental cripple. Andy may have been a brilliant investor, but he was way out of his league dealing with prostitutes and street punks. Now, a letter in a safe deposit box was probably going to put the heat on Ruby. He needed to get away, but he needed some time to get things in order.

Ruby stuffed the bloody gun into the front of his waistband and searched Andy's jacket pockets for his car keys. When he had them, Ruby pulled Andy's limp body into an empty storage closet. He didn't bother cleaning up the mess. All he needed was a couple of days, and it would probably be a week or more until some bum happened into this building and caught a whiff of the decaying body. Ruby grabbed the paper bag and opened it. The money was in the bag, just as Ruby had expected. Even Andy hadn't been sure he was going to be able to go through with murder.

Ruby ran out of the building and got in Andy's car. For a moment, he contemplated keeping it and taking it back to the Post. They could take it apart or paint it and sell it, but that was too risky. He drove it about ten blocks away and parked it. He left the keys in the ignition. With a little luck, some other street gang would find it and steal it. That might even help divert the police away from him. Yeah, that would work out just fine. All he needed to do was get away for awhile until things cooled down. Too bad he couldn't get at the letter, but he didn't have the connections to pull that off.

Ruby ran back to his vehicle and got in. As he drove back to the Post, a plan began to form. It would mean giving control of his little gang to Speedy for a while, but he would deal with that later. He had stashed enough cash away to last a while. Speedy thought he was "management" material, but he really wasn't. By the time Ruby came back to re-claim his position of authority, the other three would be more than willing to follow Ruby again. He just needed a few months.

Chapter 11

Jason walked quickly down the street toward the hangout of Ruby and his small gang. He crossed the street and slowly approached the dark building. He had watched the small group leave over 30 minutes earlier. From the pieces of conversation he had heard, he figured they would be gone for at least a few hours. It was time to find a way to give Ruby what he deserved. He didn't have enough money to buy a gun, and even if he did, all the sources he knew of got their merchandise from Ruby. If some homeless person bought a gun, it was sure to get back to Ruby somehow. He could probably steal one from a store in the neighborhood, but that would only extend Oscar's misfortune into someone else's life. No, the only way to get a gun was going to be from Ruby himself. That would provide even more satisfaction - to kill Ruby with one of his own guns.

Jason knew all the doors and windows on the ground floor were bolted, locked and secured with some type of security system. He had to get up to the second or third floor. He stopped short of the building and turned down the alley. There was no fire escape or anything that he could use to climb up to a higher level. He circled the building and came back to the front street. He turned around and thought. There had to be a way. He gazed back down the narrow alleyway from which he had just come. He tilted his head up to look at the top of the building. The roof of Ruby's building was at the same level as the one next to it.

Quickly, Jason entered the building to the right of Ruby's. This door was standing open half way. He turned on his small flashlight (one of his few possessions) and cautiously started up the stairs. He could sense rats and other rodents scampering out of his way as he continued his way upwards. He had to move slowly to avoid falling and injuring himself on the pieces of debris that lay in his way. On the third floor he proceeded down a hallway looking for a door that might lead to the roof. About halfway down, he spotted a door that looked different from all the others. He pushed and it opened slightly. With another solid shove, the door swung open enough for Jason to squeeze through. There was another flight of steps leading up. At the top of the steps was a solid metal door with no windows that was locked from the inside and had a chain secured around the crash bar and a lock fastened to the wall. Using his flashlight he moved back down the steps looking for some piece of metal. Finally, in one of the vacant, dirty rooms, he found a three foot long piece of solid piping about a half inch in diameter. He grabbed it and returned to the locked door. Wedging the pipe inside the chain and bracing it against the metal door, he pulled down on the pipe as hard as he could. The old, rusty chain and lock tore loose from the wall and crashed noisily to the floor. Slowly Jason opened the door and stepped out onto the old roof.

The wind whipped his thin jacket around him and bit into his thin body. As he stepped away from the door, the wind slammed it shut behind him. To avoid the wind as much as possible, he got down on his hands and knees and crawled toward Ruby's building. The wind was pushing at him from behind as if trying to shove him over the edge. A foot-high ledge ran all along the perimeter of the building. Jason lifted his head and peered at the building not more that ten feet away. Somehow the space between the buildings looked as wide as the Grand Canyon he had seen in some of his old school books. Ten feet! Jason remembered watching his parent's little old television long ago, before he had gone to Nam. On television the bad guys never had any problem jumping between buildings, as the policemen or detectives gave chase. Even the old detectives in bulky overcoats could easily manage the jump. But that was on TV. This was real. Jason looked down to the dark alley floor below him. So hard. If he missed and fell, he would never survive. No, he had done many stupid things in Vietnam because some sergeant was yelling at him to do it, but he couldn't sum up the courage to make the jump.

Jason fought his way back to the doorway against the pounding wind. With a sense of defeat, he retreated down the steps. On each floor he searched for something that might help him enter Ruby's building. Nothing. As he started to push his way through the door and out onto the street, he saw the large black Suburban come to a screeching halt in front of the building. Jason jumped to the side of the door and crouched down. He listened as the four doors slammed shut.

"You killed him?" a high-pitched voice asked.

"I had to," Ruby's voice answered. "He was gonna kill me. I had no choice."

"And you left his car at Louie's Texaco?" a different voice asked.

"Why do you have to leave, Ruby?" the high-pitched voice asked. "Where you gonna go?"

"Come inside. I'll explain it all again inside. It's freezing out here."

Jason listened to the five sets of feet walk toward Ruby's building. Ruby had killed someone, and he was going to leave. That couldn't happen. Jason hadn't finished his mission. And what was that about a car left at Louie's Texaco? The car must belong to the person Ruby had killed.

Jason knew there was a Texaco station on the corner of 4th and Simpson Streets. He once worked on the loading dock for a carpet manufacturer a couple blocks away. Several times he had stopped at the garage to get a soda or some snacks. He thought the manager who had owned the station was named Louie. It had to be the same place. Maybe, if no other bunch of hoodlums had discovered it yet, Jason could get to it. If he could hot-wire it, maybe he could drive it somewhere and hide it. With a little bit of luck, Jason could find out where Ruby was going and follow him. That would be his best chance. If Ruby was alone, the odds were much better. Maybe he wouldn't even need a gun. Jason had been trained to kill people with his hands as well as with various other weapons. He had to move fast.

Ruby and the others entered their building, turned on the generator-powered lights, and took their usual seats.

"Moose, go – "

"I know, I know. Go check the doors and windows." Moose didn't see the figure trotting past the window.

Ruby sat behind his desk with his head in his hands. He had sketched out a vague plan in his head in the few minutes between leaving the vacant building where Andy's body was stashed and finding Moose and Screech. After rounding up Speedy and Whispers, he had explained briefly what had happened and what he was planning to do. No one had said a word until they had gotten back to the Post and out of the vehicle. Now he needed some quiet to finish formulating his plan.

"What we gonna do?" Screech asked tentatively.

"Shut up. I gotta think."

After a few minutes, Moose returned and sat on the floor with his back against one of the cabinets where a few of their personal weapons were stored. He looked around the room at his silent friends. Finally Speedy spoke.

"How long was you shaking this Andy guy down?"

"A little over three years."

"Three years?" Speedy yelled. "And you never said anything to us about it? How much did you get from him? Why didn't you tell us? You should have known he wasn't going to give in to you forever. That's the stupidest – "

Ruby sprang up from his chair and dove at Speedy. A lightning fast right fist smashed Speedy's nose, and then Ruby planted a hard left in his stomach. Speedy slumped over. Ruby landed an uppercut to Speedy's cheek and he flew backwards off of his chair onto the floor. Speedy moaned in agony, and his eyes watered uncontrollably from the stinging pain. No one moved to help Speedy or to stop Ruby.

Ruby stood up and took several deep breaths. When he regained control, he calmly walked back to his chair. Speedy sat up on the floor holding his bleeding nose and stared at Ruby.

"You know, Speedy, I've had it with your ungrateful, pushy attitude. You think you can run this outfit better than me? Well, now you'll get the chance."

"What?" three separate voices shouted in unison.

"No, Ruby," Screech pleaded. "We don't want Speedy to be in charge." Screech was afraid of Speedy. Speedy was always picking on him, and Ruby and Moose were the only two who ever came to his defense. Screech was thin and wiry. Although his frail physique came in handy when he had to run away from trouble, he couldn't run far within the building. With Ruby gone, Screech would only have Moose to protect him. His brother was a bull of a man, but he couldn't always be around. If Speedy and Screech were alone, there was no telling what Speedy might do.

"You're the man," Whispers softly spoke from his usual place on the couch.

"Yeah," Moose added. "We don't want you to leave either."

"Don't have a choice. Here's what we're gonna do. That pansy Andy said he left a note in a safe deposit box explaining everything, including my name. Maybe he did, maybe he didn't. But I can't take the chance. I didn't tell any of you about my scheme cause then, if anything ever went wrong, you could say you knew nothing. What money I got went into the pot, and all of you seemed to have gotten PLENTY to eat. That satisfy your question, Speedy?"

Speedy silently nodded his head, but the anger in his eyes betrayed his true feelings.

"I gotta take off for a few months. Maybe there was no note. Even if there was, some other punks will probably heist the man's car. I left the keys in it to tempt them. At least that will throw suspicion away from me. If the cops come looking for me, you tell 'em I was with you all night and that I went to visit my uncle in Pennsylvania. You tell them I go there every year to hunt around his cabin."

"But you don't have an uncle, do you?" asked Moose.

"You never went huntin' before," Screech explained innocently. "What you huntin' for?"

"You stupid block of wood," Whispers explained for Ruby. "He's creatin' an alibi. Cops don't know he doesn't have an uncle, nor that he never went huntin' before. Cops can't prove we ain't lyin'."

"They can if they ask who this uncle is and where he lives," Speedy pointed out still directing his penetrating eyes at Ruby.

"I do have an uncle, and he does own a cabin in the mountains in Pennsylvania. It's in some place called

Elkton or Elk Town or Elk Run or something like that."

"How come you never mentioned him before?" Moose asked. "What's his name?"

"I don't know his real name. My father only ever called him Stubs. Said people started calling him that when he got three fingers cut off at the knuckles after a milk can or something fell on his hand. My old man split after high school and came to the city. His brother stayed home, got married and lived happily ever after, I suppose. As far as I know, he's still there. There was no need to mention him, until now. Guess it's time to go pay him a visit. Even if the cops track me down, there should be plenty of places to hide out in the mountains."

"Whatta you know about livin' in the mountains?" Speedy prodded.

"Don't worry about me, Speedy. You better worry about keeping your sorry ass out of trouble. Here's the deal. I'll take enough money to hold me over for a few months, maybe a year."

"A year!" Screech complained. "You're not gonna have to stay away that long, are you?"

Now Speedy turned his eyes toward Screech and smiled.

"Don't worry Screech," Speedy said. "I'll take care of you." A smirk crossed his lips.

"And I'll take care of you, Speedy," Moose spoke, "if anything happens to Screech."

"Nothin's gonna happen to nobody," Ruby cut in. Speedy gets to play king of the jungle while I'm gone.

When I come back, you get to decide who stays top dog."

"I don't want to go to no jungle," Screech complained.

Ruby ignored Screech and focused his attention on Speedy.

"And if the boys want me to step back in, you take a hike."

"How much money you takin'?" Speedy asked not wavering from Ruby's stare.

"Enough."

"When you leavin'."

"I need two or three days to get some things in order. I'll give you access to all the money I leave behind. Of course, I'll tell Moose how much I'm leavin', so that he can help keep an eye on it."

"Why you telling Moose?" Speedy asked, his anger re-surfacing.

"Cause I want to. Of course, I'll take the Suburban too."

"The Suburban?" Speedy complained. "How we suppose to get around?"

"Your smart, Speedy. Figure something out."

Speedy and Ruby glared at each other. Finally Speedy rose up and headed for his room.

"I gotta wash my face."

"You do that."

Screech, Whispers and Moose watched Speedy leave. They turned their heads back to Ruby, but he was already standing up and heading for his room as well.

"Guess it's time to turn in," Whispers spoke softly.

Moose and Screech just looked at each other. Things were not going to be the same.

* * *

Jason used back alleys whenever possible to get to Louie's. They also helped him avoid cops and other street gangs. He wasn't sure which he feared most. The gangs could hand out a beating, but the cops could take him to some shelter or lock him up if they wanted to. He had to get to the car before anyone else found it. He didn't even know what kind of car he was looking for.

Finally, after about 45 minutes of dodging sounds and voices, he spotted a silver Mercedes sitting near the curb a block away from the Texaco station. This had to be the car. No one would purposely park a shiny Mercedes in a neighborhood like this. He walked up the sidewalk across the street from the empty vehicle, keeping as close to the dark buildings as he could. He stopped and looked around. No one appeared to be in sight. Okay, he had found the car. It was waiting for him to take, but where was he going to go with it. He couldn't just leave the city, he had to find out where Ruby was going. He couldn't just park it on the street near his living quarters, Ruby was bound to see it and know something was up. He needed a place to go and think. He couldn't wait much longer. Sooner or later either the cops or another group of thieves would find it. He had to go somewhere. Finally he dashed across the street and tried to open the driver's door. To his surprise, it was unlocked. Sitting down on the plush leather seats, he couldn't believe his eyes when he saw the keys dangling from the ignition. He wouldn't even have to try to hot-wire it. Then he realized this was Ruby's plan. Some unsuspecting person would find the car and think they had just stumbled onto a major piece of luck. Little would they know that the owner of the car lay dead somewhere. Whoever was found with the car would be the prime suspect in the killing. Unfortunately, Ruby hadn't expected Jason to be the one to find it. Jason knew where the car had come from, and he knew he had to go into hiding fast.

Jason reached over and opened the glove compartment. Inside he found a small tool kit with a few common size screwdrivers and a small adjustable wrench. The registration card said the vehicle belonged to an Andy Redmond (now deceased). He also found a small money clip with a couple hundred dollars. Jason slammed the door shut and turned the key. The engine started up. The gas tank was almost full. Jason checked for traffic and pulled slowly out into the street. It had been a long time since he had driven any type of vehicle, and he certainly had never driven a Mercedes. Jason burst into uncontrollable laughter. Jason Shark: broke, homeless, owning only the clothes on his back, was now driving around with two hundred dollars in cash, in a car which must have cost at least twenty grand. Unbelievable.

After a few minutes, Jason began to relax behind the wheel of the beautiful car. The interior and exterior were both spotless. No crumbs or paper on the seats or floor. This Andy person must have been some real neat freak. Turning right, Jason began to move away from the dark center of the city. Since it was almost midnight on a weeknight, not many people were on the streets. Soon office buildings and storefronts gave way to low-middle class row homes. The small, square grassy plots in front of the homes were well kept. No trash littered the steps or small porches. Cars were parked on both sides of the street, leaving just enough room for two cars to pass. Suddenly, a police cruiser turned toward him a couple blocks ahead. Beads of sweat appeared on his forehead. He quickly checked the speedometer. He was only going 35 miles per hour. If he got stopped, he would be in deep trouble. As he approached the next intersection, he turned on his right turn signal, slowed slightly and made the turn. In his rear-view mirror he noticed the police cruiser slow and stop at the intersection. Two sets of eyes turned his way. Then the car moved forward. Had they recorded his license number? He had to move faster.

Making a left turn he continued to move away from the city. Just as he was approaching the entrance to Interstate 290, which would take him out into the countryside, he had an idea. Stepping on the brakes, he pulled over to the curb and put the car in park. Opening the glove compartment, he took out the small tool kit, opened his door and darted across to the other side of the street. No lights were on in any of the houses. Kneeling down behind a black Ford, 4-door sedan, he took out a screwdriver and removed the license plate. Looking around to make sure no one was watching, he ran to the back of the Mercedes and exchanged the plates. As he was about to return to the Ford, he noticed an older man walking a dog turn the corner and start down the street toward the car without a license plate. He wouldn't have time to put the Mercedes' plate onto the BMW. Jumping into the running car, he pulled out and turned right, down a narrow side street. Slowly cruising around the block, he came back to the street on which the Ford sat. He could just barely see the man and dog approaching the plate-less automobile. He watched breathlessly as the man and dog stopped one vehicle away from the Ford. The dog raised his right leg and marked his spot on a cold, metal signpost announcing something about street cleaning. When the dog finished, the two of them started jogging down the street, away from Jason and past the Ford. Jason expelled the air that he had been holding inside him. When the man and his best friend were out of sight, Jason pulled out into the street and pulled up to the curb across from the Ford. Grabbing the screwdriver and license plate, he jumped out of his car and ran back to finish what he had started. Returning to the Mercedes, he pulled out and continued toward the interstate.

Heading west, he pushed the speedometer up to 55 and continued away from the city. After about twenty minutes, he took Exit 50A and continued west on Route 90. After another twenty minutes, the adrenalin gone, his eyes began to get tired. He had to find some secluded spot to park the car where he wouldn't be bothered. He took an exit onto a two lane state road. Finally, after about thirty minutes, he spotted a narrow dirt road with a sign that read "Italian Lake". Turning down the road, dust quickly clouded his view. Before he reached any body of water, he spotted an opening on the left side of the road that was surrounded on three sides by overgrown bushes and trees. He backed in, turned off the engine and got out. After stumbling over tree roots and tall clumps of grass, he reached the back of the car. He was parked about twenty feet off the dirt road. Finding some loose branches, he covered the hood as best he could. Anyone who came down the road would surely find the car, but at least he was somewhat hidden from anyone who might use the road for a turnaround. Judging by the lack of tire tracks on the road, it wasn't used much, but he couldn't stay here much past daylight. He climbed into the backseat and lay down. He had more room to stretch out inside his cardboard home on the street, but the cushions underneath him felt much more comfortable than the hard concrete.

As the sounds of the woods began to penetrate his new home, he thought about his dilemma. He had a brand new Mercedes that belonged to a dead man and two hundred dollars in cash. He had to get back to Ruby's place to find out where he was going. He now had the means to follow Ruby wherever he went, but what was he going to do with the car until he discovered where that was.

Chapter 12

Elk Run, Pennsylvania
Thursday September 27, 1979 9:17 AM

Clint rolled over on his side and opened one of his eyes to find the clock. The digital numbers read 09:17. Paula had probably left over three hours ago, to return home and get ready for school. He hadn't heard her get up or get out of bed. After their second frolic in the large bed, Clint had slept like a baby. Now he was famished and full of energy.

He threw back the covers and swung his legs onto the floor. With a bounce in his step, he entered the large bathroom and took a long, hot shower. Today was going to be a great day. He could feel it. After drying off, he put on a clean pair of jeans and a dark green flannel shirt. He would treat Shack to a big breakfast and then take a walk around his property. Several weeks ago, Stubs had spotted a coyote moseying around an old chicken coop he had on his property. Clint didn't much care for these animals. There weren't many around, but if they weren't eliminated, they would continue to populate. That wasn't good for the deer herd. He doubted he would get too close to the scavenger, especially with Shack tagging along, but he would take his deer rifle with the scope. Perhaps he would get a long shot at him. The sun was shining through the patio windows as he walked into the kitchen.

Moving through the dining room, Clint pushed open the glass door and stepped out onto the deck. He heard shack's paws padding on the wooden surface as he came up the side of the house.

"Shack," Clint yelled as the big dog came around the corner.

Shack stopped in his tracks and lowered his head. Whenever his owner yelled like that, it usually meant he was in trouble. He couldn't remember doing anything bad, but then sometimes it was hard to figure out what people thought was good or bad. He laid down on the deck and waited for his owner to say more.

"Shack, you old mutt. Ya hungry? How 'bout some breakfast?"

Shack's head popped up at the question. Of course he was hungry. He was always hungry in the morning. Such a stupid question. Shack trotted up to his owner and sat down in front of him, awaiting further instructions.

"Come on, how 'bout some bacon and eggs. Then we'll take a walk and look for Mr. Coyote."

Shack's mouth started to drool at the sound of eggs and bacon. He wasn't overly excited about the coyote part, but the food sounded good. He led his owner back through the glass doors to the kitchen.

After a meal of bacon and eggs and toast, Clint retrieved his rifle and shells from the cabinet in the basement. He then filled his jacket pockets with packs of beef jerky and a couple wrapped packages of cupcakes. The pair went out the basement door and headed southwest. They crossed the dirt road that connected the main road to the grassy picnic area and circled the empty field. By the time they reached the northern end of the field, they had jumped two pheasants, three rabbits and a grouse, but saw no signs of any four-legged animals. Shack looked sadly at Clint when the grouse flew out, reminding him of the poor showing he made the other day with Megan. A wide path wound north from the grassy area into the woods. At the base of the mountain, the path disappeared. Clint picked up a deer path that veered off to the northwest and headed toward Stubs' home. About five hundred yards from Stub's property line, they entered the dense, swampy area. The underbrush became thicker and the thin saplings all but prevented their progress. The ground became mushy from water that seeped to the surface. Shack followed closely behind his big owner, letting the man break through the brush and create a small path. Finally, Shack got tired of getting swatted in the snoot with branches and having sharp briars bite into his wet paws. He barked once requesting a stop to this foolish idea.

Clint turned and smiled at Shack. "Things getting a little too rough for you?"

"Humph," grunted Shack. Shack turned and looked to the right where the mountain was steeper, but less thick.

Just then, there was a rustling in the brush, and a twig snapped directly in line with the path they had been following. Both Clint and Shack froze. A low growl escaped from Shack's throat.

"Quiet Shack," Clint whispered. Shack laid down on the prickly ground, but didn't move or make a sound. Clint bent down on one knee and turned back to face the sound. His rifle was slung over his right shoulder. He didn't move. He calmed his breathing and peered through the dense brush trying to pick out something that appeared out of place: movement, a pair of eyes, brown or black fur, a glint of sunlight from a buck's antlers, anything. The woods were silent and still.

Clint had learned to be patient in the woods many years ago. It had often paid off. He knew something had made the noise he had heard. Whatever it was, he knew it was something big. No small animal would have made that much noise. Finally, after about ten minutes, he saw something move about fifty yards in front and to the right of him. It was only one thin leg. The brush covered most of the animal, but Clint had seen enough to know it was a deer. He continued to gaze in the direction of the movement. Between two trees, Clint spotted part of a massive set of antlers. He couldn't get a firm count, but the rack on the male deer was at least two feet across. Now he could faintly hear the thick horns clicking and scraping against the thin saplings and brush. The deer was practically crawling along the forest floor. What a beautiful sight.

After a half hour of watching the massive creature fight its way through the dense and wet area, Clint stood and turned to Shack. "Come on boy, no coyote in here. Just grandpa buck."

Clint led Shack off to the northeast, around the dense area and up the side of the mountain. Half way up the side, Clint stopped and knelt down to peer at the soft ground. Coyote tracks. Two sets led toward the northwest, around the side of the mountain and above the swampy area where they had seen the large buck. Clint stood and stared in the direction the tracks led. Shack walked up beside him and sat down. Shack's nose nudged the jacket pocket that contained the cupcakes. The sun was high in the sky, but the cool breeze sent a chill through Clint as it found the damp T-shirt that was soaked with sweat from the earlier exertion.

"Okay, buddy. Let's take a break."

Shack barked once in agreement and waited for his snack. As Shack devoured his chocolate, Clint chewed on the hard jerky. Clint rested with his back against a tree and gazed around the forest. The woods were full of surprises. The grand buck in the swamp. Coyotes roaming the mountaintops. Pheasants and rabbits in the fields. Just a short distance behind him, Shack had gotten his surprise from the porcupine. Grouse hid beneath the brush to jump out in front of you when you got too close. In the past, he had seen the occasional black bear and fox. He wanted to share all of that with Paula. Would she get the same joy that he did? Somehow he doubted it. But, no relationship was perfect. Maybe he could help with her classes and bring some of the more able kids up into these woods, and they would receive the same joy that he did. If he couldn't share that with Paula, at least he could try to share it with her kids. Clint took a deep breath.

"Come on Shack. Time to get back to the hunt."

Shack rolled onto his back, stretched and spread his four legs in opposite directions. That felt so good. Shack wished he could eat the other cupcake he had seen his owner put in his pocket but knew it would be a waste of time trying to get it. He rolled over onto his feet and shook the loose dirt and leaves from his body. He would have to take a nice bath in the lake when they got back.

Clint led the way around the side of the mountain, following the tracks as best he could. They circled all the way around the front of the mountain. On the other side they headed up to the top. The two sets of tracks were heading southeast, toward the old cabin Clint had pointed out to Megan. Megan. She probably would have loved to be along on this excursion. As they neared the old cabin, at least six deer sprinted down the side of the mountain in front of them, leaping over bushes and fallen trees in their path. The coyote tracks led directly to the abandoned cabin. Clint slowed his pace, his eyes darted back and forth, focusing on the area approximately one hundred yards in front of him. Silently he moved up the steep incline. Shack, sensing something different, also slowed his pace. As the cabin came into view, about two hundred yards ahead, Clint slowly swung his rifle off his shoulder. A movement had caught his attention. Clint dropped to one knee and turned around to face Shack.

"Stay!" commanded Clint in a soft, but firm whisper.

Shack didn't have to be told twice. He was tired from the steep climb. He rolled onto his side and closed his eyes.

A slight wind was coming toward Clint, hiding his scent from whatever was up ahead. Avoiding small twigs and dry leaves, he slowly crept forward. As he raised his head above a slight mound, he saw the two animals about seventy-five yards ahead. They were concentrating on something on the ground. Clint watched them take turns ripping pieces of fur and red skin from a mangled dead animal lying between them. He moved to a small tree just a few feet to his left and quietly leaned his back against it. Bracing his legs on the ground and his elbows on his knees, he raised the gun to his shoulder. Through the scope, he could see the two coyotes clearly. He put his sights just behind the shoulder blade of the bigger of the two animals. He inhaled and flipped the safety off. Slowly he expelled his breath. He squeezed the trigger.

Boom! The rifle recoiled after throwing the 308-caliber bullet at the unsuspecting animal. The big animal dropped immediately. The smaller animal jumped off its feet and away from his partner. Without waiting to see if his friend was coming, the remaining coyote tore through the woods, away from the cabin, up over the top of the mountain and down toward the swampy brush.

Clint swung his rifle toward the running animal, but it was out of view before he could set his sights on it. Clint jumped up and walked quickly toward the prone animal. As he stood over it, Clint wondered if Megan could have made that shot. Probably. Clint turned back down the mountain and searched for Shack. Finally, he saw the dog peek his head out around a boulder.

"Come on Shack, the coast is clear."

Shack slowly walked toward his owner and whatever had caused him to fire that darn loud gun. Shack wished they made guns that were quieter. The surprising noise had made him pee all over his leg. Now he would surely have to go for a swim in the lake. As Shack came up to his owner, he looked down at the brown and red furry clump. He guessed that, at one time, it had been a rabbit. It wasn't a rabbit anymore. Then Shack looked at the coyote. It looked like any other dog to him, but Shack couldn't understand why this type of dog was always killing things and eating them. He was glad his owner had shot the mean animal. That way, the coyote would never get a chance to eat him. Shack proudly looked up at Clint and barked three times in congratulations.

"Yeah, well, if you get the chance, make sure you tell Megan how good I am."

Shack cocked his head to the side, trying to figure out what the man was saying. When Clint offered no further explanation, Shack glanced one last time at the dead animal with the hole in its side, and wandered toward the deserted cabin. He was sure the loud noise and the two dead animals had scared any other predators away from the area.

Clint watched Shack meander toward the cabin and then looked down at the lifeless coyote.

"At least that's one less pest in these mountains."

Clint took off his jacket and removed some plastic gloves from the pocket. The gloves covered the sleeves of his shirt, up to his elbow. Taking his knife from its sheath, he began to field dress the dead coyote. When he was finished, he took off the gloves, now dripping with blood, and put them in another clear plastic bag. Securing the bag, he put that in his jacket pocket and removed a ten-foot length of heavy rope. After securing the rope around the animal's neck, Clint put his jacket back on and began hauling the coyote up the mountain. He would have liked to check out the cabin, but the sun was starting to descend. It would be dark in an hour or two, and he had a fairly long way to drag the heavy animal. He wanted to get home in time to shower, change and hang the animal in the meat locker in the basement of the bunkhouse. Clint had installed the locker to give his guests a place to hang their game in order to keep it cold before they took it home to be butchered. Clint would probably offer the meat to Stubs. Stubs was one of the few people Clint knew who actually liked coyote meat. Maybe Paula would come over to celebrate his success. If they celebrated like they had the night before, Clint would be one happy puppy.

"Let's go Shack," Clint yelled.

Shack came around the back of the cabin and looked at his owner pulling the dead animal up the mountain. Shack decided to stay in front of Clint and lead the way home. He didn't want his owner getting any strange ideas about tying the end of that rope around Shack's neck, and having him pull the heavy load back to the house. That looked like hard work. Even if his owner offered him the remaining cupcake, Shack wasn't going to fall for that trick.

Shack led the way back to the house, and they arrived just as the sun was setting. Clint went directly to the meat locker, washed out the insides of the animal and hung it on one of the empty hooks.

"Some help you were, you worthless mutt."

"Arf."

"Go for a swim in the lake and clean yourself up. When you're done, I'll put some big steaks on the grill, bake some potatoes and invite Paula over for supper. Now get!"

Shack didn't catch all of what his owner had said, but he figured it involved swimming in the lake, eating, and Paula. Shack ran as fast as he could and jumped as far out into the lake as he could. He didn't want to miss the steak and potatoes.

Clint was whistling as he entered the basement door. This was going to be a great evening. His stomach began to growl as he thought of the juicy steaks simmering on the grill. In the bathroom of the basement, he removed his dirty and somewhat bloodstained clothes and put on an old robe he kept there for just such occasions. Running up the steps to the kitchen, he was in one of the best moods he had been in for awhile. He grabbed the phone off the hook and dialed Paula's number from memory. After four rings, her soft voice came out of the answering machine.

"I can't come to the phone right now. Please leave a message after the beep. I'll return your call as soon as I can."

"Hi beautiful. I bagged a coyote today with Shack. Not that he was much help bringing it back to the house. How 'bout you come over, and I'll cook some big steaks on the grill. Come over as soon as you can. I'm going to shower and change. Love you. Bye."

Clint took his second shower of the day and put on clean clothes. It was going on seven o'clock, and he was getting really hungry. He wasn't sure how much longer he could wait. The ringing of the phone took his mind off his stomach.

"Hello," Clint answered.

"Hi Clint, it's Megan."

That's not who Clint was expecting.

"Oh, hi. How are you doing?"

"I'm sorry, am I catching you at a bad time?"

"No. No. I was expecting someone else." Boy, that was a stupid thing to say, Clint thought.

"Oh, well, I just called to see how you were doing and thank you for the nice day yesterday. I hope you don't mind that I called."

"No, not at all. Actually, I'm glad you did. Now I can gloat a little."

"Gloat about what? Did you finally bag a one-legged bird that was caught in a vine?"

"No, wise guy. I shot a coyote today up on the other side of the mountain near that old cabin I showed you yesterday."

"No kidding!" Megan responded excitedly. "Wow, that's neat. Was it old and full of arthritis so it couldn't run away?"

Clint laughed at the easy banter the two were able to exchange.

"Well, it was standing still. And it was preoccupied eating the remains of a dead rabbit. But it was a hundred yard shot up hill." Clint felt the need to stretch the distance just a little.

"That is truly neat-oh. I am definitely impressed. So, you in the mood to celebrate? I'm not working tonight. I'll even treat the great white hunter."

A vehicle coming down the dirt driveway sounded in the background.

"Oh, I'd really like that, but I've, ah, kinda got plans for tonight."

"Oh," Megan sounded disappointed.

Clint hesitated momentarily, pondering his next words.

"Can I take a raincheck?" Clint didn't want to end the conversation like this, but he also didn't want to be on the phone with Megan when Paula came in.

"Sure, no problem. Congratulations on your kill. I'll talk to you later. Bye."

"Bye." With that, the dial tone greeted him. Why was he so disappointed?

Clint hung up the phone and headed toward the front door. A loud knock sounded. That was odd, Paula never knocked. Maybe she was being cautious after learning of his trek in the woods with Megan. Guess he couldn't blame her. He opened the door with a big smile. Then it disappeared.

"Well, guess you weren't expectin' me. Perhaps you was expectin' some young lassie with big, dark eyes and a short skirt?"

"No, Stubs. Actually, I was expecting Paula. You don't look like her either."

Stubs stuck out his chest as far as he could.

"How 'bout now?"

"Wrong color hair."

"Come in, come in. What are you doing here? Not that I mind. I'm glad you are. We should get together more often."

"I don't want to come between two hot lovers. You sure I'm not intrudin'?"

"Heck no, it doesn't look like Paula's coming anyway. You hungry for some steaks? I'm famished."

"Hey, I never turned down no steaks. Got any potatoes?"

"You read my mind. Tell you what. You grab a half dozen potatoes out of the frig and get them in the oven and I'll go get the grill ready. I got a whopper of a story to tell you."

Well, it wasn't the evening he had expected, but he was excited to tell Stubs about the hunt. They would probably swap hunting stories long into the night and kill at least a half case of beer. Maybe it would be a celebration after all, just not the kind he expected. He had even turned down an evening with Megan to spend with Stubs. Boy, what was the world coming to?

Chapter 13

Vasser, New York
Thursday September 27, 1979 9:30 am

The pain in his arm was excruciating. He tried to cry out, but no sounds came from his dry throat. His legs were tied tightly beneath him and he felt the hard barrel of the gun against his head. A bright light was shining in his face, but all he saw was darkness from his swollen eyes. Then he began to fall. Down, down until finally he landed with a thump on a soft floor. Something hard smashed against his stomach and he awoke with a start. Tossing and turning Jason grabbed at whatever was holding his legs together. Finally, he yanked the jacket away from his legs and sat up. As he focused on the roof of the car, the seat from which he fell, and the back of the seat in front of him, he began to remember where he was and what had happened the night before. The pain he had felt subsided as the blood finally rushed through his arm that had been clamped beneath him on the soft seat. Eventually he was able to maneuver back to the seat and open the door. Bright sunlight almost blinded him as he stepped outside.

Walking a few yards into the woods, Jason emptied his full bladder as he glanced around him. Apparently no one had come down the road and spotted him, but it wasn't safe to stay here much longer. Before he had gone to sleep the night before, he had started to form a plan. He just needed a little more time.

Moving back to the car, Jason quickly tore all of the branches and brush away. He got into the driver's seat and drove out onto the dirt road. Instead of going toward the main road, he turned left and headed down the dirt path toward the body of water the sign had advertised as "Italian Lake". Soon, he came to the lake and spotted a small parking area to the right. He pulled into one of the spaces and backed up as close to the water as he could. Turning off the motor, he took the keys and went around to the back. Taking a bath in the cold lake was not something he was looking forward to, but, if his plan was going to work, he couldn't be running around the city smelling like a bum. He couldn't do anything about his clothes, but he'd have to worry about that later. Taking off his shirt, he looked around for a clean place to put it. Dirt and mud surrounded the car. He pulled the keys out of his pants pocket and fumbled for the one that would open the trunk. He lifted the lid. The carpet inside was as clean as the upholstery in the car. Then he spotted a small black overnight bag. Hesitating for a moment, he finally opened it. He couldn't believe what was inside. Tearing open the zipper on the small toiletry compartment, he found a half cake of soap in a soap dish, deodorant, a small bottle of shampoo from some hotel chain, two disposable razors, and a small can of shaving cream.

Looking in the other compartments, he found a sewing kit, three Q-tips, two packets of condoms, four Band-Aids and a small pair of scissors. He debated how much time he had and decided to take a chance.

Taking the scissors to the front of the car, he adjusted the side-view mirror and bent down so he could see himself as best he could. His dark hair had grown long over both ears and down the back of his neck. As quickly as he could, he gave himself a reasonable haircut. It certainly wasn't professional, but, when he was done, he looked more like someone who should be driving a Mercedes than he had before. Using the scissors, he cut as much of his beard off as he could.

Jason returned to the trunk and rummaged through the rest of the contents of the black bag. There were two white dress shirts, two pairs of underwear, two white T-shirts, two pairs of dark blue socks, a pair of dark blue pants, and a black belt. He held the pants up to him. They appeared to be at least two sizes too big. On the bottom of the bag, he found a white terry robe with a big "H" printed on both pockets (apparently another gift from some hotel) and a pair of slippers. His excitement was growing with each second. The sun was rising higher in the sky, but the cold air reminded him of the fact that snow would soon be falling.

Jason pulled off the rest of his clothes and tossed them into the trunk. He grabbed the soap dish, shampoo, can of shaving cream and one of the disposable razors, and started toward the water. His bare feet found every small stone in his path. Stopping, he returned to the trunk and pulled out the slippers. Putting them on his feet, he re-traced his steps. As his thin ankles hit the frigid water, the shock pushed all the air out of him. Better to get it over quickly. Leaving the shaving cream and razor on the bank, he ran into the water until it was up to his waist and then sat down on the rocky, muddy bottom and let the water wash over him. Standing up and holding the soap dish in his left hand, he squeezed half the shampoo onto his head and tossed the small plastic container away. He vigorously scrubbed his head. Again he ducked under the water and tried to rinse the soap out of his hair. After washing and rinsing his hair as best he could, he concentrated on soaping and rinsing the rest of his body. The cold air and lake water, along with the threat of someone else visiting the lake, pushed him to move as fast as he could.

When he had cleaned himself as best he could, he returned to the bank for the shaving cream and razor. Smearing the cream over his face, he returned to the frigid water. He was beginning to shake from the cold air that penetrated his thin, wet body. After removing the remains of his beard, he tossed the razor away and took one last dunk in the lake. Gasping, he jumped up and walked as quickly as he could back to the shore.

Goose bumps sprang up all over his body and his teeth began to chatter. The bright sunlight didn't do much to warm him. Reaching the back of the car, he grabbed the robe and began to wipe the cold water from his body. Drying himself as well as he could, he began to put on the previous owner's clothes. They were definitely too big, but that didn't bother him. Living on the streets, one never could be too picky about what one wore. Hopefully, no one would look too close. Finally, removing the soaked slippers, he dried his wet feet and removed as much of the mud as he could. He put on both pairs of socks and then put on the black shoes. They were still too big, but the extra pair of socks took up most of the spare room. Tying them tightly, he stood up. He couldn't wear his old jacket on top of the white shirt and dress pants. He'd have to worry about that later also. Quickly, he looked into the other compartments of the black bag. In one, he found two ties, both red with different blue figures on them. He hadn't tied a tie since he went to his first high school dance. He did as best he could. In another pocket, he found another two hundred dollars in cash. This guy must have been a pretty rich traveler.

Jason made sure all his old clothes were in the trunk and closed the lid. Taking the keys from the trunk, he got back into the driver's seat, started the car, adjusted the side mirror and headed back up the dirt road. Making sure no one was coming, he made a left turn and headed back toward the interstate and the city.

About ten miles outside of the city, he found what he was looking for: a Park-n-Ride with a bus stop. Turning off the exit ramp, he headed into the parking area. Jason cruised up and down the aisles until he located an empty space between two other cars in the middle of the crowded lot. He carefully backed the car into the spot. His heart was racing now. The car would be safe here until later this evening. He wasn't sure what he was going to do tonight, or tomorrow, or the next day. Hopefully, he would find a way to figure out where Ruby was going before the cops started looking for the car. Perhaps they were already looking.

Jason reached into the glove compartment and pulled out the money clip. Flipping through the bills, he pulled out two ten-dollar bills and two twenty's. He put the loose bills in his right pocket and the clip with the remaining money in his left. Taking a deep breath, he took the keys out of the ignition, stepped outside and locked the doors. Slamming the door shut, he walked toward the bus stop. He tugged up his pants and tightened his belt one notch as he felt them start to slide down his waist. The cold air seeped through his shirts. The enclosed area for bus patrons provided some protection from the cold air. He checked his watch and couldn't help smiling. He had keys to a Mercedes, $200 in cash in his pockets and a cheap watch on his wrist that he had rescued from a dumpster a couple of weeks ago. He scanned the bus schedule taped to the side of the small booth. It was 10:15 am and the next bus was scheduled to arrive in fifteen minutes. Jason sat down on the cold, dirty bench and waited. After about twenty minutes, in which he had checked his watch at least a dozen times, he stood and began pacing back and forth.

Finally he heard the sound of a diesel engine coming down the ramp toward the parking area. A few hundred yards behind it was a state police cruiser. The bus was getting closer, but so was the police vehicle. He debated running between two of the cars and hiding. Another bus would be here in thirty minutes. What if the bus driver had seen him sitting in the booth? What if the police saw the Mercedes and began searching the lot? The bus got closer, Jason paced faster. It was too late. The bus was turning down the aisle toward the booth.

The driver was staring directly at him. He couldn't run. The police car swung down the aisle before the one the bus was taking. It would pass directly in front of the Mercedes. Jason glanced at the bus driver and then at the police vehicle. The trooper driving the car was watching him. What would he think of a man in a white shirt and tie with no coat on a cold fall morning? Jason couldn't wait any longer. With sweat beading on his forehead, he stepped up to the open bus door. At least the bus was blocking the trooper's view of Jason.

Stepping into the bus, Jason pulled two bills from his right pocket. He picked out the ten and handed it to the driver. The large, overweight man behind the big steering wheel looked over Jason, taking in the too-large clothes and absent coat.

"No change," stated the driver.

Jason looked at the ten-dollar bill and smiled.

"No problem, keep it." Jason had never in his life given a bus driver an eight dollar tip for a two dollar fare. "I was running so late, I forgot my suit jacket. The day can't get much worse."

The driver took the bill in his dirty hand and stared again at the bulky clothes. "Looks like you put on the wrong clothes too." It was a question more than a statement.

"Yeah, well, I, ah . . . lost over thirty pounds in three weeks. Haven't had time to go shopping."

"Hah!" bellowed the big man. "What's the secret?"

Jason thought. "Well, start with a messy divorce. Then don't eat anything except crackers and bread."

The big man laughed. "Never work. Mavis would skin me alive and, if that didn't kill me, the crackers and bread would. I need my burgers and fries. Take a seat, I'm late."

No problem there. Jason was more than willing to sit out of view of the patrolling police car. The sooner they were on the move, the better. As he plopped in a seat away from the side where the cruiser was, he stole a glance out of the opposite windows. The vehicle had passed the Mercedes, but Jason had not noticed if it had stopped. It was at the end of the aisle and turning toward the aisle in which the bus was stopped. Suddenly, its red, blue and white lights began to flash, and Jason heard the tires squeal. The swerving car shot past the aisle and raced toward the entrance to the interstate. Jason sighed in relief. The driver's eyes met Jason's. Jason lowered his head and contemplated his next move.

He watched the street signs pass by. They were in a section of the city known as the "Strip". The name had nothing to do with nude bodies. Both sides of the street for about ten blocks were lined with various stores and restaurants. They were about a mile from Jason's old home and Ruby's Post. When the bus stopped to pick up a few passengers, Jason got up and moved to the door.

"You work here?" asked the driver as Jason started to get off.

"Ah, no, over a few blocks. I can run over there from here. I'm really late." Jason started to step down onto the pavement and stopped. "What time is the last pickup here to get back to the Park-n-Ride?"

"Seven o'clock. If you miss it, you'll be sleeping on the street with the bums."

Jason started to respond, but caught himself. "Thanks."

He watched the bus roll down the street, then turned and walked the opposite direction. Two blocks later, he found a men's clothing store. He placed his hand in his left pocket and went inside. It had been a long time since he had purchased any new clothes. From the back of the store, an elderly woman approached. The tag on her blouse said "Anna". She didn't appear to be happy to see him.

"Hi," Jason tried. "I left home without my jacket this morning. I think I better buy another one before I freeze my . . . nose off."

Anna checked-out his over-sized clothing.

"We don't take checks here."

"Do you take cash?" Jason asked pulling the wad of bills out of his pocket. "If not, I can go somewhere else."

Anna glanced at the money. "Of course we take cash," Anna quickly blurted. "What can I help you with?"

"First a coat. I need some new suits too, but I'll have to come back later for that. Wanted to make sure I kept my weight off before I bought a whole new wardrobe."

Anna visibly relaxed and led him to a rack of insulated jackets.

Jason picked out a black one that extended below his waist. He checked the price tag.

Anna saw his hesitation. "We have a thirty percent sale on all jackets and sweaters. Pants and shirts are ten percent off."

Jason started to relax. He tried the jacket on. It was too big.

"Here, try this one." Anna handed a similar jacket in the same color. It fit perfectly.

"Okay, I'll take it."

"Very good," Anna smiled. "Anything else?" she asked hopefully.

"No, I think I'll be good for now. Ah, how late are you open tomorrow?"

"Oh, we're only open until five on weeknights. We are open Saturdays from nine until noon."

"Great, I'll try to stop back on Saturday."

Jason paid for the jacket and wore it out of the store. It was almost noon now and he was starving. He was used to going long times without eating, but he couldn't remember when he had last had a sit-down meal inside a warm restaurant. Crossing the street, he went into an Italian pizza place and ordered a large steak sandwich, fries and a large soda. He sat in the booth, eating his food and stared out of the window. He only had about seven hours to try to find out where Ruby was going and get back to the bus stop. He wasn't accomplishing anything here. Finishing the last of his fries and drink, he tossed his trash into a receptacle and returned to the street. Jason started to walk in the direction of Ruby's and then felt the remaining bills in his pocket. He didn't have to walk anymore. Jason hailed a taxi and got into the back seat. Giving directions to the silent driver, he settled back and began to think. Where would Ruby and his gang be at this time of the day?

When the cab was about four blocks from where Jason had directed the driver, he spotted the black Suburban. It was parked along the street facing in the opposite direction.

"Stop right here," Jason shouted. "Stop. Stop now."

"Alright! Alright! Keep your pants on guy. I can't just stop in the middle of the road."

When the cab finally pulled to a stop, Jason tossed a twenty toward the driver and got out of the car. Where was Ruby? The large black vehicle was parked in front of an Army surplus store. Jason crossed the street a block away and slowly walked toward the truck. He looked around for a sign of Ruby's friends. He didn't see anyone he recognized. When he got to the storefront, he slowly peeked around the edge of the building into the store. He saw Ruby and one of his buddies at the counter. Hiking boots and camouflaged clothing was stacked next to the register. They would be coming out soon.

* * *

"Looks like you're planning a long hunting trip," the old man said to Ruby.

"Yeah." Ruby was not in the mood to talk to the old man.

Speedy watched the man add up all the merchandise. Every dollar Ruby spent was less that would be turned over to him. His first order of business would be to change the name of their gang. He never did like it.

"Rubies." Who wanted to be named after a red stone? Something like "Speed Rats" would be much better. He'd get the red stones taken off of the leather jackets and get a picture of a big ugly rat to put in its place. Maybe one with its small mouth open, showing all of its pointy teeth. Yeah, now that was a real name.

"Two hundred fifty four and twenty cents."

"Rip off!" Ruby commented, but threw eight twenty-dollar bills and two fifties across the counter. The old man handed Ruby the change and put all of the items in two large canvas bags. Ruby picked them up and headed toward the door.

"Hey man," Speedy said, "how comes you had to buy all those clothes? Three pairs of pants, five shirts, two coats –."

Ruby shoved the door open and stepped out onto the sidewalk. He dropped the two bags on the street, turned, grabbed the whining man and shoved him up against the door.

"Listen to me, you asshole. I'll spend whatever I want on whatever I want. Understand? If I want to buy two whores to take with me, I'll do that too. For all I know, there won't be a store within a hundred miles of Elk Run. And, if there is, you think their prices will be as cheap as old Herman's there? HUH?"

"Okay, okay. Leave me go."

Ruby threw Speedy to the side. He fell over a scraggly homeless guy wearing a black jacket, a bright red knitted cap and only one scuffed-up black shoe.

"Get off of me, you loser," Speedy shouted. He picked the man up and hit him with a right fist to his face. If he couldn't take his anger out on Ruby, this was the next best thing.

"Come on!" Ruby shouted as he grabbed Speedy's right hand before he could land another right to the bum's face. "We don't have time for this. I gotta get my stuff together and get outta here."

Speedy left the man fall to the ground. Something was familiar about him, but he couldn't quite place him. He turned and followed Ruby to the truck. One more night and then things would be different.

"So, you think your uncle Stubs will be glad to see you?"

Jason watched the two men get into the truck and pull away. He rubbed his right cheek with his hand and jerked the cap that he had grabbed out of the trash, down over his ears. From the opening between the two buildings, he retrieved his other shoe and placed it on his cold foot. Jason turned his head and stared after the departing vehicle. That was going to be the last time Ruby or any of his henchmen were going to lay a hand on him. At least without getting something in return. "Elk Run" must be the place he was heading and someone named "Stubs" was his contact. Now, all he had to do was find a map and take a drive. From the clothes Ruby had bought, Elk Run appeared to be in the mountains somewhere. It sounded like Ruby was going to be leaving tomorrow. Wouldn't he be surprised?

Jason pushed himself off of the cold sidewalk. He pulled the remaining bills out of his pocket and counted them. He had a little over a hundred and ten dollars. Jason opened the door to the Army surplus store and went inside. He would need some different clothes: boots, heavy pants and shirts, T-shirts, gloves. If it was hunting season, he would probably need a camouflaged coat and hat in order to fit in. After checking the prices, he knew he didn't have enough money. The mission a couple of blocks away may have some shirts and pants, and maybe even a coat, but hunting style gloves, boots and hats weren't the normal type of apparel offered by the mission. Finally, he spotted a pair of boots similar to the ones he had been issued many years earlier when he entered the service. They would do. He picked out a hat and a pair of gloves and went to the counter. The old man he had seen waiting on Ruby stood up from where he was straightening boxes of shotgun shells beneath the glass counter.

"Howdy. This all you need?"

"Well, it's not all I need, but it looks like it's all I can afford. Man, I can't believe I used to get these boots for free, and now I have to pay over eighty dollars for them. Should have ripped off old Uncle Sam years ago."

"Hah," the old man laughed. "So, you're a vet?"

"Yeah. Gave the man two years of my life. Guess it coulda been worse. Most of my friends gave him their lives."

"Tell you what, I'll give you my special Vet's discount. Give me sixty for the boots. I'll throw in the gloves and hat."

"Thanks. I appreciate that. Got any discounts on the jackets? I'm thinking about tryin' my luck stalkin' some four legged animals."

"Pushin' your luck, Sport. Army or Marines?"

"Never had much time for pansy-assed jarheads."

"Hah," the old man laughed again. "Right answer. Come here."

The old man led Jason to a rack of jackets. They were thick, warm coats with a mixture of green, brown and orange camouflage. The man picked out one Jason's size, checked the price and held it out to Jason.

"Fifty bucks. Best I can do."

Jason tried on the coat. It fit perfectly. He looked at the boots on the counter and then at the old man.

"I've got a hundred and ten dollars. Can you throw in one of them green canvas bags?"

The old man looked at the man standing before him. His open jacket exposed the pants that were too big and the oversized white shirt with the sloppily tied tie. Two pairs of socks and an old red knitted cap completed his outfit. The clothes probably weren't his. He didn't know where he had gotten a hundred dollars, but that wasn't important to him. The old man's eyes became misty as he looked at Jason.

"My son was in Nam. When he came home, he wasn't the same person. We didn't know who he was, but he wasn't the kind, caring Aaron that he was when he shipped out. People spat on him, called him names, humiliated him. Uncle Sam turned him into a killer and Americans turned their backs on him. He left home a year after he got discharged. I don't know where he is or if he is even still alive. For eighteen years his mother and I tried to protect him and keep him safe. We failed him when it mattered the most."

Jason hung his head. He had heard this story so many times before. He had never thought of the pain and hurt experienced by the fathers and mothers. He

143

had always focused on himself and the others like him, never on the parents. It was one thing to lose a son to death. That was final. There was an end. No matter how hard the loss was to accept, you could at least try to move on. This man's son was not dead or alive. The pain of not knowing must be even greater. Jason lifted his watering eyes to the old man. Without thinking, Jason stepped toward the stranger and embraced him.

"You didn't fail your son. He knows you and your wife loved him and did your best. The system failed us. It's time to stop placing blame and move on."

The two embraced harder as sobs of sorrow for all the lost souls rocked through their bodies. The old man stepped back with his hands on Jason's shoulders.

"Do me a favor, will you young man?"

"Sure."

"Take the items you picked out and the bag. Keep your money and pass it on to someone who needs it more than me. I know it ain't much, but let me help the little I can."

Jason stared at the man. Not since Oscar, had anyone showed him any such kindness.

"Okay," Jason spoke softly. "Thank you."

"Thank YOU."

Jason walked out of the store with his mountain clothes in the green canvas bag. The sun was starting its descent into the western reaches of the city. He checked his watch. He had three hours before he had to catch the bus. There was plenty of time to make it to the mission.

Jason carried the canvas bag with his boots, coat, gloves and hat and headed toward the mission where he had spent so much time getting food and clothes and talking with other lonely, searching individuals. His life was changing. He was now the (illegal) owner of a new Mercedes, over three hundred dollars in cash and warm clothes. He was about to embark on a mission that would take him to some place called Elk Run. He was more excited than he had been in many years. He was finally going to get the chance to make Ruby pay for killing Oscar and smashing their dreams. He didn't really care what happened to him after that. What was important was the mission. In Vietnam, that was always the goal. Focus on the mission. Complete it successfully and you would live to face another one. He never knew what new missions would be presented to him in Nam, either. He was alive again. Fighting for a cause. Perhaps it wasn't any more right than what he had been fighting for in the rice paddies. But he had survived that, hadn't he . . . or had he?

As he neared the mission steps, he pondered the last twelve years of his life. Unable to deal with the humiliation, he had lost jobs, fought, hurt people and eventually ended up a homeless person on the streets. A bum. After a couple of years of hope, when he had known Oscar, Oscar's death had driven Jason back onto the streets. Depressed, alone, and still homeless. Perhaps he had not survived Vietnam after all. Now, somehow, he had gotten another chance. Would he blow this one too? First things first. He needed a few more clothes and a map.

Jason walked up the steps and pushed through the doors. The large room that he entered first contained table upon table of different clothes. Shirts, pants, shoes, coats, belts, winter gloves, underwear, dresses, blouses, bras, panties and much more. All used. Some in such bad condition even the homeless people who had nothing, couldn't bring themselves to wear them. Other tables contained blankets, sleeping bags, umbrellas and other items donated by schools, churches and various organizations. Shelves along the side of the room held soap, shampoo, razors, shaving cream, tampons, and various other toiletry items. It was a department store for the less fortunate. A locked metal box with a thin opening stood next to the door with a sign that said "donations". Most people who frequented this establishment didn't have much money to spend on any of the items. But even the homeless would often put in a few coins if they had them.

A room off to the right held various food items. Canned goods, boxes of cereal, drinks, cookies, candies, bread and more was scattered among the metal shelves. Donations from churches, scouting organizations and other groups were delivered almost daily. The food didn't last long. Women with small children returned each week to fill one or two shopping bags with food. It seemed that no matter how much food came in, it was never enough.

In the back was a large room with about ten tables surrounded by chairs. Volunteers in the kitchen worked from six in the morning to eight at night preparing and cleaning up after meals, three times a day, seven days a week. Sometimes the meals were just watered-down soup and a slice of old stale bread. But it was something.

Jason looked around the room as if he were seeing it for the first time. Father Franklin, who ran the shelter, was working at one of the tables. He was folding and laying out clothes that he removed from paper bags sitting on the floor by his feet.

Jason found the table that contained T-shirts. He picked out three dark shirts that were his size and stuffed them into his green bag. Moving to the table with jeans and other work/play pants, he found a pair of blue jeans, an olive green pair of old Boy Scout pants and a pair of camouflaged hunting pants. These he also stuffed into his bag. Jason finished his shopping spree by taking a couple pair of heavy wool socks, slightly used underwear and various bathroom items.

Jason started toward the door and noticed the box for donations. He felt the bills crumbled in his pocket. Stopping, he turned and walked toward Father Franklin.

"Jason?"

"Hi Father."

"We haven't seen you in quite awhile. How have you been? Looks like you've had a run of good luck." Father Franklin peered at Jason's new black jacket that was slightly tattered from the scuffle with Speedy. He also noticed the stuffed canvas bag, the white shirt and tie, the pants that were bunched up around his waist and the black dress shoes. His hair was cut unevenly just above his ears and slightly below the collar of his jacket. His face was cleanly shaven, at least in most places.

"You working for an Accounting firm now?" Father Franklin asked with a smile.

"No, a law firm," Jason laughed nervously.

"Well, good for you." Father Franklin didn't ask any more questions than he had to. Sometimes not knowing things was better. He knew things on the street were tough, but he didn't look for trouble. Jason had seen Father Franklin, who was a big man, physically throw individuals out on the street if he caught them with drugs or alcohol. The mission was open to anyone, as long as they followed a few simple rules: No fighting. No stealing. No drugs. No alcohol. Jason made up his mind.

"Father," Jason started. "I met an old man who did me a big favor. He also gave me a hundred and ten dollars. He told me to give it to someone who needed it more than he did."

Jason pulled five twenty-dollar bills from his pocket and held them out to the man.

"Can you make sure the right person gets this?"

Father Franklin stared at the money.

"Do you have a job, Jason?"

"No."

"Did someone die or something and leave you their home?"

"No."

"Do you have any other belongings than what's in that bag or what you're wearing?"

"Well, not really."

"How about food? You have food stamps or some stash of food I don't know about?"

"Ah, no."

"Well, then I don't know of anyone else who needs that money any more than you do."

"But, maybe someone needs it to buy something for their kid, or for medicine or, or, something."

"Well, there may be. But, I think whoever gave that money to you, asked YOU to find someone to give it to. Not me."

"But you meet so many more people than me. Surely you can put this money to better use than I could."

"Son, I don't know what is happening in your life, but it appears that you are traveling down a different path than the one you were on just a few months ago. I suspect that God will present you with many opportunities for you to put that money to good use."

Jason stared at Father Franklin and then at the money in his hand. He didn't want this responsibility. He should have just put it in the metal donations box. Then, Father Franklin would have just used it as he saw fit. Now, the responsibility was being given back to him. Reluctantly, he put the money in his pocket. Jason looked at the man that he would probably never see again. Once again, he was experiencing a loss. This man who had devoted his entire life to helping people like Jason, suddenly meant more to Jason than he had ever realized. Now, he was losing another friend.

"I...I'm not a very religious man, Father. I don't know if I even believe in a God. I've seen some pretty bad things. I don't understand how there can be such a loving, caring God, if he allows all those things to happen."

"We all struggle with that question at times. Even me. I can't tell you how God would answer you. All I know is that God put man on earth with the ability to make choices. He wants us to make the right choices and follow the path that He has in store for us. He promises us great riches, if we do. Not earthly riches like money and big homes and good jobs. Heavenly riches like peace and love and comfort and a sense of well being that lives on even in times of pain and suffering and, yes, even in times of confusion and doubt. I believe that He hurts and feels sorrow when we don't make the right choices. But, just like an earthly father who wants to allow his children to find the answers for themselves, He doesn't stop us, at least not usually. We must make the decisions for ourselves. Perhaps you might search more for those things that point to the existence of God, rather than for the things that suggest the non-existence. In the end, though, it all boils down to faith."

Jason danced nervously from one foot to the other. He didn't want to discuss this topic. It was too hard for him to understand. Father Franklin sensed Jason's uneasiness and smiled.

"You are a good person, Jason. Open your eyes and your heart and you will find your answers. God bless you and walk with you."

Jason looked one last time at this man to whom he had never taken the time to listen.

"Thank you Father."

Jason turned and walked toward the door. At the metal box, he stopped. Pulling out the bills, he took one of the twenties and stuffed it in the slot. Then he left the mission for the final time.

Chapter 14

Ruby pulled the truck to a stop in front of their building. He got out and looked around. This street had been his home for several years. He was comfortable here. Despite the confidence he portrayed to the others, he was unsure of what his future would hold. He had enough money stashed away in his bags to last him several years, even if he couldn't find any scams to run in the backwoods town called Elk Run. Hopefully, he wouldn't need to use much of it for awhile, if he could find his unknown uncle Stubs.

Ruby looked up and down the street at the familiar surroundings. He spotted the broken and apparently unused cardboard box of the weak homeless person that used to sleep there. He wondered where he was. He had probably died in some dumpster somewhere. Maybe some other homeless people had beaten him to death. Despite his loathing of the dirty street dweller, he had come to consider him part of the neighborhood. A part to be ignored or stepped on, but part of it nevertheless.

He wondered if there were homeless people in Elk Run. What did he care. He shook his head and followed Speedy into the building.

Screech, Moose and Whispers were in their normal places. Speedy was standing over the large desk, staring at the cushioned chair on rollers.

"Can't wait to get your crummy hands on my chair, can you Speedy?"

Speedy turned to face Ruby, a sly smile creased his face. "Nah, I'm gonna get myself a better one."

"Well, don't spend all your money at one time. Sit over there," Ruby commanded.

The other three watched the exchange. Screech shook his head and looked at Moose. The night before, they had talked about leaving the gang. But neither of them felt they would be able to survive on their own. They considered asking Whispers to join them, but they didn't know if the three of them would fare any better. He never spoke much. He just did what he was told and tried to stay out of Speedy's way. Whispers resembled a bulldog, with a wide face, thick chest and short thin legs. His blond hair hung in long strands down the side of his face and back of his head. His short, crooked nose, which had been broken in many street fights, sat between a pair of penetrating green eyes.

"Screech, " Ruby yelled. "Did you get the paper today?"

"Yeah," Screech answered, jumping out of his chair and handing the morning paper to Ruby.

"Well, anything in it about Andy?"

"Ah…I…ah…you know I can't read much."

"Jeeze, Screech, you mean between the three of you, no one can read good enough to see if there is anything about a murder of someone named Andy?"

Ruby grabbed the paper from Screech and started to flip through the pages.

"I can read just fine," Whispers stated. "No one asked me to read no paper though."

"Here it is!" Ruby yelled cutting off the bickering between the others.

Ruby read the article about the missing person.

"What's it say?" Moose asked.

"He's missing. That's all they say. They haven't found the car yet, either."

"Wonder who has the car?" Screech asked.

"Whoever has it," Speedy commented, "is gonna be in a world of hurt soon."

"It's probably been stripped and sold by now," Whispers added to the discussion.

"Well, at least they haven't found the body yet," Ruby pointed out. "Okay, tonight we party. Moose, here's a hundred bucks. You and Screech go get some refreshments and some weed. Speedy, you round up some girls. Tell them, they're spending the night. As they say: tomorrow is the first day of the rest of our lives. Tonight we celebrate the changing of the guard."

"What guard?" asked Screech anxiously. "Moose is the only guard we have. Moose ain't leavin is he? Moose?"

"You're so stupid, Screech," Speedy pointed out. "It's a figure of speech. He's talking about him and me."

"Well, Ruby ain't no guard either. He's the boss."

Speedy leaned on the edge of his chair and stared hard at Screech. "Yeah, well, tomorrow, I'm the boss. And don't you forget it."

"Enough! The three of you get. The sooner you get back, the sooner we can start the party."

Moose, Screech and Speedy got up and left to complete their tasks.

"What you want me to do?" asked Whispers.

Ruby looked at the quiet man lying on the sofa. "You have a gun on you?"

Whispers now sat up and looked suspiciously at Ruby.

"Yeah. Why?"

"Speedy's a bad one. He thinks he knows more than he does. I'm afraid he's gonna screw up bad. He's gonna beat on Screech whenever he can. He won't pick on Moose cause he knows Moose would tear him in two. He'll try to keep Moose and Screech separated. I want you to protect Screech when Moose ain't around."

"You want me to kill Speedy?" Whispers asked astonished.

"If you have to, yes." Ruby unlocked the bottom drawer of his desk and removed a metal box and a key. "Here. There is several thousand dollars in it. Moose knows how much money I have turned over to Speedy and where it's kept. Speedy will probably move it and not tell any of you where he keeps it. I'm giving this to you. Follow Speedy, as long as Speedy takes care of all of you. If . . . when he goes astray, you'll have this to help the three of you. You're smarter than Moose and Speedy. I expect you to —."

"No way man. I don't want to have that shit on my shoulders."

Ruby threw the box at Whispers, who caught it with his chest. It crashed onto the cement floor.

"You don't have a choice. Moose will look after Screech. You will look after Moose and Screech. If I find out you took that money and ran, I'll hunt you down and kill you myself. Now put that some place where Speedy won't find it."

Whispers stared at Ruby for a few moments and then shifted his gaze down to the box sitting at his feet. Finally, he reached down and picked it up. Ruby tossed him the key, and Whispers caught it with his hand. Standing, Whispers went to his room.

Ruby watched him as he shut his door behind him. Ruby shook his head. He gave the motley crew a couple of months at best. Speedy would probably eventually kill Screech. He didn't understand why Speedy hated Screech so much. Maybe Screech reminded Speedy too much of his own weaknesses. Moose would probably kill Speedy. Whispers would probably take the money and run somewhere, leaving Moose to join up with some other gang. Moose was dumb, but strong. Any gang would welcome him into their house.

Standing and going to his own room, he finished packing. He had his bag full of new clothes in the truck. He opened another black bag and ruffled through the stacks of bills. Underneath the money, he checked to make sure the Smith and Wesson 38 that he had taken from Andy was still there. Although he only had the rounds that were left in the gun, you never knew when you would need an extra weapon. Boxes of shells for his 44 Special were also hidden under the money. He threw underwear and other shirts, pants and socks on top of the money. Ruby took the bag to the truck and locked it in the back seat with his other bag full of new clothes and boots. As he shut and locked the door, he saw Moose and Screech coming around the corner. Moose carried a quarter keg of beer on his shoulder. Screech carried a tap for the keg and a box that probably held several bottles of hard liquor. Both Screech's and Moose's pockets contained several bags of other party favors. Soon Speedy would return with the female entertainment. This was going to be a night to remember.

Chapter 15

Vasser, New York
Thursday September 27, 1979 6:00 PM

Jason walked slowly toward the bus stop to catch his ride back to the Park-n-Ride. He used the time to absorb the sights and sounds of the city. He felt he was experiencing them for the first time. It had been years since he had money in his pocket and all the clothes he needed. A car awaited him to take him wherever he wanted to go. The car. What if the cops had found it? He had to find out if they were looking. Stopping at a newspaper stand, he purchased a copy of the morning paper. Jason sat on a nearby bench with his duffle bag securely lodged between his legs. Seeing nothing on the front, he turned through the pages. Then, in the local section, he spotted it:

Local Fund Manager Missing
By James Tiny, Vasser Times Reporter
    Andy Redmond, a successful fund manager at the Lincoln and Smith Financial Services Corporation was reported missing this morning by

his wife, Martha (Delrio) Redmond. According to police sources, Mrs. Redmond reported her husband missing when he failed to return home from work last evening. Sources at his firm indicated that he left work around seven in the evening, and that he was not scheduled to be out of town. His car, a 1976 silver Mercedes has also not yet been located. Mr. Redmond has been employed with Lincoln and Smith for fifteen years. After graduating from Harvard University, he began his employment with the firm as a Stock Analyst. Later he was promoted to Marketing Manager and then Regional Investment Vice President. Two years ago he was promoted to Fund Manager for the firm's largest stock portfolio.

Police are not speculating on the reason for his disappearance.

A picture of the missing man stared at Jason next to the article.

Jason began to sweat despite the coolness of the evening. He had to get to the car and get out of town fast. But where was he going to go? Throwing the paper on the bench, he picked up his bag and headed toward the bus stop again. Elk Run. Where was it? Maybe it wasn't even in New York. Suddenly, he spotted a magazine and bookstore across the street. Darting between passing cars, ignoring the blaring horns and curses from the drivers, he crossed the street and entered the store.

"May I help . . ."

"You have maps?" Jason asked not waiting for the sales clerk to finish his question.

"Sure, over on the far wall."

Jason crossed the store to the rack of maps. He briefly considered purchasing an atlas of the United States, but he was afraid the town of Elk Run would be too small to appear in the atlas. Instead, he picked out a state map for New York, Pennsylvania, Ohio, New Jersey, Maryland and Illinois. He'd look at them later.

Jason took the six maps to the counter, and the same sales clerk waited on him.

"Looks like your planning a big trip."

"Yeah," Jason replied pulling a twenty-dollar bill out of his pocket.

"I've always wanted to go over to the Jersey shores. You know, sun, babes..."

"I'm kind of in a hurry here," Jason interrupted the clerk again.

"Sorry."

The clerk finally rang up the sale, and Jason paid his bill. Not waiting for the talkative clerk to put the maps in a bag, Jason took them and left the store. Outside, he stuffed them into his duffel bag.

Walking quickly, he reached the bus stop only fifteen minutes before the last run was scheduled for the trip out to the Park-n-Ride. Sitting on the bench next to an older woman, Jason tried to think of what to do next. Now that the police were looking for the car, he couldn't afford to stay around the city. This Andy person was obviously a very rich man, and the police would not treat his disappearance lightly.

The loud bus pulled to a stop in front of the bench. Jason stood up and followed the woman up the steps. He was glad when he saw that the man sitting in the seat was not the same one from this morning. After depositing the required fare into the slot, Jason moved to the middle of the bus and sat down. He watched the city pass him by for probably the last time.

After what seemed like an eternity, the bus finally pulled to a stop in the Park-n-Ride. Only one other passenger got off. Jason waited as the bus moved slowly toward the entrance ramp to the interstate. He bent down and pretended to tie his shoelaces while the other stranger walked quickly toward his waiting vehicle. Fortunately, it was parked well away from Jason's Mercedes. The stranger appeared to take no interest in Jason, which was fine with him.

One car remained parked behind the silver car. All other spaces near it were empty. Jason picked up his pace, forcing himself not to run. He was in a cold sweat as he clumsily put the key in the door and slid in behind the wheel. He threw his duffle bag on the floor below the passenger seat. His hands were shaking as he tried to place the key in the ignition. It fell to the floor and Jason fumbled around in the dark trying to find it. Finally, his hand touched the small piece of metal. When he raised his head, he saw a car with the markings of the state police cruising down the interstate toward the Park-n-Ride exit. Quickly, Jason forced the key in the ignition and turned it. The engine started immediately. Putting the car in drive, Jason stepped on the gas. The car jumped out of the parking space, and the tires squealed. Backing off the accelerator, Jason turned the car toward the exit and gradually picked up speed. The police car was heading east on the interstate. Jason turned toward the exit, which would take him to the west-bound lanes. Jason entered the two-lane highway as the police cruiser sped past in the opposite direction.

Jason wiped his forehead on the sleeve of his jacket. He had no idea where he was going; he had to find out where Elk Run was. The fuel gauge read three quarters full. A passing sign indicated that Cleveland, Ohio was 175 miles away. After another thirty minutes, a sign indicated that there were two places of lodging at the next exit: The Budget Motel and the Squatters Inn. Jason turned off of the interstate and headed for The Budget Motel. It was less than a mile from the exit. The large building appeared to have over a hundred rooms. The parking lot was brightly lit and contained more vehicles than Jason could count while driving. A dozen cars were parked in front of the restaurant next to the hotel. Jason pulled into the lot and stopped. Several couples were in the process of entering or leaving the building. Jason thought about the fact that he had no means of identification and was driving a vehicle that he had to hide somewhere. Deciding that the motel was too populated, he did a U-turn and drove toward the Squatters Inn.

After about ten miles, Jason came to an all-night convenience store with two gas pumps. Across the road, he saw a one-floor building sitting off to the left at the end of a short two-lane driveway. A sign at the edge of the road advertised The Squatters Inn. There only appeared to be twenty units facing the front, each with its own entrance. The bright blue building appeared to be well kept, but only three vehicles were scattered across the lot. Jason turned into the driveway and approached the building. Following the road around to the back, he noticed a hallway about three feet wide running the length of the building. Another twenty units faced a steeply sloping hill in the back. Four cars were parked in front of some of the units. Jason decided to take a chance.

He parked in front of one of the units that held the number 23 on its door. There were no other cars close by. Leaving his duffle bag on the floor, Jason opened the trunk and removed the remaining two hundred dollars from the travel bag. He quickly walked around the front of the building and headed toward the office.

A blast of heat hit him as he entered the small room. Two blue chairs served as a waiting area, and a rack of brochures advertised various attractions in the area. A large fish tank sat on a black metal stand across from the door. Numerous colorful fish swam lazily around in the cloudy water. Jason turned to his left and walked up to the open counter. Various signs on the countertop advertised the different forms of plastic money that was accepted. In the small area behind the counter there was an old, scratched table with assorted papers and a box of keys. Sitting on a blue flowered sofa was a middle-aged, plump woman. As Jason approached the window, she stood, pushed her wire glasses up the bridge of her nose and greeted him with a smile.

"Hello, can I help you?"

"Yes, I need a room. Just for tonight. I'd like to pay cash. How much is it?"

"How many adults?" the woman asked as if she hadn't heard him.

"Ah, one. Just me."

"One bed or two?"

"Ah, I think I'll just use one."

"That'll be thirty five dollars plus tax. Please fill this out." The woman handed Jason a half-page form that asked for his name, address, vehicle information and the number of adults and children.

Jason printed his name and hesitated momentarily as he contemplated what to put for his address. He decided to put his original home address and phone number. He wrote one in the box for adults and left the vehicle information blank. He handed the paper back to the woman, hoping she would not question the missing vehicle information.

Taking the form from Jason, the woman scribbled some numbers on the form and turned back to the table to remove a key from the box.

"Room twelve. That will be 35 plus tax. How will you be paying?"

"Ah, cash." Jason started to pull the bills out of his pocket.

"I'll need a credit card to hold until you check out, to cover any other phone charges or incidentals on your bill."

"I don't have any credit cards, " Jason replied too quickly. "Ah, my mom always used to lecture me about the evils of plastic money. Guess it stuck. Never even applied for one."

The plump woman looked suspiciously at Jason above her glasses that seemed to constantly slide down her nose.

"I can give you an extra twenty if you'd like. I don't really expect to make any calls. I'm really beat and just want to get something to eat and hit the sack."

"Well, I guess that would be okay."

Jason handed her sixty dollars. "Why don't you just keep the change until I check out. Also, would it be okay if I got a room in the back? It would probably be quieter."

With a huff, the woman tossed the key to room twelve back into the box and pulled another one out.

"You okay with number thirty-three?" the woman asked sarcastically.

"That would be great. Thank you." He decided not to push his luck by asking for unit 23.

Jason took the key as the woman returned to the sagging couch and picked up a well-worn magazine.

Jason started toward the back of the building that housed the 40 or so units. He debated whether or not he should walk over to the convenience store and pick up something to eat. Finally, he decided to take care of the car and get settled. Returning to the Mercedes, Jason moved it in front of his room. He lifted his duffle bag off the floor, walked to the trunk and opened it. After throwing all the items that were lying loosely in the trunk into the black luggage bag, Jason entered the hotel room. One lone bed sat with it's plastic artificial wooden headboard against the wall to the left of the entrance way. Two cheap-looking dressers sat against the wall facing the bed. On the wall above the dressers was a large mirror. A television and clock radio sat on top of one of the dressers. A window to the left of the bed looked out onto the parking area and steep bank. Next to the window stood a floor lamp with a yellowish shade and a single wooden chair. Closing the door to the room, Jason opened a door off to the right. He found a small bathroom with a tub. Brownish rings circled its dull-white surface. Water slowly dripped from the silver showerhead. Another door next to the first dresser opened to expose a small closet. Jason closed the faded blue curtains over the window, dropped the black luggage bag next to the door, sat down on the soft bed, and placed his duffle bag next to him.

All of a sudden he was tired and hungry. He pushed his hand through his black hair and stared at himself in the mirror. Jason Shark. High school graduate. Vietnam veteran. Homeless person. Car thief. Soon he would be a murderer. Father Frank said something about him being on a path. Some path. He certainly hadn't planned on taking this path when he was in high school. Of course, he had chosen to enter the army. And, despite the fact that other people had driven him to it, he had chosen to move to the streets. It was also his decision to steal the car of the dead man. Yes, the path he was on was definitely of his choosing, even though he hadn't realized where the path was leading when he had made his earlier decisions. Now he had to continue to the end of the path. Poor Oscar was dead because of the scumbag Ruby. Jason owed it to Oscar to repay Ruby for what he had done. Didn't he?

Jason shook his head. He was tired. He had to get something to eat. Making sure he had the money in his pocket, Jason zipped up his coat, pulled the pair of gloves from his duffle bag and put them on his hands. He stood and left the small room. The frigid air bit into his shaven face. The wind whipped his hair in various directions. He was thankful for the warm clothes and gloves. Jason headed around the building and down the driveway toward the store.

Waiting for three cars to pass by, Jason watched a thin woman get out of an old, beat-up red station wagon that was parked in front of the store across the street. After moving to the passenger side of the car, the woman opened the two doors and three young children scrambled out into the cold night air. The thin brown coat the woman was wearing blew open in the wind exposing a faded orange dress. She wore a pair of dirty white sneakers on her feet. The children, two girls and a boy, all looked to be of elementary school age. They too wore thin coats and sneakers, but no hats. The pants on the boy stopped about two inches above his white socks. The girls also wore thin dresses. Using her arms to herd the three youths together, she pushed them toward the store.

After the last car passed, Jason crossed the street. Walking past the old station wagon, Jason looked inside. Several thin blankets with holes in them were strewn around the back seat. Shoeboxes and other discarded items littered the floor in the front and back. Jason continued inside.

The woman and three children were standing at the counter where various sandwiches were kept cold.

"Can I have a sandwich mommy?" the boy asked.

"Me too?" asked the older girl.

"I have standich?" tried the youngest.

"We'll see. Come, get out of this man's way. Let's look for the crackers."

"I'll find them," yelled the boy as he ran down the aisle in front of Jason.

"No, let me," screamed the older girl as she ran after the boy.

"I want cackers mommy," explained the little girl as she tried to run after the two older children.

"Excuse me," the woman said as she stepped past Jason, lowering her head and avoiding eye contact.

Jason watched the four people search for the crackers and then turned his attention to the sandwiches. He picked up two that contained a few pieces of turkey stuffed between a thick bun. Walking past the drinks, Jason grabbed a two-liter bottle of soda and then headed toward the aisle with chips and pretzels.

"Please mommy, I want a sandwich," pleaded the older girl. "I'm tired of crackers."

"Yeah, mommy, can't we please get a sandwich," added the boy.

"Dink mommy," stated the youngest pointing toward the soda fountain counter.

Jason watched as the woman opened a small change purse and pulled out two crumpled bills. They were both ones. She raised her left hand to cover her eyes, but Jason saw the small tears forming at the corners.

The words of the old man in the store echoed in Jason's mind. He reached into his pocket and felt the wad of bills pressing against his leg. How many times had he raised his hand to take a few pieces of change from a stranger passing by on the street? Now here he stood with an arm full of sandwiches, chips and soda, while these three children begged their mother for something to eat.

Tentatively, Jason approached the woman.

"Excuse me," Jason spoke softly.

The three children moved behind the woman. Quickly, she shoved the bills back into the purse and clutched it tightly in her hand.

"Yes?" she meekly responded, still avoiding eye contact.

"I . . . ah . . . would like to help you."

"No thank you," she replied. "Come on kids, let's go."

"But I'm hungry," cried the boy.

"Dink mommy."

"We're sorry mommy," explained the girl. "We'll eat crackers. Let's get crackers."

The woman started to push the children toward the door.

"No, wait. Please. Let me explain . . . Please."

For the first time, the woman raised her head and looked at Jason through tired, scared and lonely eyes. She stopped.

"I . . . ah . . . used to live on the streets. I would sometimes go for days without eating. The pain and emptiness would often be almost too much to bear. My teeth would often rattle inside my mouth from the cold in the winter. In the springtime, after a heavy rain, I would sit in a puddle for hours, cause I was too tired to move. Sometimes church people would bring me blankets or food, but eventually the food would run out, and the blankets would get torn and shredded. But there were shelters. Sometimes I would get hot soup and some clean clothes. But the pain and emptiness never seemed to go away. Please, a — friend — recently gave me some money. It's more than I need right now. Please let me help you."

The woman stared at the strange man. She didn't try to stop the tears from running down her cheek. The children remained quiet, hiding behind the woman's skirt. Jason reached into his pocket and pulled out two twenty-dollar bills.

"I know this isn't much, but I would really like it if you would take it. Buy your children something to eat. Maybe you can use some for gas. It's cold outside. I wish I could give you more."

Jason held the bills out toward the woman. Now his own eyes began to get moist.

"Dink mommy?" whispered the small girl.

Finally, the woman raised a shaking hand and gently took the money.

"I . . . I . . . Thank you."

The boy looked up at his mother and then turned toward the stranger.

"Thank you mister."

"Tank you mitter."

"Mommy?" the boy asked. "Can we get a sandwich?"

"Yes honey, go get a sandwich. But just one."

"Dink mommy?"

"Yes Rachael, we'll get a drink."

Jason smiled as the three children ran down the aisles.

The woman turned back to Jason.

"Thank you very much. You are very kind. God bless you."

Jason just nodded. He didn't trust himself to speak.

Walking past the woman, Jason set his items on the counter. The pain and emptiness were gone.

Back in his room, Jason removed his coat and threw it on the chair. He opened both sandwiches and put all of the meat in one thick roll. He re-wrapped the empty roll and put it in his duffle bag for later. Living on the street, Jason never knew how long it would be between meals. After finishing the dry sandwich in four large bites, Jason sat on the bed with the open bag of chips and the bottle of soda. Opening his duffle bag, he removed the several maps and began searching for Elk Run. He started with New York. He found an Elk Brook, an Elk Creek, and an Elkdale, but no Elk Run. Jason put the map aside and searched Pennsylvania. His heart skipped a beat. His hands began to shake. There it was: Elk Run. Finding the coordinates on the map, Jason scanned the area around the northern central part of the state. Finally, he located it. He guessed it was about a six to eight hour drive from *Vasser*. Controlling his excitement, he pulled out the other maps. In New Jersey, he found an Elks Terrace, but no Elk Run. In Ohio, he found an Elk City, an Elk Fork, and an Elkton. In Maryland, all he found was Elk Mills. In Illinois, he found an Elk Grove, an Elkhart, an Elks Park, an Elkton, and an Elkville. Only Pennsylvania contained an Elk Run. Had he heard the name correctly? There was only one way to find out. He had to go there. Once again, he had chosen the next stop on his path. Perhaps this was to be the final stop. He was surprisingly calm now. He put the top on the half empty bottle of soda, rolled down the top of the half-eaten bag of chips and set them both on the scratched surface of the dresser. After using the bathroom, he pulled back the covers, removed the oversized clothes, and crawled into bed. As he drifted off to sleep, visions of the woman and her three children appeared in front of his closed eyes. Darkness enveloped him.

Chapter 16

Elk Run, Pennsylvania
Friday September 28, 1979 6:30 AM

Clint's ears began to ring as he rolled over in his large bed. As much as he willed it to stop, it wouldn't. Finally, he realized it was coming from somewhere to his right. He opened his eyes and stared in the direction of the sound. There appeared to be a phone sitting there that was emitting the annoying sound. Thrusting his arm toward the device, he grabbed the phone and held it to his ear.

"Hello?"

"Hi honey."

"Paula. Hi." Clint sat up with his back against the headboard of his bed. A pain began to form in the center of his head. "How are you? I called last night. At least I think I did. Everything is a little blurry right now."

"You did," Paula laughed. "I'm sorry I didn't call you back. I was at school till after eleven working on our program for this Sunday. You remember, I'm taking the senior students to the lake for a picnic and some nature hikes."

"Yeah, I remember. You sure work a lot."

"I said I was sorry," Paula said irritably.

Clint didn't respond. His head was starting to pound even more. Things were becoming clearer as he remembered how he and Stubs had finished off a case of beer. Hopefully, Stubs was still somewhere in the house.

"What time is it?" Clint asked as he gazed through cloudy eyes at the blurry numbers on his clock radio.

"It's six thirty. I've got to leave to go to school. I just wanted to call and say I was sorry about missing the cookout last night."

"That's okay. Can we get together tonight?"

"Ah, I don't think I can do that. I still have a ton of things to plan for Sunday. Hey, would you like to help? You could plan the nature stuff. You're so much better with that stuff than me."

Clint stared at the open doorway wondering where Stubs was.

"I don't think so. I've got to get things in order around here for the first group of hunters that are coming in a couple of weeks. I'm sure you'll do a great job. You're good at organizing these things."

"Okay. Well, I better get going. I'll call you tonight." It was more of a question than a statement.

"Yeah, that would be fine. Bye."

"Bye."

The line went dead, and Clint placed the phone gingerly down on the table. Yesterday he was on cloud nine. Today he felt like crap.

Slowly he swung his legs out of the bed. He still had on his jeans and T-shirt from last night. He walked down the hallway and checked in the first guest room. The bed was unused. He checked the second guest room. That bed had also not been slept in. Clint walked into the living area. On the sofa lay Stubs. His face was buried in the cushions. His right hand rested on the floor.

"Stubs. Hey buddy. You okay?"

"Wah?" Stubs mumbled as he tried to roll onto his right side.

"Wait!" Clint yelled. It was too late.

Stubs plopped to the floor on his back.

"Ohhhh! That hurt."

Stubs pulled himself into a sitting position on the floor and opened his eyes. He turned his head from side to side, trying to determine where he was. Finally recognition showed on his face.

"Hah! Must of been a good party."

"Why didn't you sleep in one of the guest rooms?"

"Ah! What I wanna mess up those clean sheets for? Your sofa's as comfortable as my bed at home."

Clint laughed. "Stubborn old fool. How 'bout some breakfast? I'll cook up some eggs and sausage."

"Nah. I gotta get going. Gotta lot of lawns to mow today."

Stubs struggled to his feet and adjusted his shirt and pants. He retrieved his jacket from a hook next to the door and slipped it on.

"Thanks for the dinner and beer."

"Your welcome. Come by anytime. You sure you're okay to drive?"

"Yeah, no problem. Sorry I wasn't one of them pretty lady friends you was expectin'."

"Well, I had a great time swapping lies with you anyway. Besides, you probably helped me keep my virginity."

"Bull! I'll expect you to bring that coyote by later today. Tonight I'll cook you some good dog steaks at my house."

"Can't wait. See ya later."

Stubs opened the door to leave and Shack burst into the house.

"See you Shack," Stubs shouted.

"Arf."

Clint moved to the kitchen as Stubs slammed the door to his old truck, started it up and drove out the driveway.

"Hungry Shack?"

"Arf." There was that dumb question again.

Clint concentrated on making breakfast. He had a lot to do to start preparing for his first wave of guests. Later, he would take the animal hanging in the meat locker to Stubs' house, try to enjoy the steaks Stubs would prepare, and then head into the Old Timer's.

Chapter 17

Outside Vasser, New York
Friday September 28, 1979 8:15 am

Jason tried to run through the dense jungle. He moved his legs faster and faster, but couldn't move through the dark, thick muck in which he was standing. Vines held him in place, yet branches slapped him in his face, stinging him and causing blood to run into his eyes. He tasted the sweat mixed with blood that trickled into his mouth. He turned to his right to find his comrades. A man with one leg hopped in place about ten yards away. The back of his head was missing. Jason turned to his left. A man with a black jacket was running away from him. In the middle of the jacket was a bright red circle. The red color ran down his back and dripped onto the ground. The man turned his face toward Jason, and the white clerical collar tightened around his neck, causing his eyes to bulge. The man smiled. Explosions erupted all around him. Screams of pain and terror came from all directions.

"Medic! Medic!"

"Help me! Help me!"

"My arm! I can't find my arm!"

"Dink mommy."

Jason raised his head toward the last words he heard. High up in the trees he saw a woman and three young children.

"Dink mommy. Dink mommy. Dink mommy"

"Medic! Help me! I'm hit! I'm hit! Oh my God! My God! Mommy! Mommy! Don't leave me!"

A dark figure ran in front of him. Jason fired his rifle at the retreating body. A bright red circle appeared on the back of the man. The circle grew bigger and bigger. The man turned around. Oscar stared at him with a surprised look.

"No!" shouted Jason. "No. Oscar, no. I didn't mean to shoot you. Forgive me!"

"Dink mommy."

Jason looked back up into the trees. The woman's coat flew open. Her dress blew into shreds. The woman began to fall from the tree. Rain started to pour from the sky. The woman fell toward Jason. He reached out to catch her, but she fell just beyond his reach. She landed on the muddy ground and sunk into the earth.

"Dink mommy."

Explosions blasted dirt into the trees.

"Mommy, mommy, where are you?"

"God bless you my son."

Machine gun fire sounded in the distance. Jason saw the bullets streaming toward him. He tried to dive into the bushes but couldn't move. He watched as the bullets tore into his belly. He felt them exit out his back, but still he couldn't move. He felt no pain, just a hollow emptiness.

"Dink mommy."

"Medic! I'm hit! Oh God, it hurts! Help me! Help me!"

"Dink mommy."

Dozens of men came toward him, all wearing black jackets and black pants. They raised their guns toward the trees. Bright yellow flashes streamed from the ends of the guns. Jason looked up. Three children sat on the limb just above him, their round Asian faces pleading for him to help. They all wore sneakers on their feet, but the laces were untied. Jason reached his hands toward their outstretched arms. Their fingers touched. Jason gazed into their faces. Father Frank smiled serenely back at him. Jason turned to the one in the middle, and Oscar stared silently at him. Turning to the last one, he saw Ruby laughing loudly. Then, bullets ripped through their tiny bodies. Their faces disappeared. Three small children fell toward him.

"NO!" Jason yelled. He tried to catch them, but they, too, fell outside his reach on the soft earth. The ground turned red. Water rushed over them and pushed them down a steep bank.

"Help me! Someone help me!"

Jason turned his head all around. No one else was moving. Bodies lay strewn over the thick vegetation. Screams of suffering became louder and louder. Jason began firing his rifle wildly.

Jason jerked up in bed. Sweat poured down the sides of his face. Darkness surrounded him. The sheets and blankets were tangled around his legs. The screams continued, but were more faint. Jason tore at the sheets and pulled his legs loose. Standing up, he ran his hands through his sweaty hair. He glanced at the red numbers on the small clock on the dresser: 8:15. The faint screams continued. They were coming from the room next door. Jason rummaged through his duffle bag and grabbed a pair of the camouflaged pants, socks and a T-shirt. He quickly pulled the clothes on and stuffed his feet into the black boots he had set by the door. He didn't bother lacing them.

Opening the door, the cold air hit him in the face. He thought about returning for his jacket, but the screams came louder now that he was outside. Jason walked to the window where the sounds were coming from. The curtains were drawn, but through the thin material, he could still see a small child sitting on the floor next to the dresser. The room seemed to be identical to his.

"Don't hurt mommy," the little female voice pleaded.

Jason moved to the side of the window and tried to see the bed at which the child was staring. The naked back of a tall thin man was blocking most of his view. His wrinkled jeans were wrapped around his ankles.

"Shut up!" the man's voice commanded the scared child.

"Don't hurt her Hank," a female voice pleaded. "I'll do whatever you want."

"You bet your sweet ass you will," Hanks voice responded. The man called Hank raised his arm, and Jason watched as he swept it across what Jason figured was the woman's face. A cry of pain exploded from the bed.

"Mommy! Mommy!" Two other small voices sounded from what Jason assumed was the bathroom.

The man raised his hand to strike the woman again.

"If you don't shut them damn brats up, I'm gonna —"

His words were cut short by the sound of the door splintering and slamming open. Jason rushed the man and knocked him across the bed onto the floor. Hank rolled onto his back, but before he could respond to the intruder, Jason pounded his fist into the man's face. Jason pulled back his arm and let loose another blow to the man's face. His head rolled to the side as blood streamed from the cut on his right cheek. Jason prepared to strike again, but it wasn't necessary. Hank wasn't moving.

The child on the floor became silent, and her eyes grew wide in horror at the vision of the two men struggling on the floor.

"Mommy? Mommy? Are you okay?" a voice from the bathroom asked.

Jason stood up and looked at the small child and then turned toward the woman who was now sitting on the bed. Her torn orange dress was pulled down to her waist, exposing her small breasts. Jason raised his eyes to those of the woman he had first met in the convenience store.

The woman lowered her head and tried to cover her nakedness with her torn dress.

Jason moved back to the door and closed it, but the strong, cold wind blew it back open. He pulled a chair from the corner of the room and propped it against the door to keep it shut.

"Are you okay?" Jason asked.

"Dink man, mommy" explained the girl on the floor.

Tears dripped from the woman's eyes onto her torn dress.

"Yes, now I am. Thank you . . . again."

"Are your other kids in there?" Jason asked pointing toward the bathroom.

"Yes."

Jason moved to the bathroom door and opened it.

"You can come out. Your mommy needs you."

The two older children slowly edged their way out of the small room. They looked at their mother sitting on the bed and then at the man lying on the floor.

"Did you kill him?" the boy asked.

Jason looked at the prone figure. Hank's chest rose and fell slowly. "No, he'll live."

"I wish you'd kill him," the boy stated.

"Toby!" the woman chastised. "Don't say that."

"But mom —"

"Don't you ever say that about anyone!"

"I'm sorry," Toby apologized.

Slowly, the girl that had remained hidden behind her brother, walked over to the bed. She crawled up beside her mother and wrapped her small arms around the beaten woman. The tiny girl on the floor quickly pulled herself onto the bed and joined her sister. Toby stood frozen in place, staring at the bleeding man on the floor.

A blast of wind blew the splintered door open and knocked the chair over on its side. The boy jumped onto the bed and crawled beside his two sisters. All four left out a weak cry.

"My name's Jason. Perhaps we should get out of here. If you'd like, you can go to my room. I should be leaving anyway."

"Sleepy mommy," the tiny girl informed her mother.

"I . . . I . . . We . . .can go to my car."

Jason looked at the woman's face, which was red and bruised from the man's fist. He noticed blood trickling down her chin from a split lip.

"My name is Norma. This is Toby and Hannah and Sally."

"Hi," the three said quietly.

"You're bleeding," Jason stated. "Let me take care of your cuts, and then you can rest in my room. It will be warmer than the car. Checkout time is not till one. You can stay there till noon and leave before the maids come."

Norma looked at Hank lying on the floor.

"Come," Jason said offering his hand, "I'll take care of Hank." Jason looked around at the half dozen empty beer bottles. "He won't wake up for a while."

Norma returned her eyes to Jason and then to the three children nestled beside her. Both girls' eyes were already closing. She nodded slightly.

"Come on kids. We're going to go to Jason's room."

"NO!" Toby yelled, fear showing in his eyes.

"It will be okay," Norma answered calmly. "Won't it?" she asked pleadingly.

"Yes, it will be okay. Come."

This time, Norma took Jason's hand and slowly got out of bed, holding her torn dress up with the other.

"Toby, carry Hannah," the mother instructed.

Toby picked up his sister and followed Sally and his mother through the door. The wind and cold air quickly sent goose bumps up all their arms. Jason followed from behind and reached around them to open the door to his room. The warmth hit them immediately.

"Why don't you clean up in the bathroom," Jason suggested to Norma. "I'll go take care of Hank and be right back."

"Are you going to kill him?" Toby asked excitedly. "Can I watch?"

"Hank is a bad man," Jason explained, "but, no, I'm not going to kill him. Some day, someone will, but not me . . . or you." Turning back to Norma, Jason asked, "Do you have any other clothes in the car?"

"Yes —"

"I'll get them," Toby volunteered.

"Okay," Jason took control. "Toby, you go and get your mom's clothes. Sally, you make Hannah comfortable in the bed and then help your mother in the bathroom." Sally and Toby did as they were instructed.

Jason looked at Norma and smiled. "They're good kids."

"Yes, they are. Thank you again."

"Don't worry about it. I've known a lot of men like Hank. They DO deserve to die."

Turning away before Norma could respond, Jason left the room and re-entered the one where Hank lay. Jason checked the man's pulse to make sure he was still alive. He was. Picking him up, Jason carried him into the bathroom and dumped him into the tub. He left the man's pants tangled around his legs, but removed his belt. Jason worked the belt around Hank's body, trapping his arms behind his back. He tied the belt as tight as possible. Looking around the room, Jason spotted an extension chord running from the table lamp to the electrical outlet. Another one stretched from the television to a second outlet. Jason returned to the bathroom and hog-tied the man's arms and legs. Jason tied them tight, knowing that eventually a maid would find him. He took the pillow off of the bed and removed the case. Jason put the pillow under the man's head and tied the case around his mouth to keep him from yelling. Making sure he was breathing through his nose, Jason went to the door to leave.

He tried to put the splintered pieces of wood back together as much as possible. Despite his efforts, the busted latch still didn't hold against the force of the wind. Jason went back into the room and searched for something to lodge between the door and the jam. In the bottom drawer of the dresser, he found a telephone book. Its front page was made of a thick cardboard-like material. Tearing the page from the book, he continued to rip it into quarters. He folded two of the pieces as small as possible and returned to the door. Jason held both pieces against the jam and pulled the door shut with his left hand. The door wedged tightly against the folded paper.

Jason returned to his room and quietly opened the door. All three children were asleep on the bed. Jason shut the door and stepped inside. The bathroom door opened and Norma stepped outside. She was wearing a thin white cotton top that stopped short of her faded blue jeans. There was no bra underneath. Jason raised his gaze to Norma's face. Despite the redness on her cheeks, the dark bruise forming on her forehead and the cut on her lip that was still seeping blood, she was beautiful. Without thinking, he told her so.

Norma lowered her head in embarrassment and dabbed at the cut on her lip with the white towel she held in her left hand.

"I'm sorry. I shouldn't have said that. You must think . . .I mean . . . " Jason couldn't finish what he knew she must have been thinking. He walked to the far end of the room, fearing that she would leave the security of the room.

"No one ever told me that I was beautiful."

Jason turned back to face the thin woman. "You're kidding? You are very beautiful. But, I don't want you to . . . "

"I know," Norma said quietly. "You are a good man, Jason. You've helped me so much. I don't know how to ever thank you."

Now it was Jason's turn to hide his head in embarrassment. This woman had no idea who he was, who he had been, who he was going to be when he found Ruby.

"I'm sorry," Norma said. "I said something wrong."

"Yes. Yes, you did. I'm not a good man. You don't know what I've done. What I'm capable of doing. What I will do."

Norma wrapped her arms around herself. "You're scaring me."

"No, I didn't mean to you or your children. I've killed people before. In Nam. There's this guy —" He couldn't finish.

Norma lowered her arms and walked toward him. "My brother was in Vietnam. He didn't come home. He's missing. Did you kill children? Like everyone says?"

"No. I didn't. But I saw others do it. Children. Women. Old men. They just —"

Norma raised her hand and gently placed her fingers on his lips.

"That wasn't you. That isn't you. This is you." Norma swept her hand toward her silent, sleeping children.

Jason's shoulders shook uncontrollably and tears flowed down his cheeks.

"I don't know who I am."

Norma moved next to Jason and put her arms around him.

"Hold me please?" Norma asked.

Jason awkwardly placed his hands on Norma's shoulders. He then moved them down her back and gently squeezed her to him. The warmth of her body penetrated his, and he felt a calmness pass through him. He gently stroked her back as she rubbed the back of his neck. All the tension seemed to evaporate from his body. Slowly, they slid to the floor and rested their backs against the bed. One of the children snored softly. Their eyes closed and peace settled over the two lonely individuals.

Jason woke with a start. A strange woman's head was resting on his lap. As his mind cleared, he remembered where he was and the woman's name. He raised his head and tried to focus on the clock on the dresser: 12:15.

Jason gently shook Norma's shoulders. She slowly raised her head. Their eyes met, and their lips touched. Their kiss lingered, and Jason tasted a sweetness he had not experienced in a long time. With great effort, he softly pushed her away.

"Norma, I have to leave. You should go too. Get as far away from here as possible. When they find Hank next door, there will be all sorts of questions. You could be in a lot of trouble. If they learn that I beat up Hank and find me, I'll be in trouble. I've got to leave quickly."

"You go. I'll get the kids awake and leave soon. Hank won't want the cops involved. He's got a record, and the cops are probably already looking for him."

"You know him?"

Norma lowered her head in shame again. "Yes. He is . . . was . . . a friend. Last night. After you left. We drove over here and parked in front of one of the open rooms. We come here at least once a month. No one normally bothers us. Hank knew it. He found us and offered to put us up in the room. He left around midnight. When he came back this morning, he had the beer and started drinking. Well, he probably just continued drinking. That's when he pushed Hannah onto the floor and made Toby and Sarah go into the bathroom. You came before he —"

"I know." This time it was Jason who gently placed his fingers on Norma's lips to silence her confession. "Maybe . . . someday . . . I'll come back."

Norma smiled. "I'd like that."

Chapter 18

Ruby awoke feeling a heavy weight on top of him. As his eyes began to focus, he realized a bare shoulder was nestled beneath his chin. With his left hand, he pushed the naked woman off him. A soft moan escaped her lips, but she did not awaken. Sitting up, he noticed that he was also naked. A slight pounding in his head began to remind him of the evening's activities. Ruby stood and searched for his clothes. After putting them on, he took one last look at the naked woman. He had seen her before on the streets, but didn't know her name. Opening his door, he went out into the lobby area that had served as his office. Speedy was slouched on the chair behind the desk. Several glasses partially filled with beer sat on the desk. Another naked woman with red hair was asleep on the floor, her back resting against the desk. Moose, Screech and Whispers were nowhere to be seen. They were probably recovering in their own rooms. Ruby checked his watch. It was just after ten. Taking one final look around, he left the building and walked to the truck. Checking the back seat, he found everything as he had left it. Ruby got behind the wheel, started the engine and drove off. He did not look back.

Chapter 19

Elk Run, Pennsylvania
Friday September 28, 1979 3:00 PM

After breakfast, Clint had cleaned up around the house and then paid the bills that had been piling up on his desk. He checked the bunkroom to make sure everything was in order. Once the hunting seasons began, he would have little time to himself. He called the grocery store, gunsmith and beer distributor. With all the paperwork completed, Clint walked to the meat locker to clean and skin the dead coyote. Shack came running up to him from the woods.

"Well, mutt, you wanna help skin a coyote?"

"Grrrrrr." Shack wasn't sure what his owner was asking, but he wasn't too excited about doing anything with a coyote. Despite his reservations, Shack followed his master to the meat locker.

Clint entered the large room and went to one of the four metal lockers. From the narrow compartment, Clint removed several items. He put on a pair of rubber pants with suspenders, a pair of knee-high rubber boots and a matching pair of rubber gloves.

Shack stood just inside the doorway and looked at the strange looking man that was once his owner. Cocking his head, he barked once softly. He walked over to Clint and sniffed the black boots and pants. What a strange smell. Shack backed up until his butt bumped into something. He turned quickly to make sure there wasn't another strange-looking thing behind him. Seeing only the wall, he sat on his haunches to watch what his master would do next.

Clint ran the hose from the large stainless steel sink over to the hanging animal. As he sprayed the inside of the animal with a stream of cold water, he wiped the dirt and leaves from the cavity with a cloth. Reddish-brown liquid and debris flowed onto the floor and down the drains.

Shack ventured over to the streaming water and decided to take a drink. The bitter taste caused him to gag and shake his head in frustration. That was terrible. The water in the lake was much better. Shack decided to move to the door and lie down while his owner washed the coyote. He wondered why the animal needed a bath when he was dead.

When the insides of the animal were clean, Clint chose a sharp knife from the counter drawer and began removing its hide. With this done, he lifted the heavy carcass off the meat hooks and placed it on the metal table. After removing the heavy rubber clothing, Clint began carving up the animal.

Shack watched in anticipation as Clint cut the meat into steaks and roasts. Maybe his owner would cook some of the steaks on the stove on the deck, like he had the night before.

By the time Clint had finished butchering, it was nearly five o'clock. With the meat neatly wrapped and boxed, he placed it in the cooler until he was ready to go to Stubs'. After hosing down and cleaning the butchering area, Clint started toward the door.

"Come on Shack. Time to clean up."

Shack looked at the closed door where his master had hidden the boxes of meat. He wondered why his owner wasn't taking any of them with him. Despite his disappointment, Shack followed Clint back to the house.

When they reached the top of the steps, Clint walked part of the way down the deck and stopped. He turned to face the animal that was hot on his heels. "You hungry?"

Shack wondered if this was a trick question. He glanced back toward the building where his owner had left the boxes of meat. Finally, he sat on his haunches and waited to see what his owner had in mind.

Clint opened the top of a wooden box that sat up against the wall. He took the metal pot from inside and scooped up the dog food. Pouring it into Shack's dog dish that was sitting next to the box, he turned back to the dumbfounded animal.

"Here, you've been eating too good lately. Besides, I'm not cooking tonight. I'm going over to Stubs' for some juicy coyote steaks and then to Sadie's. You're on your own."

Shack looked at the unappealing pile of hard nuggets and then at his owner. Life sure wasn't fair. His owner was going to eat cooked coyote, and he would have to eat these dull hard things that tasted like mud. He knew they tasted like mud because he had accidentally swallowed some of the slimy stuff when he was coming out of the lake yesterday. Shack snorted his displeasure and walked back up the deck and down the steps. He would come back and eat the so-called food later after his owner left.

"Love you Shack," Clint yelled.

Shack refused to answer.

* * *

It was after six o'clock when Clint pulled up in front of Stubs' house. The older man came out to meet him carrying two cans of beer. Clint wasn't sure if one was intended for him, or if Stubs had just brought a spare in case his first one ran out before he got back into the house. Clint stepped out of the truck and shut the door.

"'Bout time you got here," Stubs yelled as he handed Clint one of the cold cans. "I'm starving. The grill's hot, and I got my special sauce all ready for them steaks."

"Yeah, well, I hope you got room in your freezer for this stuff," Clint said pointing to the three boxes of wrapped meat. He noticed the well-used grill sitting in the corner of the front porch.

"Got plenty of room. You take the two biggins. I'll get this little one here." Stubs picked up the smallest of the three boxes and headed back to the house. "How comes you didn't bring Shack along?"

Clint set his can of beer on top of one of the boxes and lifted both of them in his arms. "I'm heading into Sadie's when we're done. He's not too welcome there."

"Ah. Makes sense. I'll go with you."

Stubs left the door open for Clint and set his box down on the table. Throwing his empty can into the garbage, he retrieved another one from the refrigerator. "You want another one?" he asked as Clint struggled into the kitchen and added his boxes to the table.

"Jeez, Stubs, you got a whole in your stomach? Nah, I'm okay, for now."

Clint opened one of the larger boxes and removed two big steaks.

"Here's tonight's dinner."

"Great. I'll start soaking them. You can take the rest of that out to the storage room and load the freezer."

"You want me to vacuum or dust while I'm here too?"

"Nah, maid comes tomorrow."

Clint took the boxes out to the storage room, which was once a bedroom. He began loading the packages in Stubs' chest freezer. There were only a dozen or so packages in the freezer when he opened it. These, he made sure were back on the top when he was done. By the time he returned to the kitchen, he could smell the meat cooking on the grill.

"Now I'm ready for another beer," Clint yelled at Stubs who was outside cooking. He noticed a pot on the stove half filled with corn and simmering slowly. Through the glass window of the oven, he spotted four large potatoes baking. Suddenly his stomach growled reminding him that he hadn't eaten since around ten that morning. He thought of Shack munching on his dry dog food and felt guilty. Tomorrow he would have to make it up to him.

"Good. Bring me one too."

Clint removed two cans from the refrigerator and went outside. Stubs was busy flipping the steaks and adding his special sauce, so Clint set the can down on a table next to the grill. Clint sat down on one of the two wooden chairs on either side of the window that looked into Stubs' living room. The cold September sky was void of clouds, and Clint began to relax staring at the bright stars twinkling overhead. It was a beautiful night. One that Paula would love.

"So, you got a thing for that pretty little waitress down at Sadie's?"

Clint turned his attention to the man working over the burning coals.

"How many beers have you had already?"

"Don't know. Can't remember how to count. Now, quit avoiding my question."

"And exactly why is this any business of yours, you old coot? Do I ask you questions about your female associates?"

"It's my business cause you're my neighbor. I gotta keep my eye on you, cause you don't have the priverledge of my vast experience. And I ain't tellin' you nothin' 'bout my female assoshates till you answer my question."

"Megan is a very nice girl, and she certainly can handle a shotgun."

"Then you better not piss her off."

"Are them steaks done yet?" Clint asked trying to change the subject.

"Still didn't answer my question. Go get a couple more beers. I'll be right in with these steaks."

Clint shook his head in disbelief. He hadn't even seen Stubs pick up the beer. Clint stood up and took his half-empty can with him. He got Stubs another can from the refrigerator and found the plates and utensils to set the table. By the time Stubs entered the warm kitchen, Clint had put a helping of the corn and a potato on each of the plates. Stubs plopped a steak on each of the plates and set the empty dish in the sink.

"Lets eat," Stubs declared.

Clint didn't argue.

* * *

By the time Clint and Stubs had finished eating and had cleaned up the dishes, it was after nine o'clock. Stubs had finished a six-pack in the couple of hours that Clint had been there. Clint hadn't even tried to keep pace with the more experienced drinker, but still he felt a slight buzz. It was time to go celebrate yesterday's hunt.

"You coming old man?"

"Old man? You watch your mouth, or I'll wup you right here on my porch." With that, Stubs stumbled down the single step, but managed to catch himself before he landed on his nose.

"You sure you're in shape to go to Sadie's?"

"Of course. I been practicin' for the last six hours. I'm in perfect shape to go to the bar."

Clint opened the passenger door for Stubs and then went around to the driver's side.

"Buckle up," Clint suggested as he purposely stepped on the gas pedal harder than necessary.

"Hey, watch it," Stubs yelled as he bounced around on the seat and finally got the strap buckled.

* * *

Clint pulled into the dusty lot and parked in the last spot of the back row, beside a black suburban. A dozen other vehicles filled the small lot.

"Plaish is packed tonight," Stubs observed.

"Yeah, hope they have some beer left. You might start going through withdrawal."

"There'll be hell to pray if they don't."

The thin man sitting at the bar watched the two men enter. One was large with a massive chest and large arms. His thighs threatened to rip the seams of his jeans. A slight belly was the only sign of a life of leisure. This was not a man to tangle with. He turned his attention to the other newcomer. He was older with bloodshot eyes. From his stagger, it appeared that he had already been hitting the bottle for several hours. Ruby's eyes went wide, as he noticed the three fingers missing on the man's right hand.

Clint and Stubs found two empty seats at the bar, and Sadie was there immediately with two filled glasses.

"My friend's just havin' water tonight," Clint proclaimed seriously.

"Water?" Stubs complained. "That water better have some alcohol in it, or it's gonna get poured on your head."

Sadie laughed and went to wait on some of her other customers. "I'll be back."

Clint surveyed the loud crowd. Some of the people he recognized as locals. They seemed to be the quieter ones. He noticed a thin man on the opposite side of the bar staring at them, but the man turned his gaze toward his glass when their eyes met. At a table near the bathrooms, Clint recognized a group of four who were loudly trying to sing along with the tune playing on the jukebox. One of them was Bob, the man who had caused all the trouble a couple of nights ago. As the man turned his head, he caught Clint watching him. Their eyes locked. Finally, the man smiled and raised his beer in a toast to Clint. Clint returned the gesture and then continued to scan the crowd looking for Megan.

"She's in the back helping Ralph cook," Sadie offered as if she had read Clint's mind.

"Who is?"

"Queen Elizabeth. Give me a break, Clinton."

"He's got a thing for the Queen," Stubs pointed out.

"Shut up and drink your water."

Stubs eyed his glass suspiciously. After satisfying himself that Clint was lying about its contents, he downed half of it.

"Ahhhhhh. Best water I've ever had."

"Yeah, well, go easy. I don't want to have to carry your butt out of here."

"Never happen."

Clint turned to the man on his other side and asked where he was from. It turned out he was from somewhere in central Pennsylvania and was in the area checking out cabins that were for sale. They spent the next hour swapping hunting stories and buying each other drinks. The music continued to blare and Clint found himself tapping his feet to the beat. Half of the patrons had left, and things were starting to wind down. Bob and his three cronies were now quietly eating the food Sadie had delivered. The stranger on the other side of the bar was also still there. Stubs was returning from the bathroom. He was either having a hard time putting one foot in front of the other, or he was attempting to do a jig to the fast-beat song that was playing. He finally made it safely to his seat.

"What do you call that maneuver?" Clint asked.

"That's danshin. Want me to give you some leshons?"

Clint started to answer, but noticed Megan coming out from the back room. Beads of sweat dampened her forehead, and her normally curly hair was almost straight in the back. The top two buttons of her blouse were open, and Clint glimpsed the edge of her white bra. His heart skipped a beat, as she came over and took the vacant seat left by the man who was searching for a cabin.

"Howdy stranger. Buy a girl a drink?"

Her dark eyes and broad smile lit up the room.

"I don't know. Looks like you and Ralph were workin' up a pretty good sweat. What exactly were you doin'?"

Megan swatted Clint on the shoulder. "Wouldn't you like to know?"

Just then *The Devil Came Down to Georgia* began playing on the jukebox.

"Come on," Megan shouted grabbing Clint's arm, "lets dance."

"Oh, I don't —"

"Go ahead junor," Stubs coaxed. "I'll join ya."

Within seconds, Megan had Clint spinning and twirling on the dance floor. The faster the fiddle played, the faster his feet seemed to move. He couldn't keep his eyes off of the lovely girl beside him. It was probably good that he didn't too, or he would lose his balance and fall head first into the large-screen television. Stubs was doing a jig to his own beat, and the few remaining patrons were clapping and cheering him on. Clint was lost in his own world — just him and Megan. When the music stopped, Clint pulled Megan to him, wrapped his arms around her and their lips locked in a long, moist kiss.

Suddenly, there was a loud crash. Clint turned quickly to see Stubs roll off of the table where Bob and his friends were sitting.

"Stubs!" Clint yelled. He rushed over to help his fallen comrade.

"Ahhh. Who put that table there?"

"Stubs, are you okay?"

"Yeah, yeah, I'm fine. Darn table."

Stubs pulled himself up with the help of Clint and another man.

"Ah, excuse me," the stranger said, "but is your name really Stubs?"

Stubs stood up straight and looked at the stranger. "Well, I think it is, but right now I'm not too sure. Who are you?"

Clint eyed the stranger suspiciously.

"Well, my name is Ruby. I'm your nephew."

"My nephew? You're Jack's boy? How is the worthless shit? What are you doin' here? How'd you get here? Where you stayin'?"

Ruby's face turned a deep red at the insult of his father. His father was worthless, but this drunken fool had no right to criticize him.

Ruby helped Stubs up onto the bar stool and sat beside him. Clint and Megan followed, stunned by the surprise reunion. Clint sat next to Ruby, and Megan pulled a stool close to Clint. She rested her hand on his leg. Suddenly, Clint wasn't interested in the conversation between the two relatives.

"Actually, I don't know how Dad is. I haven't seen him in about fifteen years. I've been living up in *Vasser*."

Clint's attention was brought back to the two men.

"You want another beer?" Ruby asked.

"Does a bear crap in the woods?"

"I don't know. I haven't spent much time in the woods."

"Hah! Goodun. Buy me a beer nephew."

Clint watched as Sadie filled two glasses. A scuffle from the side caught his attention. The four men were standing and moving toward the door. He watched as one of them threw a couple of bills on the table. Bob gave Clint a smirk as he walked by. As they left, Clint turned his attention back to Megan. She was staring at him with a wide smile.

"Don't you ever stop smiling?"

"Not when I'm with you."

Clint shook his head. He couldn't understand why this woman had such an effect on him. He knew he should feel guilty about being here with Megan while Paula was at home working . . . Well, maybe that was the problem.

"Hey Clint!" Stubs yelled.

"What old man?"

"My nephew's gonna take me home. He's gonna stay in the spare room. Think you can get home okay without me?"

Clint looked at his friend and then at the man called Ruby. Something didn't seem right. Things were moving too fast here.

"You sure that's smart?" Although the question was directed at Stubs, Clint's eyes never left Ruby.

"Hey, he's famalee. Curse it's allright."

Clint turned his gaze back to Stubs. "Okay. I'll stop by early tomorrow."

"Not too early."

Clint watched as Stubs and Ruby left. Then, he turned back to Megan. Sadie and Ralph came out of the kitchen to join them. The four of them were alone.

"Where's Stubs and that stranger?" Ralph asked.

"The stranger said he was Stubs' nephew," Sadie explained.

"Said he was from *Vasser*," Megan added.

"Well don't that beat all," Ralph commented. "How'd he end up in Elk Run?"

"Don't know," Clint answered. "That's what worries me."

"You don't think he's really his nephew?" Megan asked.

"Don't know that either," Clint responded

The three looked at Clint expectantly.

"Ah, I'm just bein' paranoid." Clint turned his attention back to Megan. "You never did tell me what you and Ralph were doin' back there that made you sweat so much."

"Watcha talkin' about?" demanded Sadie.

"We were cooking," explained Ralph innocently.

"You better mean you were cooking potatoes Ralph Ungst, or I'll be cooking you in a big black pot!"

Clint and Megan broke out laughing at the sight of Sadie chasing Ralph around the bar.

"They sure are happy together," observed Megan.

"Yeah, that they are," agreed Clint. "Well, I guess I better get goin'. Thanks for the dance."

"Thanks for the kiss. I'm sorry we got interrupted . . . again."

Clint started to get off the stool. Megan stood up at the same time and reached her hands up behind his neck. She pulled Clint's head down to hers and their lips met. This time they kissed for a long, uninterrupted time. When Clint finally came up for air, he was light headed.

"Wow. I . . . ah —"

"Good night sweet man. Will I see you tomorrow?"

"I hope so."

Clint turned and walked to the door. Stopping, he turned one last time to look at the beautiful woman standing at the bar.

"Good night." Clint opened the door and stepped out into the cold night air. He felt alive. He whistled some tune he had forgotten the name of, as he walked down the dark lot toward his truck. Only one other vehicle, besides his own, remained.

Chapter 20

Jason pulled the map off of the passenger's seat for what seemed like the hundredth time. He had been driving for over eight hours, only stopping once to eat and once for gas. Both times he had to take an exit and find an out-of the way place where there were few cars and people. That added a lot of time to the trip, but it was a precaution he had to take since he was driving the stolen car of a murdered man. Thankfully, he had seen only two police cruisers and they were both traveling in the opposite direction. Jason glanced at the map again. The exit he wanted was just ahead.

Jason's heart began beating faster as he pulled up to the stop sign at the end of the exit ramp. There in front of him was a green rectangular sign pointing toward the left. It read: "Elk Run – 15". Jason made the turn and started on the final leg of the journey. He had been starting to dose off during the last hour, but now he was wide-awake. What was he going to do when he got to the town? Where would he stay? How would he find this person named Stubs? What would he do with the car? He had to hide it somewhere it would not be found, at least not for a long time. These thoughts circled in his mind as he drove over the narrow two-lane road. He began to take notice of the surroundings. Thick forests came to within a few feet of either side of the road. An occasional dirt road retreated into the darkness, sometimes ending in front of a cabin or home. Suddenly, several dark forms on the edge of the left side of the road caught his attention. He slowed and finally had to stop as six large deer trotted across the road in front of him. He sat behind the wheel and watched as they disappeared into the blackness. Finally, he continued down the road. Several more times he slowed to stare at other deer standing on the side of the road. Some watched him drive by. Others just ignored him and continued munching on whatever it was they found nourishing in the thick grass. A large lake appeared off to the right. A two-lane macadam road ran up to it and apparently all the way around. Then a sign appeared informing him that he was now entering the town of Elk Run. He slowed and pulled to a stop alongside the road. He couldn't see over the top of the hill a couple hundred yards ahead of him, but he could tell there was some sort of man-made lights intruding on the dark night sky. He turned around to look at the lake off to the right.

Putting the car in gear, he made a u-turn and then turned left onto the road that led to the lake. As he approached the lake, which was on his left, he noticed several parking areas on the right that held picnic tables and grills. The road wound around the lake and followed the contour of the water. He passed a sandy beach-like area and then started up an incline. As the road continued around the lake, the incline got steeper and he could no longer see the water on his left. At the peak of the hill, he was three-quarters way around the lake. Jason stopped the car and got out. He walked to the edge of the road and looked over the side. The bank dropped almost straight down about twenty yards. The edge of the lake was only a couple of feet from the base of the bank, but tall strands of grass appearing several feet out into the lake indicated that the water was shallow there.

Jason got back into the car and continued down the road. He began descending the hill until he was back level with the lake. He pulled off to the side of the road into a large parking area when he noticed a cement ramp descending into the water. Two small boat docks were rocking in the water a few yards away. Jason got out of the car and walked part of the way down the ramp. He could hear and smell the cold water lapping against the boat ramp. Jason walked back to the car. He knew what he had to do.

Jason made sure all his clothes were in his duffle bag and set the bag in the grass a safe distance from the ramp. He stuffed all the maps and the dead car owner's clothes into the black overnight bag and locked it in the trunk. Getting back into the car, Jason used the power controls on the side of his door to open all the windows, lined the car up with the ramp, and backed up about twenty yards. He opened his door, got out and stood with his left hand gripping the inside of the door jam and his right on the steering wheel. He made one last check around the lake for any headlights. He saw none. Pushing with all his might on the door jam and the steering wheel, the car began to move forward. It continued to pick up speed as Jason pushed the car and jogged to keep pace with it. He was at the edge of the ramp. The car was moving faster. Half way down the ramp, Jason gave one final shove and dove out of the way of the car. He landed on his right shoulder and rolled over several times. Something hard crashed into his left heel as he came to an abrupt stop on the cool, damp ground and he felt pain shoot up his left leg. Jason sat up just as the back end of the car entered the water. He held his breath. The car tilted up in a vertical position and seemed like it was stuck in mid-air. Finally, after what seemed like minutes, the car slid onto its side and sunk into the water. A loud splash sent water running up the ramp. Then the night was silent as the car disappeared from view.

He was going to miss the car. It sure was easier getting around in a Mercedes than it was walking or taking the bus. But, it was only a matter of time before someone would stop and question him. They were probably looking for both the Mercedes and the missing license plate from the old ford by now. He wasn't sure how he would get around in Elk Run, but he was used to walking through jungles and the terrain he had seen over the last twenty or thirty minutes didn't look any more challenging than what he had experienced in Vietnam; and it was certainly cooler here than in Nam.

Jason stood up slowly, testing his aching ankle. Although it pained him, he could still walk. It didn't feel like anything was broken. He picked up the duffle bag and slung it over his shoulder. Then he started his walk toward the lights of Elk Run.

The night air was cool and the sky was full of stars and empty of clouds. Silence surrounded him. He couldn't ever remember being in a place so quiet and peaceful. He imagined all sorts of wild animals standing calmly in the woods watching him stroll down the unlit road.

As he topped the hill, he saw several houses and some type of store or business sitting quietly about two hundred yards down on the left side of the road. Jason barely made out the word "Old" on a sign hanging from the establishment. On the left side of the building, stretching out towards Jason, was a macadam parking lot about 30 yards long and 10 yards wide. Two vehicles were sitting near each other at the end of the small parking lot furthest from the lighted building. Several small forms seemed to be sitting around the two trucks. He continued walking. Suddenly, a door opened at the establishment. The light from inside silhouetted a large man in a light-colored jacket. He casually walked toward the two trucks.

Jason's attention was drawn to the vehicles as he noticed the forms moving slightly. Both trucks were parked with their front ends toward the steep bank that ran the length of the parking lot and continued behind the building. Jason could now read the sign clearly, which advertised the "Old Timer's Inn." A green Explorer was parked with its driver's side close to the end of the parking lot. The other vehicle, a red pickup, appeared to be one space away. Two forms, which Jason could now make out as men with green camouflaged jackets and hats, were crouched near the back fender of the Explorer. Two other men, dressed almost identical to the first two, were crouched near the front fender of the pickup. All four were out of sight of the man walking toward the vehicles. As the single man approached the first vehicle, the two men slowly moved around the front of the truck, to the passenger's side. They were circling behind the unsuspecting man as he passed the pickup truck.

Ambush! The thought brought back all the painful memories of Vietnam. Without thinking, he began running. He tried to yell, but nothing came out of his mouth. The man who was walking alone was now passing the first truck. He appeared to glance at the vehicle, but did not stop moving. He was now at the back of what was probably his own vehicle. Jason was still fifty yards away and the slope in the road caused him to lose sight of the events that were taking place.

* * *

Clint glanced at the red pickup truck. Something about the duel cab vehicle looked familiar, but he could not remember where he had seen it before. Nothing much was registering in his mind at the moment, except the last kiss from Megan.

As he crossed the back of his truck, he reached into his pocket to pull out his keys. His head was down as he rounded the vehicle and started toward the driver's door. He never saw the short two-by-four that crashed into his stomach. Clint bent over in pain, the wind knocked out of him. A fist came up from underneath him and landed on his right cheek. The force lifted his head up into the air, but it was not strong enough to knock him over. Clint stared at the man in front of him: Bob. Clint gasped for breath and pulled his right hand back to land a punch in the man's face. His arm wouldn't move. As the man in front of him landed another shot to Clint's right cheek, his head twisted to the side. Now he noticed the small man holding his arm with both his hands. Another set of hands grabbed his left arm and the two of them pinned him against the tailgate of his truck. Bob starting pummeling Clint in the stomach and face. Clint tried to raise his feet to kick at the man hitting him, but he couldn't make his legs move. Clint tasted blood in his mouth and felt a thick liquid flowing into his right eye. He struggled to remain conscious. All he saw was a blur.

* * *

Jason was running now, his duffle bag discarded. As he came out of the gully in the road, he was only ten yards away from the terrible scene. Two men were holding the big man against the truck. One was pounding the defenseless man in the stomach and face. The fourth was silently standing off to the side watching. Jason sprinted the last five yards. Finally the sound that had been building inside him, escaped from his throat in a blood-curdling cry. Jason slammed into the man who was dishing out the punishment. The two landed on the dirt ground and Jason did not give the man under him a chance to get up. All the anger he had held inside him for so many years exploded to the surface. Jason smashed his right and then his left fist into the man's face. The man stopped resisting. Jason stood up and lifted the man with both hands. Holding him with his left, Jason landed one final right punch to the man's nose. He crumbled to the ground and did not move.

* * *

Clint watched as the man who was hitting him was driven past him and two figures landed on the ground. Clint sensed the two men's grips on his arms loosen. He summoned all his remaining strength and pulled his arms free. Then he quickly jerked his elbows backwards. He felt them land in the men's upper bodies. Turning around, Clint focused on the man on his left. Clint smashed a large fist into the man's face and then followed-up with a left to his midsection. Before he could land another punch, the man on his right drove his head into Clint's chest, driving him backwards. Clint lost his balance and fell on his back on the ground. The man was on top of him now, landing punches to Clint's stomach and face. The last thing Clint saw was a bloody fist coming toward his face. Clint tried to turn his head away from the blow. The dark night overtook him.

* * *

Jason turned around as he heard the bodies fall to the ground. A smaller man was on top of the man who had been ambushed, landing blow after blow. Jason ran toward the two men on the ground. He kicked the man on top squarely in his side. The force drove the man off of the man lying on his back. As Jason started toward the man he had just kicked, the other man who had been holding the defenseless person against the back of his truck drove a fist into Jason's right ear. The blow glanced off the back of his head and Jason kept his balance. Turning toward the new threat, Jason swung a left hook into the man's face, which was already bloody. The man staggered backwards. Jason drove his head into the man's stomach and pushed him up against the tailgate. The man let out a small gasp of pain. Jason finished him off with a right and left hook to his face. The man slumped to the ground. Suddenly pain shot through Jason's body as a fist landed in his left lower back. Another fist landed to his right lower back. As Jason tried to turn around to face his assailant, he saw another large man running toward him from the now well-lit building. This man was huge. Jason braced himself for what he knew was going to be a terrible blow.

* * *

Ralph was wiping off one of the tables near the door when he had heard a cry that sounded like a wounded animal caught in a trap. Not sure of what he was hearing, he casually opened the door and stepped outside. He looked down the road, but did not see anything. Turning toward the parking lot, he couldn't believe his eyes. Two men were lying on the ground. The one on top was pummeling the other who was on his back. One last punch from the man on top silenced the other's movements. Then Ralph saw Clint being driven to the ground. Ralph jumped into action.

"Sadie, call the sheriff! Quick!"

Ralph sprinted as fast as he could toward the end of the lot. He saw the man who had been pummeling the figure laying on his back kick another man off of Clint. Ralph watched helplessly as the person who had helped Clint was struck on the side of the head, but then pushed his assailant against the back of Clint's truck and landed shots to his face. The man who had been kicked got up off the ground and jumped to save his friend. Before Ralph could get there, the man had landed two punches to the kidneys of the man who had saved Clint. Ralph ran smack into Clint's savior's assailant before he could land a third punch. Ralph lifted him off of the ground and threw him into the bank beside Clint's truck. Ralph continued after the man. Before he had a chance to regain his feet, Ralph picked him up with his left hand and landed a right fist to his face. The man went out like a light.

* * *

Clint opened his swollen eyes to see beautiful colored lights flashing all around him. There was a dull pain in his chest. His hands hurt, and a sticky liquid was seeping into his lips. He felt the cold, hard ground underneath him. Gradually, his eyes began to focus on the figures hovering above him. Clint tried to get up, but a firm pressure on his shoulders held him to the ground.

"Just stay put old buddy," Ralph's calm voice sounded in his left ear.

Clint turned his head toward the voice. He tried to open his mouth to speak, but his mouth was so dry, no sound came out.

"Clint?" a sweet female voice asked to his right. "Clint? Are you alright?"

Clint turned his head to the other side and stared into Megan's dark eyes. The smile was gone and fear and concern were written on her face. He tried to wet his lips with his tongue so he could speak.

"Need . . . a . . . beer."

The familiar smile returned to Megan's face.

"You'll have to settle for water." Megan put a cold plastic bottle to Clint's lip and gently poured a trickle of clear liquid into his mouth.

Clint swallowed thankfully.

Megan gently stroked Clint's face with her hand. Despite the cold night air, her hand was soft and warm. Several car doors slammed and Clint heard a set of feet approach from behind him.

"Okay, Ralph. We got all these assholes in the cars. They're gonna spend a few days in the pokey. Course, some wiseass lawyer will probably have them out on bail, but with Clint and Jason's testimony, they'll be back in before long. I'll radio for an ambulance..."

"No!" Clint broke in. "No ambulance. Not spending any time in a hospital. I'll mend just fine at my house."

"Now Clint —" Ralph started.

"No ambulance," Clint repeated.

"You sure Clint?" the old sheriff asked.

"Yeah, I'm sure. I feel better already. Who's Jason?"

"That'd be me," a strange voice answered from the direction of his feet.

"This is the guy who happened to come along and probably save your life," Megan explained appreciatively.

Clint tried to sit up again. This time, Ralph's firm grip loosened and he helped raise Clint into a sitting position. Clint stared at the stranger who was slightly bent over at the waist.

"Got a lot of questions for you, but I'll just say thank you for now."

"You're welcome."

"Well, I'll leave this stubborn mule in your hands, Ralph," the Sheriff said. "If you need anything else, you just call."

The sheriff retreated to one of the two cars with the flashing lights. Clint turned his head and watched them drive away.

"Help me up."

Ralph and Megan slipped their arms under Clint's and pulled him to his feet. The pain in his chest shot through him and he couldn't suppress a groan.

"Looks like a cracked rib to me," Ralph observed.

"Nothing they can do for that at the hospital. Must have been from that stick of wood they hit me with," Clint commented. The details of the past few minutes were coming back to him. He remembered being held against the tailgate of his truck and being pummeled by a third man. Then he remembered a blurry figure slamming into the man, allowing Clint to free himself.

"Where did you come from?" Clint asked his newfound friend.

"I was walking down the road up there. I saw them waiting for you, but I couldn't warn you in time. I'm sorry."

"Sorry? Man, if you hadn't come along when you did, I'd be planted in those weeds over there. I don't know how I can ever repay you."

"You two can work that out later," Sadie interrupted, speaking for the first time. "Right now, we're going to get you inside and clean up your ugly face."

"Ah, Sadie, you hurt my feelings."

"I oughtta hurt more than your feelings for refusing the ambulance. Now you gotta deal with me as your nurse, and I ain't gonna be as gentle as those pretty things in at the hospital."

"I think I want Megan to nurse me."

"No way! Come on!"

Clint was able to walk back into the Inn on his own, but each step sent another shot of pain through him. Once inside the warm building, Clint sat down at one of the tables. Jason sat on the other side and Sadie and Ralph went into the kitchen to get some supplies. Megan pulled a chair next to Clint and rested her hand on his thigh.

"I can't believe those guys did this to you! Jason, I'm so glad you came along when you did. Where were you coming from?"

Jason had been thinking about his story since he had run the Mercedes into the lake. "I've been hitchin' east from Ohio for a couple of days. Guess I just ended up on the right road at the right time."

Clint looked at the man again. He wondered how someone hitch hiking from Ohio would end up on a back road to Elk Run. Clint figured stranger things could happen, but something didn't sound right. Whether Jason was telling the truth or not, for now, Clint didn't care. He hated to think how the night would have turned out if Jason hadn't shown up when he did.

"So, you don't have a place to stay?" Clint asked.

"Not yet. Is there a hotel around somewhere?"

"Not in Elk Run, there isn't," Megan answered.

"You'll stay at my house," Clint stated flatly.

"Oh, I couldn't do that —"

"Nonsense. You'll stay with me. I've got two extra bedrooms and an entire bunkroom that's empty. You can have your pick."

Jason thought it over. He didn't want to take any handouts, but it was late and he didn't want to offend this man who seemed very observant, despite the beating he had taken. "Okay, I accept. But, if it's alright, I'll stay in the bunkhouse."

"That's better," Clint laughed. The pain returned.

Sadie and Ralph returned from the kitchen with a pot of warm water, some towels and a first aid kit.

"Take your shirt off Clinton," Sadie demanded.

"Oh Sadie, now? In front of all of these people?"

"Careful, or she'll ask for your pants next," Ralph pointed out. "Then you'll be really embarrassed."

Clint started to unbutton his shirt, but Megan pushed his hands aside and helped him. The feel of her long, soft fingers against his bruised chest caused a warm feeling to spread over him. He almost forgot the pain in his chest. Almost.

Megan slowly pulled the torn and bloody shirt off his strong shoulders and down his back. When she had run into the parking lot and saw Clint lying silently on the ground, she had almost screamed in fear. She had thought he was dead. How had this man come to mean so much to her. As she laid the shirt on the table, their eyes met. Feelings, inexpressible in words, transcended the short space between them.

"Okay, now step aside," Sadie instructed.

Jason watched silently as the attractive woman removed Clint's shirt. He could tell there was some kind of romantic bond between the two of them. His thoughts drifted back to Norma, and how she looked when she had stepped out of the bathroom. He wondered if he would survive his encounter with Ruby. Ruby! Now that he had found Elk Run, how was he going to find this Stubs character? The town was obviously not very big, but there were probably a lot of cabins spread all over the area. He had no means of transportation, and he couldn't just ask someone if they knew the man. Despite their gratitude for his helping Clint, they would still become suspicious.

"There," Sadie spoke. "Now at least you look a little presentable."

Jason looked at the large man sitting opposite him. The dirt and grime had been wiped off of his face and the cuts had been cleaned and covered with a clear salve. An ace bandage had been rapped around his large chest.

"Ralph," Sadie demanded, "go get Clinton one of your clean shirts."

"Something in wool would be nice," Clint requested.

"Beggars can't be choosey," Ralph responded. "You'll take what you get."

"Yes sir." Ralph left to get a clean shirt.

Sadie and Ralph lived above the bar. There were six rooms upstairs that once served as a resting stop for passers-by and provided a home-away-from-home for many hunters in years gone by. When Sadie and Ralph purchased the establishment, they decided it was too much for them to maintain the inn and the bar and the restaurant. So, they converted it into a living area, which now had two bedrooms, a living room, dining room, kitchen and two bathrooms. There was an outside entrance around back, where they had a small garage and parking area. There was also an inside set of steps leading from the kitchen area. It was these that Ralph took to go upstairs.

"Do you drive, Jason?" Clint asked.

"Ah, yeah."

"Good, you can drive me home."

"Do you want me to come along?" Megan asked.

"Oh, I don't think that's necessary." Clint answered. He saw the disappointment on Megan's face. "I mean, it's not that I don't want you to. I'm just tired and —"

"I understand," Megan responded. After a moment she added, "but I will come over in the morning. If that's okay."

"Sure," Clint affirmed. He wasn't sure if it was okay or not. He didn't know if Paula was going to come by or not. Paula. Clint wondered if he should call her and explain what had happened. If he didn't, she would probably be upset that he hadn't called. Clint checked the clock on the wall. It was almost midnight.

224

Paula was probably asleep by now. He would wait until tomorrow to tell her.

Sadie watched the exchange between the two. She knew Clint was in a turmoil over what to do about Megan and Paula. Oh well, he was a big boy. He would have to figure that one out on his own.

A door slammed and Ralph came back into the room.

"Here's my best wool shirt. Don't get any blood on it."

"I'll try my best." Clint stood up and took the shirt from Ralph.

"Let me help," Megan asked, but did not wait for permission. She took the shirt from Ralph and gently helped Clint put it on. As she buttoned the buttons, her hands again brushed his hairy chest. When she was done, she kissed him on the cheek.

"There! Now, go straight home and go to bed. I'll stop by in the morning."

"Yes mama." Clint smiled.

"Here's his keys, Jason. I found them on the ground behind the truck."

"Let's get going. I'm beat!"

Ralph, Sadie and Megan watched the two leave the building. Suddenly, Megan felt very alone. She knew she wouldn't sleep much tonight.

Clint struggled to lift himself into the passenger's seat. Every movement caused him to grit his teeth against the pain. Jason tossed his large black duffle bag, which he had retrieved earlier after the cops had questioned him, in the back and started the vehicle.

"That way," Clint pointed in the direction of his house. He had a lot of questions for the man sitting beside him, but Clint was too tired to be sociable. He focused on directing the newcomer along the dark country roads. Soon, they passed the road leading to Stubs' home nestled among the forest trees. All looked dark and quiet.

"Good thing Stubs left earlier tonight. Man, to think he could have been with me when those jerks jumped me." Clint's anger began to rise as he envisioned the worst.

Jason almost lost control of the truck at the sound of the man's name.

"Hey, watch it," Clint complained as the jerky movement reminded him of the pain in his chest.

"Sorry. Who's Stubs?" Jason tried to ask casually.

"My neighbor. He lives alone since his wife died. No kids. I brought him into Sadie's with me. Luckily he left earlier with another stranger who happened to show up at the Inn." Clint realized what he had just said. Two strangers showing up in Elk Run on the same day. A lot of outsiders came to the area to hunt this time of year, but how many times did two people just show up at the Inn on the same day, with no interest in the outdoors. One was looking for his long, lost uncle and the other just happened to be hitchhiking through.

"Weird."

"What's weird?" Jason asked, fearing the answer.

"You and that other stranger, Rudy or something like that, showing up at Sadie's on the same day. That's weird."

"Yeah, guess it is." Jason decided not to comment further. "Rudy" had to be "Ruby". At least he now knew where he probably was. As Clint directed him down the driveway to his own house, Jason concentrated on the location of Stubs' house. It didn't appear to be too far away. Jason wouldn't need a vehicle to reach Ruby. Now all he needed was a weapon. Jason's thoughts were interrupted at the sight of the large house that loomed in front of him. A large black dog was standing guard on the porch.

"That's Shack. He won't bite, especially if you give him anything chocolate. You can leave the truck here in front. I'll move it tomorrow. Right now, I just want to hit the sack."

Jason turned off the engine and handed Clint the keys. Opening the door, he retrieved his bag and stepped onto the ground. Immediately the growling black dog greeted him.

"Oh stop it Shack. This guy just saved my butt. You better be nice to him."

Shack dropped his tough-guy routine. His owner apparently thought the stranger was okay, so Shack sat on his haunches and waited expectantly for the man to pet him. Instead, the stranger just walked past him. The stranger's eyes never left Shack. Shack sensed the man's fear and wondered what he was afraid of. Maybe there was a monster in the woods somewhere. If there was, Shack didn't want to waste time outside. He hopped up and down alongside the man as the two of them walked onto the porch. The two stopped and waited at the door for Shack's owner to open it. The stranger continued to stare at Shack. Shack's attention was diverted to a strange groaning sound coming from his master. Shack turned his head, and watched the big man walk awkwardly toward the door. Shack twisted his head to get a different view of the man and try to see what was wrong. Shack couldn't figure out why his owner was moaning and walking funny. Maybe he drank too much of that beer stuff.

Jason finally awkwardly reached down and cautiously stroked the big dog's neck. The dog responded by nuzzling Jason's leg with his big jaw. Jason had never been very comfortable around dogs or any other large animal. The memory of the time he was attacked by a German shepherd on his way home from elementary school was still vivid. This one appeared to be safe and Jason began to relax. The timid dog began to whine softly as Jason continued to stroke behind his ears.

"Looks like you two are going to get along just fine. Go ahead in. The door's open."

"He seems like a good dog. What did you say his name was?"

"Shack."

At the sound of his name, Shack looked expectantly at his owner. He was confused when his owner didn't say anything else. His owner must be sick or something.

Jason opened the door as he was instructed and stepped inside the house. It was warm and cozy. Once again, Jason was amazed at the turn of events in his life. Less than a week ago, he was alone, sleeping in a box in a crowded city, with the cold cement underneath him. Now he was standing in an expensive house, in the middle of the mountains, next to a friendly, black dog. Amazing.

"You sure you don't want to stay in one of the guest rooms here? There is plenty of room."

"I don't mind staying in the bunkhouse, if that's okay."

"No problem. Whatever you're comfortable with. If you don't mind, I'll just give you the keys and point you in the right direction." Clint went to a drawer in the kitchen and removed a set of keys. He started to remove one, but with each effort, pain jerked his body. He decided to just give the complete set to Jason.

Clint held the ring of keys out to Jason. "This one opens the main door. You probably won't need the others. The bunkhouse has plenty of beds. Pick whichever you want. There's a bathroom and a kitchen. I'm not sure what's in the frig and cupboards, but help yourself to whatever you can find. The heat is probably turned down, but the thermostat is just inside the door. Probably take a while to warm up, but in a couple of hours, it will be toasty. Come over here."

Clint led Jason through the dining room and out onto the back deck. He flipped a switch and lights illuminated the path down to the bunkhouse.

"There it is. You'll be okay?"

"Yeah, no problem. Can I help you with anything before I go down there?"

"Nah. I'll probably be asleep before you get down off the deck. Shack, you want to stay here or go sleep in the bunkhouse with Jason?"

Shack looked back and forth between the two men. Apparently the new man's name was Jason. It sounded like Shack had a choice to make: stay here or go to the bunkhouse. From the looks of his owner, Shack figured he should stay with his owner in case he was needed. Shack lay down on the floor indicating his choice.

"Guess you're on your own."

Jason laughed awkwardly. He liked the friendly animal, but he wasn't sure he was ready to spend the night alone with him.

"That's okay. I'll be fine."

"Okay. Well, have a good night then."

Jason adjusted the heavy bag on his shoulder and stepped out on the deck.

Clint watched as Jason started down the steps and then closed the door. He left the door unlocked as usual and left the outdoor light on. He started toward the bedroom but stopped as he remembered the bland dinner he had left Shack.

"I assume you ate all your dog food tonight."

"Grrrrrrrr," Shack responded.

Clint opened the refrigerator door and withdrew the remains of the chocolate cake Paula had brought over several days ago. Paula. He wondered if she would come over tomorrow. He wondered if Megan would be here if she did. Suddenly, he was too tired to think about it. He unwrapped the cake and set it on the floor.

"Enjoy."

Shack raced to the sweet dessert before his owner changed his mind.

Clint stopped at the bathroom before continuing to his bedroom. Struggling with his shoes and finally getting his pants off, he plopped on his back. He drifted off to sleep quickly. His last thoughts were of Megan's soft fingers on his chest.

Chapter 21

Elk Run, Pennsylvania
Saturday September 29, 1979 10:10 AM

Ruby woke from a restless sleep to the sound of pans banging in the kitchen. After arriving at his uncle's house the night before, Stubs pointed Ruby in the direction of the spare bedroom and indicated where the bathroom was. The old man barely stayed awake on the drive to the house to give Ruby directions. As far as Ruby was concerned, the man was basically a drunk. That didn't surprise Ruby much, since he remembered his own father, Stubs' brother, drinking himself to sleep most nights. At least that was what happened on the nights his father was at home. It was for that reason alone that Ruby avoided drinking as much as possible. A binge now and then was okay, and smoking the wacky weed was okay, but Ruby vowed never to get hooked on the liquid substance.

After Stubs had gone to bed, Ruby had silently checked out the old house. He had found a shotgun and rifle standing in a closet. Ammunition for both weapons was stored on a shelf above the guns. In the back of the cupboard above the refrigerator, Ruby found a tin box that contained five hundred dollars in cash. He made a mental note of that for future use. There were pictures of Stubs and a homely looking woman, who Ruby figured was the man's dead wife. He found nothing else of value and went to bed. He had lain awake for a long time listening to the silence. There were no sirens or doors slamming. No strange voices. Once he heard something howling that sounded like a creature from an old movie. Chills had gone down his arms at the sound. Perhaps coming to this godforsaken place was not a good move. He finally drifted off to sleep and dreamed of a plush hotel with an indoor swimming pool and beautiful women rubbing lotion on his body.

"Hey Ruby! Wake up sleepy head. Breakfast is ready."

Reluctantly, Ruby pushed back the blankets and got out of bed. He pulled on his pants, socks and a sweatshirt and walked to the kitchen. The smell of steaks made his stomach growl. Suddenly, he was very hungry.

"Something smells good," Ruby commented.

"Hope your hungry. Figured steaks and eggs would be a fitting welcome to the mountains for a city boy like you."

Ruby wasn't sure if the comment was meant as an insult or not. Without responding, he sat down on the worn chair in front of the plate that Stubs had put on the table. Stubs filled a second plate with food and sat across from Ruby.

"Eat up. There's plenty more."

"What time is it," Ruby asked as he took a mouthful of the scrambled eggs and juicy meat.

"Little after ten. I don't usually sleep this late, but I figured you'd want to sleep in."

"Sleep in? Hell, I usually sleep till noon."

"Ah! Waste of time! You should get up early and experience as much of what the day has to offer as you can."

Again, Ruby felt the man was criticizing him. He stuffed another piece of meat in his mouth to avoid putting the man in his place. Stubs was getting on his nerves already, and he hadn't even been in Elk Run for twenty-four hours. At least the food was good.

"The steak is great," Ruby commented, keeping his growing anger in check.

"Glad you like it. I think coyote meat is the best there is."

Stubs spit the remains of the food in his mouth onto his plate.

"Coyote? What're you trying to do, old man, poison me?" Ruby pushed the plate across the table and jumped up out of his seat. The chair fell over backwards. Moving to the refrigerator, he opened it and looked for something to wash away the taste of the wild animal. All he found was row upon row of beer cans.

"Don't you have anything to drink besides beer, you old drunk?"

"Why you foul-mouthed young punk. Show some respect for your elders. And if you don't like it here, leave. I'm only tryin' to be hospitable."

Ruby slammed the refrigerator door shut and turned back to face the old man. Their eyes locked and neither one broke contact. Ruby wanted to smash the man's face. How dare he feed him some wild animal without telling him what it was. He had to get out of the house before he got into more trouble. Finally, Ruby turned and went back to his bedroom.

"Could of at least brought me another beer," Stubs yelled at the retreating figure.

Ruby lifted his bag onto the bed and removed his pistol from inside. Shoving it into his belt in the small of his back, he quickly pulled on his boots and grabbed his jacket from the floor.

"I'm goin' for a walk," Ruby stated flatly as he walked through the living room and shoved open the door.

"Don't get lost!" Stubs shouted at the departing man. "Damn smart-alick kid," Stubs whispered to himself.

Ruby stomped across the porch and headed up a path into the woods. After going about fifty yards, he stopped and bent over with his hands on his knees. He finally got his breathing under control and looked around him. The path led from Stubs' house and angled to the right up a steep hill. Large trees loomed above him on both sides of the path. He began to feel lost, despite the fact that the house was still in view behind him. He couldn't go back. He either had to sit here and gather his thoughts or continue up the path. He decided to keep moving. There was no reason for him to go back and the overcast sky was already making him cold. The walk would keep him warm.

At the top of the hill, he had to stop again to catch his breath. He felt terribly out of shape and his legs were weak and tired. At least the path headed downwards. After about a half hour, he continued his walk.

He was beginning to relax as the contour of the ground began to level off. His boots made a sucking sound as he continued along the path. Soon, the path began to get narrower and it became difficult to follow. The large, round trees disappeared, and instead he found himself surrounded by hundreds and hundreds of small saplings that slapped at his face and arms. The brush underneath became thick and threatened to wrap itself around Ruby's legs. Ruby's heart began to pound. He felt trapped. The path had disappeared. His boots were sinking into the wet, mushy ground up to their tops. He had no idea which way to turn. How was he going to get out? Suddenly, a loud crash ahead of him caused the hairs on the back of his neck to stand up straight. He pulled the pistol from his back and pointed it in the direction of the noise. A huge, brown animal crashed through the dense brush. Horns protruding from his head seemed to be three feet long. As quickly as it had appeared, it was gone.

Ruby began to shake uncontrollably. He felt a warm liquid running down the inside of his legs. Ruby fell onto the wet ground and covered his head with his hands. After a few minutes, Ruby's shaking stopped, and he lifted his head off of the cold surface. Slowly he stood and looked around him. Maybe it would have been safer to stay in *Vasser* and take his chances with the police. He had no idea which way the house was. His heart started beating rapidly again, and he struggled not to panic. Finally, he decided to move in the opposite direction from the large animal. He replaced his weapon in his belt. He pulled one foot and then the other out of the murky ground. Ruby made slow, but steady progress, even though he had no idea what direction he was heading.

After a while, the ground started to become more solid as it sloped upwards. Ruby broke through the last of the thick underbrush into a more open area. Once again, thick, tall trees loomed all around him, but there was no path to guide him anywhere. Ruby's legs were aching terribly. His pants were soaked through from the waist down. Water had penetrated his boots and his feet were beginning to get cold while he stood still. Ruby decided to continue moving up the steep hill. He wanted to get as far away from the swampy area as possible, and he hoped he would be able to see Stubs' house from the top of the hill.

Ruby was gasping for breath as he fell to the ground at the top of the hill. He rolled onto his stomach and crawled to a large stump. Pulling himself up onto the stump, he sat with his arms on his knees. Sweat dripped from his forehead onto the leaf-covered ground.

After catching his breath, Ruby raised his head and looked down the mountain in front of him. He was startled to see a large house about two hundred yards away. In front of the house sat a green explorer and a pickup truck. Past the house was a lake. Some kind of animal seemed to be swimming near the shore. Off to the right was a long two-story building and a large open field. Ruby continued to turn around. In the distance he saw another smaller house. In front of it sat his black Suburban. Ruby sighed with great relief.

A car door slammed back in the direction of the first house. Ruby swung around in time to see a woman with blond hair get out of a red car and stroll toward the house. She stopped as she neared the pickup truck and turned sideways to look inside. As she did, her open coat revealed ample breasts. Ruby smiled. Maybe there was something worth staying for in Elk Run. He continued to watch the sway of her hips as she approached the door. She seemed to hesitate momentarily and then went inside. Ruby decided he would ask his uncle about who his neighbors were. Painfully, he moved his tired and aching body toward his uncle's cabin. There was a smile on his face.

Chapter 22

Elk Run, Pennsylvania
Saturday September 29, 1979 10:45 AM

Clint woke to Shack's barking. He swung his legs over the side of the bed and cringed at the pain that seemed like it would never leave him. Twice during the night he had to get up and toss down a couple of aspirins. He finally got some rest when he decided to sleep propped up against the headboard of his bed. Now he was wide-awake as Shack continued his barking from the hallway.

"Oh Shack, what is it? Right now I wouldn't care if someone came in and robbed me blind."

"Well, it's a thought, but I don't know what I'd do with all this stuff."

Shack stopped his barking and began whining. Clint stood and walked out into the hall to greet Megan.

"Ooh! Do you feel as bad as you look?"

"Probably."

Megan's eyes shifted to Clint's boxers and hairy legs. "Of course, not ALL of you looks that bad."

"Ah, I guess you caught me with my pants down."

"I'm not complaining."

Shack remained sitting on the floor while Megan gently stroked the back of his neck. He turned his head sideways to look at the strange looking man standing in his underwear a few feet away. His owner had all different shades of black, red and blue marks on his face. Shack wondered why he had made his face look that way. He remembered one day a long time ago when a bunch of little people came to their door looking like his owner, but they also had all kind of strange costumes on. His owner had given them some chocolate candy, and they had gone away. Shack wondered if his owner was going to go out to get some candy. He would have to put some more clothes on.

"I think I need a long hot shower."

"Is that an invitation?" Megan prompted, a mischievous smile on her face.

"That's tempting, but I'm afraid you'd hurt me," Clint smiled. He did not relish the thought of Paula showing up while he and Megan were in the shower. "Feel like making some breakfast?"

"Oh, I guess I could do that," Megan answered somewhat disappointed. "Yell if you need any help. Come on Shack. What are you hungry for?"

"Arf." Shack led the way back into the kitchen and sat down in front of the refrigerator, as if he was going to choose what he wanted from inside.

Megan picked a plate off of the floor and placed it into the sink.

"Looks like one of you guys ate on the floor last night. Suppose that was you."

Shack lowered his head and whined softly. He hoped that didn't mean he wasn't going to get any breakfast.

Megan found a half empty pack of bacon in the refrigerator and some sausage in the freezer. She began simmering the sausage and then remembered that the stranger named Jason was staying in the bunkhouse.

"Hey, why don't you go wake up Jason?" Megan commanded Shack.

Shack whined again. He was sure he was going to miss out on the food.

"Don't worry. We won't eat till you get back."

Shack reluctantly walked to the glass doors in the dining room. Megan followed him and opened the doors.

Shack ran across the deck and down the steps. He didn't want to be gone any longer than he had to. He did, however, stop to relieve himself before continuing to the bunkhouse. When he arrived, he barked as loud as he could.

* * *

Jason was tying his boots when he heard the barking outside. The dog that was so friendly last night sounded angry this morning. Cautiously, Jason walked to the door and opened it a crack.

Shack stopped barking when the door was opened. He stared at the man peeking out of the door. Shack sat down on his haunches and waited for the man to ask him to come inside.

"What is it Shack?"

Shack whined. He didn't have time to play games right now. Food was cooking in the kitchen. He stood up and began walking away. Stopping, he turned to face the stranger and barked once. Shack figured he had done his job. He turned back toward the house and trotted away.

Jason watched the big dog return to the house. Clint must be awake and had sent Shack to come and get him. Jason went outside. The sky was overcast, but Jason took his time. After spending so much time in the city, Jason marveled at the clean, crisp air that filled his lungs. Soft ripples disturbed the surface of the pond. The trees at the edge of the woods swayed gently in the breeze.

* * *

The hot shower had relaxed many of Clint's muscles and much of the pain had disappeared. His rib still hurt every time he moved, but the other minor aches were now bearable. Sitting on the edge of the tub, Clint slowly dried himself off as well as he could. He was unable to reach his back. After pulling on clean underwear and pants that he had brought with him into the bathroom, he decided to solicit Megan's help.

"Oh Nurse?" Clint yelled.

After a few moments, Megan replied.

"Yes."

Clint heard her footsteps coming down the hallway. There was a soft knock on the door and it slowly opened.

"You decent?" Megan asked.

"Mostly."

"Darn."

"I need a little help."

"That's why I'm here. Your wish is my command." Megan stepped into the large bathroom and smiled at the half-naked man.

"My first wish is for you to dry my back and re-wrap this ace bandage around me."

"Yes master." Megan took the towel from Clint as he stood and turned around. Gently, she wiped the water from his strong back. She gently rubbed the remaining water from his neck. Then she attempted to dry the hair on the back of his head. With the towel in her right hand, she slipped her left around his body and rested it on his chest. As she continued to mop his damp hair, she moved the fingers of her left hand over his strong chest. Her chest pressed upon his back. She felt Clint's nipples come erect. His breathing became heavy. Her own body began to tremble with excitement. Megan dropped the towel to the floor, and Clint slowly turned to face her. He ran his hands up the back of her legs, across her firm buttocks and up her back.

"Ruff. Ruff. Ruff. Ruff. Ruff." Sounded from the deck at the back of the house.

Clint and Megan burst into laughter at the same time.

"Man, what timing that dog has," commented Clint.

"If a porcupine is after him, he's on his own."

"Maybe you better just wrap me up for now. Jason is probably with him."

"Ooooookay." Megan reluctantly picked up the bandage from the top of the hamper and began wrapping it around Clint's chest.

"You're good at this."

"I've had lots of practice."

Clint creased his brow and looked quizzically at Megan.

"With DOGS, idiot."

"Oh."

Megan finished wrapping Clint's chest, and then helped him on with his shirt.

"Ruff. Ruff. Ruff. Ruff. Ruff. Ruff. Ruff."

"I better go let the wild animal in before he breaks down the door."

"Thanks. I'll be right out."

Megan left the bathroom and went to let Shack back inside. She found him standing outside the deck doors, slimy slobbers were running down the outside of the glass.

"I don't do windows, Shack."

Shack sat on his haunches and cocked his head at the woman talking on the other side. He hoped there was still food left.

"Come on in Shack," Megan said as she opened the door. She stepped outside on the deck to see if Jason was following. She saw Jason casually strolling up the path from the bunkhouse. He seemed to be basking in the beauty of the surroundings. She knew how he must feel. When she had come back from New York, she had spent hours just sitting outside staring at the surrounding trees, breathing in the clean, fresh air and waiting for some animal to stroll by. Jason finally reached the steps and started up toward the deck.

"Hi Jason. It's beautiful out here, isn't it?"

"Sure is. It's so quiet."

"Yeah, well, at least when Shack isn't yelling for food. Come on in, breakfast is ready."

"Oh, jeez, you didn't have to make me breakfast. I could —"

"Jason, relax. You're like a part of Clint's family now. You probably saved the guy's life. Besides, Clint kind of makes it a habit of helping others. It's not really charity or anything. He just, kinda, does things. He never expects anything in return. He'd probably give you the shirt off of his back. My dad says he's probably helped half the people in Elk Run. Rich, poor, everyone. So, relax. People always seem to find a way to pay him back.

"Who's paying who back?" Clint asked as he strolled into the kitchen.

"You'll be paying me back, big time, if I have to clean this window for slobber lips over there."

Shack shrunk down onto the floor as all three of the adults turned to stare at him. He wasn't sure why he was in trouble, but it looked like he was.

Jason pulled the door shut behind him and smiled as he followed Clint and Megan into the kitchen. There definitely was something going on between the two of them. Jason liked them. They made a nice couple.

"You guys sit down. I'll fix your plates. Come on Shack, you too."

Shack didn't hesitate at the sound of his name. He was sitting beside the stove before Megan got there.

"I can help," Jason offered.

"Okay, you can get some plates and utensils."

Clint gave directions to Jason and took a seat at the table.

"This is nice. A maid and a butler."

Megan laughed. "Remember there are paybacks."

Jason said nothing. His thoughts were on a day many years ago when he and Oscar had talked about getting a house together. Oscar had also told him he could be a butler in the house. Jason remembered why he had come to Elk Run. He had to find Ruby before he began to forget his debt to Oscar. He needed a gun. Then he would find his way over to Stubs' house, and it would all be over.

Jason took the first plate of food from Megan and set it down in front of Clint.

"Here you go Masta." The smile was forced.

After finishing breakfast, Jason suggested that Clint go relax on the deck. He and Megan would clean up. Clint offered no resistance.

"Hey, Jason, do me a favor?" Clint asked.

"Sure. What do ya need?"

"Down those steps," Clint explained pointing to a door off of the kitchen "is a refrigerator with a bunch of beer in it. How about loading the cooler on the deck and bringing it back up?"

"Okay." Jason retrieved the cooler from the deck, opened the door to the basement and went down the stairs. Once down there, he turned on a light and took in the sight of the large room. This definitely was a hunter's haven. His gaze settled on several large gun cabinets. He felt the set of keys in his pocket.

Perspiration appeared on his forehead. He had never robbed anyone before and starting with the man who had opened his home in hospitality did not sit well with him. But, how else was he going to get a gun? He pulled the keys from his pocket and tried the first cabinet. Finally, the door opened. It was empty. He tried the second and third. They too were empty. His hands began to sweat. He had been downstairs for several minutes. Soon, Clint and Megan would get suspicious. Finally, the last cabinet opened. Inside were several rifles. They would not work. On the shelf above the guns were boxes of ammo and a handgun. Jason had no idea what kind it was. As quickly as he could, he opened the boxes of ammunition. One box of shells seemed to fit the pistol. He jammed the gun into his belt and pulled his shirt over it. He took a handful of shells from the box and stuffed them into his pocket. Locking the door to the cabinet, he ran over to the refrigerator and filled the cooler three quarters full with cans. Jason opened the freezer door and found a half full bag of ice. Bouncing the bag on the floor to loosen the cubes, he finished filling the cooler with ice.

"You okay down there?" Megan's voice sounded from the top of the stairs.

Jason slammed the door shut and closed the cooler. He wiped his forehead with the sleeve of his shirt.

"Yeah, I'm comin'."

Jason turned off the light and went back upstairs. Megan was starting to rinse the dishes. Jason walked quickly out onto the deck and set the cooler down next to Clint.

"Thought you got lost." Clint was smiling but his eyes were penetrating.

"Sorry. Man, that's some room you got down there. I kind of looked around. Hope you don't mind."

Clint relaxed. "Nah. I'll give you the grand tour later." Clint winced as he bent over and pulled out a cold can. "Well, maybe tomorrow, if you don't mind."

Clint popped the top of the can and turned to look at Jason. "You are planning on staying around for awhile, aren't you?"

"Well...I...ah...probably. For a while. It sure is beautiful around here."

"Yeah, it is. Stick around. I could certainly use some help around here for awhile."

"We'll see. I better go get a jacket. I'll be back to help Megan."

Clint watched Jason return to his bunkhouse. The opening of the deck doors interrupted his thoughts.

"I think your dog wants out."

Shack squeezed past Megan, darted across the deck and down the steps. He didn't stop until he was a safe distance into the woods. After doing his business, Shack decided on a swim.

"When you gotta go, you gotta go," Clint observed.

"And a woman's work is never done."

Megan shut the door and returned to the kitchen.

Jason jumped as he heard the big animal race past him and retreat into the woods. Jason continued to the bunkhouse, not looking back. He could feel Clint's eyes on him. Jason hoped the man had not spotted the bulge under his shirt. When Jason was safely inside his temporary home, he went to his duffle bag and hid the gun in the bottom. Reaching into his pocket, he removed the shells and also put them in the bottom. Jason retrieved his jacket and headed back to the house.

Jason heard a noise coming from the lake. He turned in time to see the large black dog walk up the bank and shake the water from his back. Walking about ten yards away from the water, the dog barked once at Jason and turned to face the water. Suddenly, the dog took off on a run. About a yard from the edge, the dog leaped into the air. He landed with a loud plop in the water and began swimming around. Jason wondered if the belly flop had hurt. He continued his walk to the house.

Megan was busy drying the large frying pan when she heard a noise from behind her. Turning around, she saw a tall, attractive blond woman standing just inside the door. Their eyes met in an awkward stare. Paula was the first to speak.

"You must be Megan."

"Yes." Megan put down the dry pan and the dishtowel. She walked toward the woman and extended her hand. "Hi."

"I'm Paula. Is, ah, Clint here?" she asked shaking the woman's firm hand.

"Oh, yeah. He's out on the deck."

"Thank you." Paula dropped the woman's hand and moved to the dining room. Opening the door, she stepped out on the deck and spotted Clint sitting on a chair with a beer in his hand.

"Oh my God! What happened to you?" Paula rushed to the man with the bruises on his face and knelt beside him. She gently touched his face with her soft fingers.

"I kinda had a run in with some guys at Sadie's last night."

"Why didn't you call me? I would have come over." Paula heard the door slide open and turned to see Megan step onto the deck. "Oh, I understand."

Clint turned to see what Paula was staring at.

"Oh, no, you —"

"You don't have to explain." Paula stood up and stepped back from the chair. The sounds of footsteps on the stairs caught her attention.

"Hi," Jason said as he stepped onto the deck.

"Paula, this is Jason. Jason came along last night and rescued me from the guys who were beating on me. Megan was at Sadie's when it happened. She came over, this morning, to see how we were. We just finished breakfast. You hungry? I can get you something." Clint started to get up. He relished the thought of getting away from this confrontation.

"No, sit down," Paula commanded. "I already ate." She couldn't take her eyes off the man's beaten face. "Oh God, Clint, why do you go to that place. Is there anything I —" Paula turned her gaze back to Megan and decided the young, pretty woman with dark hair had provided all the nursing Clint needed.

"Please, sit down Paula."

"Yes, sit down, I was just leaving," Megan commented.

"Ah, Megan. I thought you were going to take me for a walk up in the mountains. I've never seen anything so beautiful." Jason wasn't sure why he had suggested the walk. For some reason, he didn't want Megan to leave. She and Clint seemed to be so happy together. Besides, perhaps he would find a way to get over to the house where Stubs lived.

"Ah, yeah. Come on. I can at least lead you to some grouse." Megan caught a glimpse of Clint smiling as she turned and started walking up the deck. She heard Jason following behind her.

Clint and Paula watched the two disappear around the corner of the house. Clint had several comments he wanted to make, but felt it was safer to remain silent. He turned his eyes to Paula as she moved to sit on the chair next to him. Her eyes began to mist as she stared at his bruised face.

"It's not that bad," Clint offered. "The worst is over. In a few days, you won't —"

"It's not the bruises." Paula lowered her head and tears dropped slowly onto her lap. "You're in love with her, aren't you?"

"Megan? No. Honey, I — She's — No, I love you," Clint offered weakly. He felt he loved Paula. He didn't know how he felt about Megan, other than he was so happy when he was around her.

"You don't show any interest in my work. You keep going to that bar and drinking yourself into oblivion. We never go anywhere. You spend all your time in the woods . . . or with Megan." Paula's shoulders shook from her silent sobs.

"Paula, I — I am interested in your work. I think you are wonderful. You are so good with those kids. Why, if it weren't for you, most of those kids would be in jail or in some home somewhere. You always seem too busy to go away anywhere. As for Sadie's and the woods, I enjoy those things. You want me to stop hunting and going to Sadie's?"

Paula wiped her eyes on the sleeve of her jacket. "No. I know that's part of who you are. It's just— I just don't — Oh Clint, I love you so much, but I need more. I need someone to share my life with. You and Megan seem so much alike."

Paula jumped off the seat and began walking away as tears began to spill uncontrollably down her cheeks. Clint sensed the pain he had caused and struggled to get up.

"Paula, wait."

Paula stopped several steps away. She turned and propped her elbows on the deck rail. Her head rested in her hands as she continued to cry.

Clint walked up behind her. Gently, he placed his hands on her shoulders. Paula shook them off and leaned further over the rail.

"Paula, please, don't cry." Although he didn't believe he was in love with Megan, everything else Paula had said was true. His mind was a jumbled mess. This woman meant so much to him, but when he tried to envision their lives together a year, two years, ten years from now, no picture came to his mind. Then he thought of Megan. He saw them traipsing through the woods: hunting, fishing, and laughing over a beer at Sadie's. Was that love? Or was that just something you did for fun? He felt like his mind was about to explode.

"Paula, I'm sorry."

Paula turned around slowly and looked into Clint's eyes. Her mascara was running down her cheeks. Finally, a small smile creased her lips.

"I know you are, my sweet man. But we can't help who we are. I guess it's time we move on." Paula raised her finger to her lips and passed a kiss to Clint's.

"Take care of yourself, Clint. Good-bye my friend."

Paula gently pushed past Clint and walked down the deck. Clint watched her turn the corner and disappear.

"Damn!"

Clint moved back to his chair and sat down. Roughly, he grabbed a beer from the cooler and tore the tab off. He downed half the can in one swallow.

Padded footsteps sounded on the stairs. Shack stopped with his front paws on the deck. He had watched Paula leave as he came up from the lake. He sensed that something was not right, so he wasn't sure whether he should approach his owner, or return to the water.

Clint turned and stared at the big dog.

"Want a beer, mutt?"

Wow, this was a rare treat. His owner didn't offer him a drink of that funny yellow stuff very often. It tasted kind of funny and sometimes bubbles went up his nose. If he drank too much of it, he got dizzy for some reason and had trouble walking. He would have to be careful. He didn't want his face to turn colors like his owner. Shack went over to the dish that was normally filled with water. Using his paws, he tipped it over, spilling the clear liquid on the deck. Picking up the empty dish in his mouth, he walked over and held it out to Clint.

"Ah, a dog after my own heart."

Clint took the dish and emptied a can into it. Setting the dish on the deck, Clint pulled a second can from the cooler for himself and sat back to stare at the sky. The cool breeze began to calm him. Clint emptied half of the second can into Shack's dish and finished the rest himself. Dropping the empty can on the deck, Clint closed his eyes. Forgetting about Paula and Megan, he listened to the birds and squirrels that seemed to surround him. Before long, he fell asleep.

* * *

Jason and Megan reached the top of the first ridge behind Clint's house. Megan led the way. Jason panted heavily behind her.

"Stop. Stop, please," Jason gasped. "My God, whatcha jogging for?"

"I'm sorry," Megan laughed. "I just feel so invigorated in the mountains in the fall. Come on, let's sit on this stump over here."

Jason drug his tired legs over to the large stump and sat facing back down the hill. A couple hundred yards away sat Clint's house. Jason wiped his forehead on the sleeve of his jacket and took in the beautiful surroundings. His breathing gradually returned to normal.

"So, Mr. Jason Shark, who are you?"

"Huh?" Jason asked, startled by the question.

"Who are you? Where do you come from? Where are you going? What do you like? What do you hate? Do you work? Do — "

"Stop already!" Jason smiled. "What are you, a reporter?"

Megan returned the smile. It was easy for Jason to see what Clint liked about this girl.

"No, I'm just making conversation. I am curious though. You magically show up one night and stop four goons from beating up a man I care a lot about. You seem like a nice guy. I'd like to know more about you." Megan shrugged. "But, you don't have to tell me anything if you don't want to."

Jason continued observing the colorful surroundings. Different birds were shouting or singing in the trees. A squirrel stood on his hind legs about twenty yards away and began nibbling on an acorn that he held in his tiny paws. The crisp smell in the air relaxed Jason's tense muscles.

"Ain't too much to tell. I graduated from high school and went to Nam. Just kinda been bouncing around since I got back."

"You were in Vietnam? I . . . I can't even imagine what that must have been like. A friend of mine got drafted. He wasn't a close friend, but we were in classes together in high school. I heard he was killed his first week there. I was in college. My mom wrote me and told me there was a closed-casket funeral. One day we were doing silly dances at our senior prom. The next, Allen was dead. He was just a smart, kind, happy boy. How does that happen?"

Jason stopped watching the squirrel, which had retreated up a large oak tree and was busy chasing another furry creature around the branches on the tree.

"It happened to a lot of boys. Too many. I don't know why. Some say our government made it happen. Others blame those of us who came home alive. Sometimes I think people would be happier if every one of us who went over there, had come back dead. Then they could yell at the government and not have to look the survivors in the eyes. Maybe my life would have meant more if I had died."

"No!" Megan responded loudly. "Don't you ever say that." Megan grasped Jason's hands in hers.

"If you had died, would it have allowed Allen to come home? If you had died, would Clint still be alive, or walking? I can't even imagine what your life has been like since you came back. My guess is that you've probably made some decisions you regret. I can hear your anger. But I'd also guess that Clint is not the first person you've offered your help to. How many people are a little better off because you've touched their lives? I know I'm one of them."

Jason looked into the lovely woman's eyes. They were intense. They reflected what she believed in her heart. Jason thought of Norma. Then he thought of Oscar. Oscar was dead because of Jason. Yes, he had touched other's lives. Norma was better off. Oscar was dead.

Jason pulled his hands away.

"You're a good woman. Clint likes you a lot. I can see it in his eyes. He's a lucky man."

A car door slammed below them. Jason and Megan turned their heads at the same time. They watched as Paula backed up her car, put it in drive and went around Megan's. She disappeared down the driveway.

"Guess it's clear to go back," Jason observed.

"Sure you don't want to go up further? There is a beautiful view from up top."

Jason stood and took a few steps toward the top of the mountain. To his left, he spotted a house with smoke coming out of the chimney.

"Who lives there?" Jason asked hopefully.

"That's Clint's neighbor Stubs. He's a nice old man. His wife died, and he lives alone. You know, it's strange. The same night you showed up, Stubs' nephew did too. I think his name was Ruby or something like that. I believe he's staying with Stubs. Maybe the five of us should get together for dinner or drinks at Sadie's."

"Yeah, maybe we could do that," Jason lied. "I think you've given me a good enough workout for one day. Let's go back and see if the patient needs anything."

Chapter 22

Elk Run – Stubs' house
Saturday September 29, 1979 1:30 PM

Ruby pushed open the door to Stubs' house and stepped inside. His boots squished as he walked across the floor to his bedroom. From outside the back of the house, he heard the sound of someone chopping wood. Ruby had to admit that, for an old drunk, Stubs sure had a lot of energy. He decided to change and get a shower before facing the man again.

The hot shower had refreshed him somewhat, but the muscles in his legs ached. Putting on clean clothes and a pair of sneakers, Ruby went out into the living room. Stubs had apparently finished chopping wood and was relaxing on the old sofa. A beer can sat on the table next to him.

"Enjoy your walk?"

"Yeah," Ruby lied. He wasn't about to admit to this old man that he had gotten lost in a swamp. "Saw some huge animal with gigantic horns. Also saw a big house nearby. Who's your neighbor?"

"Ah! You musta been in the swamp. That's Old Ruthless. And the horns are called antlers."

There he went, correcting him again. This old man treated him like a kid. Ruby walked quickly to the kitchen and yanked open the refrigerator door. He didn't want to start drinking, but there wasn't much else to choose from.

"Bring me a beer," Stubs yelled from the other end of the house.

Ruby grabbed two cans and slammed the door shut. Walking into the living room, Ruby dropped one of the cans in Stubs' lap. He then took a seat on the recliner and pulled back the tab on his own can.

"Hey, watch it kid, you'll shake it all up." Stubs pulled back the tab and began sucking the foam as it squirted out of the top. "The house was probably Clint's. You know, the guy who I came to Sadie's with."

Ruby stared at the man as his anger began to grow. He tried to control it by focusing on the subject of Stubs' neighbor. "Nice house. What's the guy do to make all the money to build a house like that?"

"Well, don't actually know what he did to make all the money to build that house. Had it when he came here. 'Bout five years ago. Doubt he got it robbin' banks, though."

Stubs eyes looked accusingly at Ruby. Ruby thought about his duffle bag loaded with cash. Had the old man searched his belongings while he was wandering around in the woods? Ruby's piercing eyes returned Stubs' glare. Ruby's hands grasped the arms of the chair.

"What's he do now?" Ruby questioned.

Stubs shrugged. "Now he runs a huntin' camp. Guys, some gals, come in for a week at a time, pay him to hunt on his land and stay in his bunkhouse. I need another beer."

Stubs got up and went to the kitchen for another drink. Ruby used the time to gain his composure. So, the man next door was a hunter. He must have several guns in his house, as well as a lot of other valuables. Maybe he would have to find a way to pay a visit to the big house.

"There was a blond chick came to the house," Ruby continued as Stubs resumed his seat on the sofa. "That his wife?"

"Hah! That's a good one! Naw, that'd be Paula. Them two have had a thing goin' for several years. But they're like whisky and beer. Separate, they both taste great. But God didn't make them to mix together. Know what I mean?"

Ruby had to think about the strange explanation. In the end, he figured it meant that the two didn't get along too well. That was good.

"This Paula dame ain't into hunting?"

"No way! She's a teacher. Teaches what they call disadvantaged youths. You know, mentally disabled, troublemakers, kids who hate their parents. She's real good at it too. Least, that's what I hear."

Ruby thought about what the old man was saying as he sipped slowly on the cold beer. He wanted to ask where the blond woman lived, but didn't want Stubs to become suspicious. As he thought about the woman and the house next door, his eyelids became heavy. The old man was saying something, but Ruby could barely hear the words. He felt the can being pulled from his hand, but did not have the energy to offer any resistance; not that he wanted to.

Stubs took the can from Ruby's hand and downed the remaining liquid. There was no sense letting any of the cold beer go to waste. As he walked to the kitchen to dispose of the empty cans, he wasn't sure what to think of the strange man sitting in his living room. Stubs didn't doubt that Ruby was his kin. Stubs could see the resemblance to his brother. He felt obligated to help the young man however he could. What concerned him was the large amount of money in the man's bag. At first, Stubs had felt guilty rummaging through Ruby's belongings. But, after finding the money, the gun and the cartridges, Stubs became angry and worried. Stubs had no doubt that the money was not earned. No one carried that amount of cash around with him. Stubs wasn't sure what to do. He debated driving over to Clint's to ask his help. Clint was a smart man. After retrieving another beer and checking the clock, Stubs decided he was hungry. He would make himself something to eat and then go over to Clint's. Clint had said he would stop by this morning. It wasn't like Clint not to do what he said he would.

Chapter 23

Elk Run – Clint's house
Saturday September 29, 1979 3:15 PM

Stubs pulled his beat-up truck to a stop in front of Clint's house. He had left Ruby sleeping soundly. Stubs had offered Ruby something to eat, but the younger man had simply grunted and shifted his position from the recliner to the sofa.

Before Stubs could open the door, Shack was sitting patiently in front of the vehicle. Stubs opened the door and stepped out.

"Hey Shack, how you doin'?"

"Arf. Arf." Shack responded. Shack liked when the old man called Stubs came over. He always brought cupcakes with him. He watched anxiously as the man got out of the truck and walked toward him. To Shack's surprise, the man simply patted him on the head and continued past him to the door. Shack turned his head to follow him. Without warning, a whine escaped his throat. That was so uncool. Stubs stopped and turned around.

"Oh, guess I forgot something," Stubs smiled. He reached into his coat and pulled out a pack of chocolate cupcakes. Before Stubs could open the wrapper, the big dog staggered over to Stubs and sat with his front paws on Stubs' feet. His tongue was hanging out of the side of his mouth and he seemed to have trouble keeping his head still. His tail was slapping against the porch post. Stubs tossed one of the cakes into the air. Shack jumped into the air and tried to grab the treat. It bounced once on his nose and rolled down the side of his head to the ground. A big blob of chocolate stuck on his ear. Stubs placed the second cake on the porch and turned back to face the door. "You're awfully uncoordinated today." He rang the bell.

A strange man with thick black hair and dark eyes opened the door. The two stared at each other for a few moments.

"Who er you?" Stubs asked.

"I'm Jason. Who are you?"

"Stubs. I'm looking for Clint. I know that's his dog, and I think this is his house. Is he in there?"

"Oh, yeah. You're his neighbor. Come in. He's out on the deck."

Stubs stepped through the door and followed the stranger to the back of the house. They went through the sliding doors and stepped onto the deck. Stubs stopped in his tracks as he caught sight of the man slouched in the chair.

"Holy cow! What happened to you?"

"Schtubs old man! Glad to see ya. Come on, have a sheet. Jason, get Schtubs a beer. You still drink, don't ya?"

"I will after you tell me who painted your face with their fists. And who's the new guy?"

Stubs sat down on the chair next to Clint and watched as Jason picked up the empty cooler and headed into the house to replenish it with beer from the basement. The garbage can that normally sat in the kitchen was propped against the deck banister. It was two-thirds full of empty cans.

"Looks like there's been a party here. How comes you invited the dog and not me?"

"Shorry neighbor. It was kinda unplanned."

"So, you gonna tell me who rearranged your face, or do I have to beat it outta you?"

"Don't make me laugh, old man. It hurts too much." Clint held his side as he chuckled at the man's quick wit. "Member the guy and his pals that made a pass at Megan couple days ago?"

"Yeah, vaguely."

"Well, they hung around Sadie's last night and jumped me."

"Shit! I can't believe it!"

"Well, here's the poof," Clint answered pointing to his face. "Jason happened to be passing by and saved my ass."

"Where's the scumbags now?"

"Locked up. Jason's kinda hard to get to know, but he sheems to be a good guy. He's stayin' in the bunkhouse."

Jason opened the sliding doors and returned with a cooler of beer. At the same time, Shack came wobbling around the corner of the house and banged into the banister. The dog let out a small growl at the wooden posts and decided to plop down on the deck without attempting to walk any further.

"Looks like you better cut the dog off," Jason observed.

"Yeah, think your right," Clint answered. "Sides, now that Schtubs is here, we'll probly run out of beer. Can't waste any on the furbag."

Jason popped the top on two cans of beer and handed one to Clint and Stubs. He opened a third for himself and settled into a chair.

Stubs took a long sip of the cold liquid and turned to face the stranger. "Clint says you happened by Sadie's at a most opportune time. You just driven through?"

"Actually, I was just hitchin' through."

"Hitch hiking? From where?"

Jason was beginning to get uncomfortable with the questioning. "From Ohio. I'm heading to the Jersey shore. Never been to the beach. Always wanted to go there. Guess it was some kind of divine intervention that brought me here. Clint says you got a visitor yesterday too. A cousin or something?"

"Hah! My brother's kid. Calls himself Ruby. What kinda name is that?"

"'Bout the same kind as Schtubs," Clint observed loudly.

"You're drunk!" Stubs pointed out to Clint as he turned to face the big man. "Somethin' ain't right about that boy. He's got a bag full of money sittin' in my house and I don't think he won it in the lottery. Wanted to talk to you about what to do 'bout it, but I can see you're in no condition to offer any advice at this point."

Jason's face turned red. That was probably what was left of Oscar's money. His anger returned, and he forced himself not to speak. He wasn't sure what would come out. Thankfully, Stubs changed the subject.

"You see a doctor?"

"Yeah, Doc whatshisname shtopped by this afternoon. Ralph sent him. Shaid my rib was only bruised and my face would be as pretty as before in a couple of days."

"Better hope your lady friends don't find some other handsome fellows while you're healing," Stubs commented. "How 'bout another beer, Jason?"

"You mean like you?" Clint asked Stubs.

"Ah, they're too young for me. Now, Jason here, that's another story." Stubs started on the can Jason handed to him.

"Well, Paula's already told me to take a hike."

"Ah, now I understand the reason for the beer bash. Don't fret 'bout Paula. You two was never meant for each other anyhow. Now, Megan! She's good for you."

The three men continued talking and drinking for several hours. Around eight, Jason decided it would be a good idea to get some food in their stomachs. With Clint's and Stubs' directions, he found and prepared four venison steaks and several baked potatoes. Even Shack seemed to feel better after eating something. Around ten, the phone rang. Jason went to the kitchen to answer it.

"Hello,"

"Hello," a woman's voice responded. "Is this, ah, Jason?"

"Yeah, who's this?"

"It's Paula. Is, ah, Clint there?"

"Ahhh, yeah. Kinda," Jason laughed. "Hold on a minute." Jason went out to the deck to get Clint.

"Yo!" Clint spoke after maneuvering his way to the telephone.

"Clint? Are you okay?"

"Hi Paula. Yeah, I'm fine. What's up?"

"Well, I'm sorry to bother you, but something has come up. You know I was supposed to have my field trip tomorrow up at Rainbow Lake?"

"Yeah, why? You're still having it aren't you?"

"Well, I hope so. The problem is that they're closing access to the lake."

"Who is? Why?"

"The state police are. Some fishermen discovered a car in the lake. Over by the boat ramp. The news report says it's some kind of Mercedes. They think it's related to a homicide that happened in *Vasser* a few days ago."

Clint was trying to force his mind to clear. His old detective instincts were taking over. A homicide occurred in *Vasser*. A few days later, Stubs' nephew shows up, and Jason comes walking down the road . . . from the direction of Rainbow Lake. He realized he was jumping to conclusions, but there were too many coincidences.

"Clint? You still there?"

"Oh, yeah. Sorry. Whattaya gonna do about the field trip?"

"Well, that's why I really called. I was wondering if I could use your field and pond. I'll probably be up all night rearranging my plans, but I don't know what else to do on such short notice. I don't want to take advantage —"

"Oh, stop. Of course you can use the field and pond. Heck, you can use the whole mountain if you want."

"Thank you Clint. You don't need to feel obligated to help. Jack and Marci will be there and some of the parents are coming also. I really appreciate it."

"Don't worry about it. In fact, if you want, I'll even take those that can make it, on a walk up to the old cabin."

"Well, that would be nice, but you should probably just get your rest. I know you're in a lot of pain."

"Hah. Right now, I don't feel anything at all."

"Yeah," Paula commented quietly, "I figured that."

Clint didn't respond. He knew if he said what he wanted, it would only hurt Paula or make her angry. "What time you plan on arriving?" he said instead.

"Probably around ten. Is that okay?"

"That'll be fine. Anything else I can do to help?"

"No, you've been a big help. Thank you very much."

"No problem. I'll see you in the morning. Goodnight."

"Goodnight."

Clint sensed Paula wanted to say more. He hung up before she had a chance. He stared at the phone a moment. The anger he felt at Paula's comment disappeared quickly as he thought about the car in the lake, Jason and Ruby. What was the connection? Had Jason been driving the car? Ruby had admitted he had come from *Vasser*, but he had his own vehicle. Then again, Stubs had said Ruby had a bunch of money in his bag. His mind was reeling, but with the amount of beer he had drunk, he couldn't focus enough to put the pieces together.

"You okay?"

Clint turned and watched as Jason closed the door to the deck behind him.

"Yeah." Clint watched Jason's face as he explained why Paula had called. Jason's eyes betrayed him. Clint could tell that Jason knew about the car in the lake. Clint wanted to push him about the homicide, but knew he was not in any condition to interrogate Jason effectively. Besides, he couldn't believe this man who had risked his own well being to break up the fight at Sadie's, had anything to do with murder. Clint would push him more tomorrow.

"You know," Jason finally said, "I'm not used to drinking this much. If you don't mind, I think I'll just go crash in the bunkhouse."

"Ah, you rookies just can't handle it, like us old timers." Clint followed Jason out onto the porch. "Looks like Shack has had enough too."

Shack was sprawled out on the deck where he had collided with the banister. It didn't appear that he would be waking up soon.

"Looks like the rookies are calling it quits, Stubs."

"You don't say," Stubs answered as he tossed another empty can into the garbage can. "I should probably head home too, since I'm my own designated driver. What'd Paula want? She change her mind and decide she can't live without you?"

"Nah, she's smarter'n that. Actually, she says some fishermen found a car in Rainbow Lake and the police are closing down access. She wants to use my field and pond for her field trip tomorrow. Said the police think the car was involved in a homicide in *Vasser*."

"No shit!" Stubs exclaimed. "I bet that no good nephew of mine had somethin' to do with that. Bet that's where he got all that money."

"Now, don't go jumpin' to any conclusions old man. But, maybe, it would be better if you stayed here tonight. I'll go over to the house with you tomorrow and we can talk to Ruby about the money and car together."

"No way! No young punk is gonna scare me out of my own house. Sides, he's not used to all this outdoor life. He was sleepin' when I left and is probably in bed already. I'll be fine."

"You sure? You know it's no problem for you to stay."

"Yeah, ah, you know, you did drink a lot," Jason added. Jason knew Ruby was dangerous. If Stubs told Ruby about the car, there was no telling what he would do. Jason didn't want anything to happen to the old man.

Clint caught something strange about the tone of Jason's comment. For some reason, Clint didn't think Jason was just concerned about Stubs' ability to drive home.

"Hah! I'm fine. Didn't even drink a case yet." Stubs stood and started to clean up the debris.

"Ah, don't worry about the mess," Clint instructed. "I'll get it in the morning. You sure you don't wanna stay?" Clint's eyes locked on Jason's. There was something Jason wasn't saying, but Clint's mind was still not focusing properly.

"Nah, I'm fine."

"Well, maybe you at least want to take Shack with you."

At the sound of his name, Shack opened his eyes. He raised his head slightly and looked from Clint to Stubs. Then he let out a long breath through his nose and lowered his head back to the deck.

"Don't think Shack would even make it to my truck. I'll be fine."

Stubs led the way around the side of the house to his truck. Clint and Jason followed behind him. As Stubs got into his vehicle and drove down the lane, Jason turned to face Clint.

"I guess I better turn in," Jason said after a few moments of silence. "You sure you don't want me to help clean up tonight?"

"Nah, leave it till tomorrow." Clint still wasn't ready to confront Jason about the car and Ruby.

"Okay, then. Goodnight."

"Goodnight." Clint watched the man disappear around the side of the house and heard his footsteps descend the stairs. Clint tried to arrange his thoughts, but his mind wouldn't function properly. He decided he needed rest. After a stop in the bathroom, Clint stripped off his clothes and got under the covers. His thoughts jumped from Paula to Megan to Jason to Ruby and then to Stubs. He was missing something. He drifted off to sleep.

Jason almost ran to the bunkhouse. Things were happening too fast. The car was found and he could tell by the look on Clint's face that he knew Jason had something to do with it. If Stubs told Ruby about the car, Ruby might run. What if Ruby knew there was a stranger staying with Clint? What would Ruby do to Stubs, if confronted about the car and the money? He feared for the old man, but knew there was no way he could find his way to Stubs' house in the dark. Tomorrow, early, he would have to get to the old man. And he would end Ruby's life. Tomorrow he would vindicate Oscar. Jason tossed and turned in his bed. He wondered what his life would be like after that moment when he pulled the trigger and watched the life flow out of Ruby's body. Jason reached under the mattress where he had hidden the pistol and felt the cold metal of the weapon. He tossed and turned long into the night before he finally fell into a restless sleep.

Chapter 24

Elk Run – Stubs' house
Saturday September 29, 1979 8:30 PM

Ruby awoke with a start as he felt himself falling. His eyes began to focus, and he realized he was hanging off the side of the sofa. Darkness surrounded him in the lightless room and gave Ruby an eerie feeling. Carefully, he pushed himself off of the worn cushions and fumbled for the switch on the lamp sitting on the table next to the sofa. Finally the light came on, and Ruby sat back to let his eyes adjust. Despite feeling refreshed from the nap, the muscles in his legs still ached. He was hungry. The old furnishings in the house were depressing. He was bored and missed the excitement and action of the city streets. Perhaps he had made a mistake coming here.

By now, some unsuspecting soul had probably been picked up driving the stolen car owned by the murdered man. Ruby was glad he was not in that predicament. The cops would be looking to close the case quickly. Chances were that the unfortunate thief would already have a police record and therefore be a good candidate to hang the crime on. Maybe he should go back. Ruby laughed. Wouldn't Speedy be surprised?

First things first, however. Ruby was hungry. He stood up and made his way to the kitchen. On the way, he turned on every light he could, which was not many. Opening the refrigerator, he contemplated his choices. Besides the rows of beer cans, there was a plate with the leftover coyote meat from this morning's breakfast. No way was he going to eat that stuff. Ruby pulled open a metal drawer and found a pack of lunchmeat and a pack of cheese. He took the two packages and a jar of mustard to the counter and put them down. Finding a half loaf of bread in one of the cupboards, he proceeded to make himself two sandwiches. Ruby returned to the refrigerator to find something to drink. Not surprised, the only cold liquid was beer. What the heck! He grabbed two cans, took his sandwiches, and walked back into the living room.

As he ate the quickly prepared dinner, his hunger dissipated, but his depression only worsened. Birds and other animals yelled at him in strange sounds from outside. He found himself missing the bickering and yelling of his four cronies. There was one thing he could do to improve his spirits.

Ruby dropped the second empty can on the floor with the first and stood to retrieve his stash of marijuana from his bag. His head started to spin from drinking the two twelve ounce cans so quickly. After gaining his balance, he walked into his room and rummaged through the pockets of the duffle bag. Finally he found what he was looking for. On the way back to the sofa, he decided to grab another beer. It was tasting better with each can.

He took the final drag from his first joint and sucked the remaining drops from his third can of beer. The depression that had overcome him less than hour before, was gone. It was replaced by anger: anger at Speedy for what he was probably doing to the gang; at Stubs for his drunkenness and his ridicule; at the depressing surroundings; at Andy for pushing Ruby to commit murder; at the sounds coming from the woods outside. That damn noise!

Ruby jumped up from the sofa, knocking over the end table with the lamp. The bulb burst and the light in the house got dimmer. Ruby pushed over a kitchen chair as he tore open the refrigerator door and yanked out another can. He saw the meat sitting on the plate. The face of a dog-like creature growled at him. Ruby took his fist and smashed at the face. The plate flew at him from inside the refrigerator. The rack that had held the plate and about a dozen cans of beer bent and fell to the floor. Cans of beer rolled around on the worn linoleum. Ruby slammed the door shut and yelled back at the noises coming from outside. He ripped off the tab and downed half of the cold liquid. As he stepped back, his foot landed on several loose cans. Losing his balance, Ruby fell back against the table and then rolled onto the floor.

"Damn it!!!"

Ruby pulled himself up and, with both hands, lifted the table off its legs and flipped it over. The table crashed against the counter and knocked cereal boxes, cupcakes, and several other items in different directions.

Ruby picked up another loose can and popped the top. He took a big gulp and threw it against the refrigerator. Stumbling back to the living room, he found the second joint and fell back on the sofa. After several puffs, the room began to spin. The yells from outside continued to torment him. Creatures with horns and claws and fur jumped at him from all directions.

"I'll shut you up," Ruby yelled as he pushed himself up from the sofa and headed to his bedroom.

* * *

Stubs pulled his truck to a stop behind Ruby's large Suburban. As he stepped outside he heard the familiar sounds of the night. They always relaxed him.

"Bet you stole the truck too," Stubs muttered as he staggered past the large vehicle and headed toward the door.

Just as he was about to reach for the door, it flew open in his face, knocking him to the ground. A wild man ran past him, a pistol in his hand.

"Ruby!" Stubs yelled. "What the hell are you doin'?"

Ruby stopped at the sound of his name. He turned to see the old man lying on the ground, propped up on his elbows. Blood from a gash above his eye trickled down the side of his face. Ruby was confused. He thought the man was his uncle, but he looked like someone from the past.

"You! You homeless bum! What are you doing here?"

"What the hell are you talking about boy? I live here. You been drinkin'."

Ruby shook his head; the vision of the homeless man from the streets was gone.

"I'm not your boy, old man!"

Stubs slowly stood up and stared at the strange man in front of him.

"I'm sick of you old man! I'm sick of your drinking. I'm sick of you calling me boy! I'm sick of this place!"

"Then leave!" Stubs shouted back. "Run away like you did when you killed that man with the car and stole his money."

Ruby's mouth dropped open. "What car?" he barely whispered.

"You know damn well what car I'm talkin' about. The Mercedes up in Rainbow Lake."

"Mercedes?" Ruby couldn't believe what he was hearing. He began to weave from side to side. The man in front of him became blurry as the figure moved toward the house. Ruby vaguely saw the door swing open and the man disappear inside.

"Don't run away from me, old man!" Ruby staggered toward the house and, after several tries, yanked the door open. He stepped inside and heard a noise from the direction of the kitchen.

Stubs had stumbled over the overturned table and chairs and finally reached the closet where he kept his shotgun.

"What did you do to my house, boy?" Stubs pulled the loaded gun from the closet and turned to face the mad man.

Ruby saw the figure turn from the closet. He couldn't quite make out what the old man had in his hand, but it appeared to be a gun of some sort.

"You'll never call me boy again old man!" Ruby raised the pistol and fired two shots. The man dropped to the floor.

Ruby turned and fled out of the house. The door slammed shut behind him and the sound of a shotgun blast echoed across the mountains. Then the night was silent. No animals yelled at him. The creatures in his head were gone. Ruby stumbled and fell. He got up and continued running into the night, until the darkness swallowed him.

Chapter 25

Jason pounded on the flimsy aluminum door. The cold wind and wet snow whipped around his body and found its way down the back of the collar of his thin army-issued jacket. His feet ached from the cold seeping through the soles of his worn out combat boots.

"Hey Stubs!" Jason yelled. "Open the damn door. I'm freezin' out here".

Only the sound of some children's cartoons answered him as he pulled open the screen door and tried the knob on the paint-chipped wooden door.

"Stubs! You know you shouldn't leave your door unlocked. How many times have I told you that?"

"What's that smell?"

"Where the hell are you?"

As Jason stepped inside the door, he almost tripped and fell over the floor lamp lying at his feet.

"Stubs! Where are you?"

Jason glanced into the bedroom. The pillows from the bed lie crumpled on the floor, as did the lamp that once sat on the cheap nightstand. Jason turned and approached the open door to the bathroom.

"Stubs! Where are you?"

Jason stared at the dark red shower curtain. As he reached for the curtain, his heart pounded in his chest. The sound of water dripping from the faucet and smacking against the porcelain tub, echoed in the room

"Stubs?" Jason whispered as he slowly pulled open the curtain.

The breath, which he had been holding within him, exploded from his mouth as he gazed at the empty tub.

"Stubs! Where are you?"

Jason stormed out of the bathroom and stomped into the kitchen.

"Stubs! Where are you?"

He froze as he gazed at the figure slouched over the table.

"Stubs? Is that you?"

The gray-haired head of the man was face down on the table. A red liquid poured out of a large hole above the temple.

"Stubs? Is that you?"

The left arm of the old man had been severed at the elbow and laid on the table. His right leg, from the knee down lay next to it.

"Stubs. What happened to your arm and leg?"

The red liquid poured onto the metal table and ran off the edge onto the floor.

Drip. Drip. Drip. Droop. Droop. Drump. Drump. Thump. Thump. Thump. Thump.

Jason jerked up out of bed. Sweat poured down the sides of his face. The thumping sound continued. Finally, he realized that it was coming from the direction of the door. Jason swung his feet off the side of the bed, retrieved the gun from under the mattress and slowly approached the door. Peering cautiously through the small window, he was relieved to see the large black dog pawing at the base of the door.

Jason opened the door and Shack quickly squeezed inside. Turning to face the man, Shack sat on his haunches and stared at the man holding the gun. A soft whine escaped his closed snout.

"Stubs!" Jason whispered.

"Arf!" Shack returned.

Jason sprinted to the bed and pulled on his socks and boots. He found the shirt on the floor where he had discarded it the night before. Jason checked the gun to make sure it was fully loaded. Reaching into the bottom of the bag, he pulled out a handful of shells and stuffed them into his coat pocket. Putting on the coat, he ran to the door.

Before Jason had the door half open, Shack raced out in front of him. The big dog ran half way up the hill at the side of the house and stopped. He turned back to face Jason, expecting the man to follow

Jason shoved his hands into his coat pockets and took in his surroundings. The sun had been up for about an hour. The mist on the lake was slowly evaporating into the cold morning air. A lone bullfrog bellowed his song from the opposite bank. Turning to his right, he noticed a lone vehicle parked at the end of the open field. A tall, blond woman was unloading boxes and placing them on a small table. The slight breeze ruffled her hair. Even from this distance, Jason saw her sad eyes. He turned to face the waiting animal and felt the cold metal of the weapon of death in his pocket. Jason's eyes wandered to the deck, still littered with empty cans. He had no idea how this day would end, but, somehow, he knew his relationship with Clint would not be the same. Perhaps, he would not even survive until the sun set. For a moment, he was sad. Would he ever see another sunset? Would he ever lie in bed and listen to the sounds of the woods surrounding him? Oscar would like this place. But Oscar would never experience it. Ruby had made sure of that. Now it was time to make things right.

Without another thought, Jason quickly walked toward the dog. He began contemplating what he would say when he finally faced the man who had killed his best friend.

Jason was already huffing when he reached the dog, but Shack didn't wait for him to catch his breath. Shack began trotting up the side of the hill, past the big home. Jason tried his best to keep up, but failed.

"Shack, hold up," Jason gasped. He flopped on his back and stared at the dark blue sky. He let the cold breeze dry the sweat pouring off his forehead. His shirt was already soaked with sweat under the heavy jacket.

After a few minutes, Jason felt a hot breath against his closed eyes. Opening them, he stared into a bright red tongue dangling a couple inches from his face.

"You have bad breath, dog."

"Arf," Shack responded. Shack nuzzled Jason with his nose, urging him to get up.

"Okay, lets go."

Jason struggled to his feet and followed the dog further up the side of the mountain. Jason recognized many of the surroundings from his short hike with Megan. Finally, after what seemed like an eternity, the two made it over a crest and Jason spotted the large tree stump he had sat on with Megan. He gasped as he plopped down to rest.

After several minutes, Jason rose from the stump and started down the side of the mountain to his left. He stopped as he noticed that Shack wasn't in sight. Turning around he saw the dog walking slowly away from him, up a slight incline.

"Shack! Whattaya doin'?"

Shack stopped and slowly turned his head back to face Jason. A low growl came from his throat.

"Come on, there's no time to chase rabbits or whatever you see. We gotta get to Stubs."

Shack whined and turned his head away from Jason. He did not move. Another growl, louder, drifted back to Jason.

"I'm goin' to Stubs', Shack. You do what you want." Jason continued toward the cabin sitting in the distance.

Shack moved his head from side to side. A strange smell was coming from the old cabin sitting in the distance. He thought he had seen something through the window, but now it was gone. He turned back and watched Jason disappear beyond the crest of the hill.

Chapter 26

Elk Run – Clint's Old Cabin
Sunday September 30, 1979 9:45 AM

Ruby rolled slowly onto his side. He felt the cold, hard, wooden surface underneath him. Dirt covered his hair and body. He tasted it in his mouth. Slowly, the memory of the night before returned to him: the colliding feelings of giddiness and anger and loneliness and bitterness; the penetrating noises from outside the depressing cabin; the face of the old man staring at him; the homeless man from the streets of *Vasser*; the gun shots; the woods; the dirt; the trees; the mountain; and, finally, this old, abandoned, dark, cold cabin.

Ruby slowly got to his feet. His head immediately started pounding, as if it was caught in a vice. The vice was getting tighter. He pressed his hands against both of his temples, trying to push the pain away. He groaned in agony.

Ruby straightened up and walked to the dirt-covered window. Immediately he dropped back down to the floor and sat with his back against the wall. Searching around him, he spotted the pistol and grasped it in his hands. The pain got sharper.

A large, black dog was slowly walking toward the cabin. If the animal entered the cabin, he would shoot it. The dog had been about fifty yards away. He didn't know if the creature had heard him, seen him or smelled him.

After a few minutes, Ruby turned around and slowly raised himself up enough to peer out of the corner of the window. He caught sight of the back of the dog disappearing over the side of the hill. The dog was heading in the direction of Stubs' cabin.

Chapter 27

Elk Run – Clint's House
Sunday September 30, 1979 9:50 AM

Clint rolled over onto his side and stared at the red numbers on the clock. It took a while for them to come into focus. The throbbing pain in his head began to jog his memory: the scene with Paula crying on his deck ... drinking ... Stubs ... more drinking ... Ruby's money ... the Mercedes in Rainbow Lake ... the look on Jason's face when Clint told him about the car ... *Vasser* ... homicide.

"Damn!" Clint shouted as he jumped out of bed. The pain in his head and chest made him dizzy and he almost lost his balance. Staggering to the bathroom, Clint found a jar of aspirin and popped three into his mouth. Washing them down with water from the sink, Clint almost ran down the hallway. He had to talk to Jason.

Why hadn't he insisted that Stubs stay the night. Jason knew Ruby. He knew Ruby had killed the man in New York. Ruby was a dangerous man, and Jason knew that. Why hadn't Jason warned Stubs?

Clint went out onto the deck and collided with the garbage can overflowing with beer cans. He ran down the steps and headed toward the bunkhouse.

"Shaaaaack?"

"Poor dog is probably in the woods puking his guts out," Clint spoke to the squirrels chattering in the trees.

Clint ran to the bunkhouse and pounded on the door.

"Jason! Jason, wake up!"

When no one answered, Clint opened the door and stepped inside. Everything was quiet.

"Jason? You in here?"

Clint stepped into the sleeping area and saw the bed in which Jason had been sleeping.

"Damn it, where are you?"

As he turned back toward the door, light reflecting off of a shiny object caught his eye. It was lying near the open bag on Jason's bed. He walked over and gazed down. Picking up the shell in his hand, he felt a terrible dread. Clint paused only momentarily before reaching his hand into Jason's bag and feeling around. He found several more rounds of ammunition.

Shoving them into his pocket, Clint ran toward the door and out into the sunlight. As he ran toward the basement door, he pulled his keys from his pocket. He entered the basement, unlocked the door and flipped on the light switch.

Clint moved quickly to the cabinet where he kept his personal guns. Opening it, he felt on the top shelf for his pistol. As he had expected, it was gone.

Slamming the door, Clint started toward the stairway but stopped and returned to the open cabinet. He grabbed his lever-action, 308 Winchester rifle and a box of loaded shells from the floor of the cabinet. Popping out the clip on the rifle, he filled it with four rounds of ammunition and tossed the box back onto the floor. He slammed the clip back into the gun and made sure the safety was on. Slamming the door to the cabinet shut, he finally headed back up the stairs.

Before he reached the front door, his phone began to ring. He debated whether he should stop to answer it, then considered the possibility it may be Stubs.

"Hello," Clint spoke tentatively.

"Hi! Got your pants on?"

"Megan. Ah, as a matter of fact, I do."

"Oh, that's too bad. Can I come over anyway?"

"Actually, no. I think we have a problem." Clint quickly explained the details from the night before; as least as best as he could recall. He also left out the part about the drinking.

"What can I do? I can meet you at Stubs — "

"No! Just stay by your phone. I'll call you as soon as I can. Gotta go. Bye."

Megan stared at the silent phone. Stubs was in danger, Jason was probably confronting Ruby, and the man she thought she loved was heading directly into the middle of the whole mess. She couldn't just sit quietly by the phone.

Chapter 28

Jason heard the crashing of the four-legged creature coming behind him, but did not stop. The going was easier, now that he was headed downhill. Shack passed Jason and continued toward the cabin in the distance.

As Jason neared the small structure that Stubs called home, the ground became softer, and his boots began sinking into the swampy earth. He veered off to the right to avoid the marshy ground.

Suddenly, he stopped. Shack was barking from the direction of the front door. Jason knelt on the ground. If Ruby was around, he would surely hear the noise outside. Jason had to surprise the man. He wondered what he would say to Stubs if there was nothing amiss. Could he still kill Ruby if Stubs was a witness? Somehow, he sensed that he would not have to answer that question.

As the barking continued, Jason moved closer to the house. He kept in a crouch as much as he could and crawled on the ground when he had to skirt between open areas. Fifty yards from the side wall, he decided to move to the back of the house and try to find a rear entrance.

Jason dashed the remaining twenty yards and planted himself against the wall. He had to keep an eye on both the front and back of the house. Someone could come from either direction. Sweat trickled down the back of his neck. His mind flashed back to Vietnam: a Vietnamese hooch; the Vietcong waiting somewhere in the shadows.

Jason darted silently toward the back of the building. He peered around the corner, expecting to be face to face with short, black-clad Asian soldiers. There was no one there. Jason moved quickly under the window that looked out toward the dense woods behind the house. He raised his head slowly and peered under the faded curtains hanging inside.

The living room floor was littered with beer cans. Several dark spots could be seen on the rug next to the overturned cans. The house was silent. The barking had stopped. It was obvious that no one was around. At least no one who was alive.

Jason sprinted to the opposite side of the house and peered around the corner. Ruby's black truck was parked in front and behind it sat Stubs' pickup. Hurrying along the side, Jason turned the corner and looked for Shack. He was nowhere in sight.

Jason walked toward the front door. His pistol was gripped tightly in his hand and pointed toward the ground. When he reached the door, he took one last look around for Shack.

"Stubs? It's Jason. You in there?" He didn't expect an answer and he didn't get one.

Jason placed his hand on the knob of the screen door and pulled it open. The inside door was ajar. Stepping through the doorway, Jason saw the overturned table and the chairs lying on their side.

"Stubs?" Jason called softly. He could barely get the word out of his mouth. It was a different home. A different town. A different friend. But he knew the ending would be the same.

Jason took a few more steps into the house and saw the man sitting on the floor next to an open closet in the kitchen. Stubs' back rested against the wall peacefully. Blood covered the old man's face and chest. Jason took a step toward him.

Ferocious barking and growling stopped Jason in his tracks. He turned back toward the door. It was a sound like he had never heard before. There was a single gunshot and the growling turned to a loud screech. Then everything was quiet.

Jason tore out of the house and across the yard. Avoiding the swamp, Jason ran up the hill as fast as his legs and heart would allow him. He knew what he would find.

Chapter 29

Elk Run – Clint's Field
Sunday September 30, 1979 9:55 AM

Paula finished arranging all her materials and stepped back to view the finished product. Normally, she always felt alive and excited at the start of one of these events. She loved her kids and loved to see their excitement as they experienced and learned new things. Learning seemed to mean so much more to these kids. Perhaps it was because it came so much harder for them. They experienced a much greater sense of achievement than other "normal" kids did.

But today, the excitement was gone. Clint was gone. Although, in her mind, she knew it was for the best and knew it was bound to come sooner or later, it still left an emptiness in her heart. Clint was such a dear and special man. But they were on different paths.

A movement in the distance, from the direction of Clint's house, caught her attention. She turned and took a few steps toward the house. A man, it appeared to be Clint, was running toward the bunkhouse. She watched as he disappeared from view behind the building.

Taking a few more steps toward the bunkhouse, which was only about fifty yards away, she stopped and waited. Why was Clint running? Something must be wrong. Maybe it was that man named Jason. Although he appeared to be a nice guy, she didn't trust him. He seemed to be hiding something. What if Clint was in trouble? Maybe she should call the sheriff.

She started to turn away when Clint came running back out of the building. He raced toward the basement of the house. Paula watched as he pulled something from his pocket and went inside. The door closed behind him.

Something was definitely wrong. She started walking toward the house.

"Pauuullllaaaaa?" a man's voice yelled from a distance behind her.

Paula stopped and turned around. Jack and Marci were walking up the field yelling her name. Several other cars were pulling into the field. The kids were arriving.

Paula turned back toward Clint's house.

"Paula. There you are," Jack yelled. "Where do you want me to put the barbecue stuff? We also have the ropes for tying knots and the maps and compasses. Where are the stations going to be? How 'bout the tug-o-war game? Where's that going to be?"

Paula turned back to face her two assistants. They were dedicated and sweet people, but they couldn't make any decisions on their own.

"Put the tug-o-war rope in the middle of the field. We'll use the three grills over on the right."

Paula continued to give instructions to her two helpers. Several of the kids came running toward her and hugged her tightly. Paula smiled and basked in the warmth of the small children. Thoughts of Clint faded from her mind.

Chapter 30

Elk Run – Clint on the Road
Sunday September 30, 1979 10:20 AM

Clint pushed the truck as fast as he could down the winding road toward Stubs' house. If only he had insisted Stubs stay at his house last night. Why didn't he? Why had he drowned his sorrows in beer? Maybe he would have put the pieces together sooner. Maybe Paula was right.

Clint slammed on his brakes and then swerved to miss a fox that darted across the road. Slowing down, he continued toward Stubs' house.

As he pulled into the driveway, he saw Stubs' truck parked peacefully outside. Ruby's large Suburban was sitting in front. Maybe he had jumped to conclusions. If Ruby had done anything to hurt Stubs, he wouldn't wait around. He would have taken off in a flash; especially if he knew about the car in the lake.

Clint pulled to a stop behind the old truck. He turned off the engine and started to get out. Glancing back at the rifle, he grabbed it and got out of the vehicle.

Clint strolled past the two vehicles toward the front of the house. Stopping at the Suburban, he felt the engine. It was cold. Clint continued to the front door. He stopped with his hand on the knob. Clint turned and searched the woods. No sounds greeted him. No birds singing their sweet songs. No squirrels chattering from the branches overhead. No large animals wandering through the brush. Just a not-so-peaceful quiet.

"Stubs?" Clint yelled through the screen door and noticed the inside door ajar.

"Stubs?" Clint pulled open the screen door and gently pushed open the inside door. He stopped at the sight of the disheveled house. He raised the rifle to his waist and flicked off the safety. A rifle was not a weapon to be used at close quarters, but it was all he had.

Stepping into the room, he glanced around. There were no noises. He took another step and turned toward the kitchen.

"Stubs!"

Clint dashed to the old man's side. Kneeling on the floor, he placed the gun next to the discarded shotgun. Clint pushed his fingers against the man's neck. Miraculously, he felt a faint pulse.

Clint jumped up and reached for the phone sitting on the counter. He dialed the sheriff's office from memory.

"Sheriff —"

"Rooster! It's Clint. I'm at Stubs' house. He's been shot. Looks like head and chest wounds. Light pulse. Get an ambulance over here."

"Bad guys around?" the sheriff responded. From the sounds of Clint's voice, he knew there was no time for small talk.

"Somewhere, but don't know where. Gotta go." Clint hung up the phone. He had known and dealt with Sheriff Jack "Rooster" Blocker for many years. He was a no-nonsense guy. Clint knew he would get the medics here quicker than calling 911 and he would also bring some assistance to find Ruby . . . and Jason.

Clint went to the sink and grabbed a towel from the counter. Drenching it in water, he went back to Stubs. Gently he wiped the dried blood off of his face and forehead. Using his fingers to search his head, he found a graze wound on the top of his head. He figured this was the source of the blood on his face. Clint pulled open Stubs' shirt and found a bullet wound just below the shoulder.

"Ahhhhh!" Stubs yelled as Clint touched his shoulder.

"Stubs! You're going to be okay."

"That bastard shot me."

"Who? Who shot you Stubs?"

"My . . . damned . . . nephew," Stubs whispered.

"Okay, you just relax. An ambulance —"

The sound of the ringing phone interrupted him. Clint jumped over to the phone and picked it up.

"Yeah?"

"Clint! Help me. There's a wild man outside. He's coming toward your house."

"Megan, what are —. Lock the doors. In the basement in the open gun cabinet —"

Only the dial tone responded.

Chapter 31

Megan slammed the phone down when she saw the strange man heading for the house. She ran to the front door and locked it. Turning, she dashed to the doors leading to the deck and locked them as well. She wondered if the windows were locked, but couldn't waste time checking them.

She ran down the steps to the basement. Looking around, she quickly found the gun cabinet with the door unlocked. Checking inside, she found Clint's shotgun. She pulled it out and searched around for shells. Finally, she found a box on the bottom of the cabinet. She shoved three shells into the gun and put a handful in her pocket. She hoped she wouldn't need any of them.

As she started up the stairs to the kitchen, she noticed the basement door that opened to the outside. She quickly ran over to it and locked it.

"I sure hope you don't have any other doors to this place," she spoke to the empty house.

Megan ran up the stairs and walked through the kitchen. Goosebumps ran down the back of her neck. The man she had seen was no longer in sight through the large window in the front of the house. *Where was he?*

Megan fell to the floor and scooted backwards until her back bumped into the sofa. She held the shotgun close to her. She heard something scraping on the deck along the side of the house. Footsteps followed, heading toward the back. Megan stared at the glass doors. The drapes were open. She could see through the doors to the bright sky and tall trees outside. She realized that someone on the deck would be able to see clearly into the house, where she was sitting.

The footsteps reached the corner of the house. Megan was frozen on the floor. Her back was against the sofa. Although she knew she should move, she couldn't. Tears fell uncontrollably. Her hands shook. The shotgun felt like a heavy weight holding her in place on the floor. The footsteps continued

* * *

Paula jumped at the sound of the gunshot. It was the second shot she had heard in the last hour or so. At first, she figured it was someone hunting. Now, her thoughts returned to Clint and his strange behavior earlier. She turned and gazed up at the large home. She didn't see anyone.

"Paula?"

"Yes Rachael? What is it?"

"Why is someone shooting? I'm scared."

"Oh honey," Paula answered bending over and hugging the young frightened girl, "its just someone hunting. There's no reason to be scared. Would you go get me a cup of lemonade?"

"Sure!" The girl's face lit up and she turned and ran to the drink station.

Paula stood up and turned back toward the house. A woman was standing at the glass doors to the deck. In a moment, she was gone from sight. *Well, guess Megan is here. She can take care of Clint.*

Paula angrily turned and went back to join the kids forming two tug-o-war lines. She failed to hear the sirens sounding in the distance.

Chapter 32

Elk Run – Woods Above Stubs' House
Sunday September 30, 1979 10:32 AM

Jason scrambled up the steep bank toward the sound of the gunshot. At times he had to crawl, but he continued to move upwards. Finally, about thirty yards from the top, he had to stop. Resting with his hands on his knees, he sucked in one deep breath after another. Finally, he was able to continue on. After taking a dozen steps, a dark form, lying in the brush, caught his eye.

"Oh Shack," he cried painfully.

Jason ran to the still animal and fell on his knees. Anger and sorrow swept over him.

"Why? Why God? Why?"

A branch snapped in the distance. Slowly Jason turned his head toward the sound.

Standing not more than twenty yards away was the man who had caused so much pain and suffering. Jason gripped the pistol in his hand tightly.

"Who are you?" the crazed man asked.

Jason glared back at Ruby. He was afraid to speak for fear nothing would come out.

"Ah, gee. Guess I killed your dog. He wasn't a very nice dog, you know."

Jason pulled up his gun to fire, but Ruby's gun cracked first. Jason fell on top of Shack. He had felt the bullet rip through his thick jacket but it seemed to only have grazed his arm. Jason struggled up and, taking one last look at the silent animal, began crawling slowly up the hill after the man who had disappeared over the crest. This time, his pistol was aimed in front of him.

Chapter 33

Elk Run – Stubs' House
Sunday September 30, 1979 10:45 AM

"Clint?" Stubs whispered softly.

Clint moved back to his old friend and knelt beside him.

"Yeah, Stubs. You just be quiet. Help is coming."

"Clint. You . . . have . . . to stop him."

Clint turned his head toward the door. Megan was in trouble. He wanted so much to run and protect her. But his friend needed him also.

"Clint. Go."

"Stubs, I can't just leave you."

"I'll be . . . okay." Stubs' head fell back against the wall.

Clint heard a siren in the distance. He looked at the silent man in front of him. He checked for a pulse again and found it.

"Stubs. The ambulance is here. I hear it. You hold on. We got a lot of drinking to do yet."

Stubs nodded his head slightly, but was too weak to speak.

Tearing himself away, Clint grabbed his gun from the floor and dashed for the door. The only sound he heard was the wailing of the siren getting closer. He started toward his truck and then changed his mind. It would be quicker through the woods.

Clint's feet pounded on the ground, matching the beat of his heart. His bruised rib yelled for him to stop, but he kept going. Clint darted around the swampy ground and headed up the hill. His legs began to ache, and his head continued to throb. Still, he continued up the steep hill.

Just before he reached the top, he heard a strange sound coming from his right. He pivoted in the direction of the sound, brought his rifle to his shoulder and flipped off the safety, all in one fluid motion. He shuddered at what he saw.

"Shack! No!"

Tears fell uncontrollably as he ran to his best friend. He plopped down beside the still dog.

"Shack! Shack!"

The dog's eyes opened slowly. Clint saw the poor animal's shallow breathing.

Feeling the side of the animal, where the fur was matted with a dark, thick liquid, Clint found the bullet wound. Shack jerked at Clint's touch. Blood was still spilling slowly from the wound.

Clint yanked off his jacket and shirt and began unwinding the ace bandage from his ribs. He pulled a handkerchief from his coat pocket and pressed it against the wound. Again the dog jerked. As gently as he could, Clint wound the bandage around the animal's body to keep the makeshift dressing in place.

* * *

Shack felt the man's strong hands lift him and put him back down. Pain flowed through his body. Pain almost as bad as he felt when the hard object pounded him in his side and knocked him to the ground. Then the man lifted him again. And again. Why was his owner causing him so much pain? What had he done wrong?

He had sensed that something was wrong with Stubs this morning. Sometimes he got these weird feelings. Sometimes they were good weird feelings. But sometimes they were bad. This morning they were bad.

He had finally gotten Jason to come with him, but he couldn't find Stubs. Then, he had seen the dirty man coming down the hill toward Stubs' house. Somehow, he knew the man was bad. Another one of those feelings.

He had to protect Jason, and Stubs, wherever he was. He had run toward the man as fast as he could. The man had turned and fled back up the hill. That made him feel good. He growled and barked as loud and ferociously as he could. Just when he thought he had made the man run away, the man turned around and pointed something at him. Shack saw smoke spurt out of the man's hand. Then the hard object had smacked him in the side and knocked him into the brush. Oh how that had hurt. Now, his owner was hurting him again. What was wrong with these humans?

* * *

Clint finished wrapping the bandage around Shack. He petted the quiet animal on the head.

"Shack, I gotta go. I'll be back. I promise. I'll bring Megan. She'll help you. Hang in there boy . . . Please!"

Clint pushed himself off the ground and ran blindly up the last few yards of the hill. His gun was gripped tightly in his hand.

Chapter 34

Elk Run – Clint's House
Sunday September 30, 1979 10:50 AM

Ruby ran down the hill toward the big house. He wanted to go back to Stubs' and get his money and truck, but that would have to wait. He needed to get a vehicle and get out of here. He would worry about money later. There was plenty more back in *Vasser.*

Ruby slammed against the small truck parked in front of the house. With any luck, the doors would be open and the keys in the ignition. He tried the door.

"Damn!" The door was locked and there were no keys.

Ruby glanced at the big house. There were probably guns inside. Nice guns. Guns that would bring a lot of money back in the city. But, first he needed a vehicle.

Ruby ran around the front of the truck and spotted two large buildings sitting to the left of the house. The buildings were big enough to hold several cars or trucks.

Ruby ran to the one that had no door on it. There were several lawn tractors and mowers and two snowmobiles. He went back to the other building and pulled on the large garage door. It opened.

Pushing the door up out of the way, he couldn't believe his eyes. An old pickup truck sat there just waiting to be taken. He moved to the driver's door and gazed inside. The keys were sticking out of the ignition.

Ruby smiled and got inside.

Chapter 35

Elk Run – Clint's House
Sunday September 30, 1979 11:00 AM

Megan stared helplessly as the pair of legs appeared at the glass doors. Suddenly a man's body filled the door. An uncontrollable scream escaped from her mouth.

"Megan! Megan! It's me, Jason."

* * *

Paula and the other children around her let go of the thick rope at the sound of the scream coming from the house on the hill. The adults and kids pulling from the other side fell in a heap on the ground.

Everyone in the field turned to look in the direction of the woman's voice.

"Miss Paula, who's that man on the porch."

"What does he have in his hand, Miss Paula?"

"There's another man on the hill."

* * *

Ruby turned the key in the ignition. It made a grinding sound but would not start.

"Damn it!"

Ruby tried the key again. He got the same results.

* * *

Clint skidded to a stop at the sound of the engine in his old truck turning over. His left foot slipped on a damp tree limb that was lying just beneath the cover of leaves. The stock of Clint's rifle slammed against the ground. His finger, which was resting outside of the trigger guard, slipped across the guard and slapped against the trigger. His head banged against the hard earth. Pain from his ribs shot through his body.

* * *

All of the kids in the field screamed at the sight of the man falling onto his back and the loud boom that echoed across the hills.

Paula spotted the man lying on the ground. She recognized the jacket.

"Clint!" she yelled, and raced toward the house.

* * *

Jason jumped at the sound of the rifle shot. He turned and ran back up the side of the house. He tried to focus on the figure moving on the ground about a hundred yards up the hill. He stopped before reaching the corner, listening to the soft thumping of footsteps on the front porch of the house.

* * *

Megan watched as Jason turned and ran at the sound of the rifle blast. It had to be Clint who fired. The wild man did not have a rifle. She forced herself up off of the floor and ran to the front window. Clint was lying on the ground. She froze again. She wanted to run to him, to hold him. But where was the wild man?

* * *

Ruby turned at the sound of the gunshot. He jumped out of the truck and ran out of the building. He didn't see anyone, but knew the sound had come from the hill above the house. He ran toward the front of the house to get a better view of the hill.

* * *

Jason heard the sound of footsteps coming closer. He waited.

Finally he stepped out from the side of the building and raised his pistol in both hands. Ruby was ten yards away. The man stopped in his tracks.

"Hello Ruby."

Ruby looked curiously at the stranger, who was vaguely familiar.

"Who are you?"

"You don't recognize me?"

"You look familiar."

"You remember the man who used to live on the street near your building? The man you kicked and beat and spit on? The man you called a loser?"

"You! How did you —"

"How I got here ain't important. I'm going to kill you."

319

"For giving you a few bruises?" Ruby felt the gun in his hand hanging at his side. He knew he couldn't raise it quick enough to get a shot off. He had to divert this man's attention somehow.

"No, not for the bruises. I could have lived with that. But you took my hope away. You killed the most important person in my life. Then you stole his money and rubbed it in my face every day of my life."

Ruby thought for a few moments, and then it hit him.

"You talkin' about that cripple?"

Jason gripped the gun tighter. It was all he could do to not pull the trigger. Why didn't he? Why didn't he just fire now? End it. Kill Ruby. End it. Out of the corner of his eye he glimpsed Megan standing a few yards from the window. Her mouth was open. Her disbelieving eyes echoed all the doubts he had about killing another human being this way. This was not Vietnam. This was not war. He was not even defending himself . . . yet.

"He wasn't a cripple. He was a caring man with dreams. His dreams were about to come true, and then you ended them. You killed a man with one arm and one leg and then took all his money and spent it on girls, trucks, booze, drugs and anything else you wanted for pleasure."

Ruby sensed something in the man's eyes. He didn't have the look that Ruby had seen in other men who were about to pull the trigger on another person. Ruby didn't think this man would fire his weapon . . . unless Ruby did something to provoke him.

"You're right," Ruby admitted as sadly as he could make his voice sound. "I did kill the man."

Ruby started to raise his hand ever so slightly.

"I was drunk."

Ruby raised the gun a little more.

"I wasn't thinking straight."

Ruby gripped the gun tighter.

"But, there was no money."

"Liar!" Jason yelled. There was over $ 300,000." Jason extended the gun further toward the wild looking man who had killed his friend. "End it," a voice inside him yelled.

"Please," Ruby pleaded. He sensed the change in the man's eyes. "Honestly, there was no money. Or, if there was, I never found it. You gotta believe me. I didn't want to kill him. I was drunk. I didn't take his money."

* * *

Clint rolled over onto his side and pulled the gun toward him. He glanced toward the house and saw two men standing less than ten yards apart. He ejected a shell from the chamber and pushed another one in. Raising the gun to his shoulder, he focused on the one on the right. It was Jason. He moved the gun to the other: Ruby. Out of the corner of his eye he saw a third figure running up the side of the deck toward him.

* * *

Paula ran as fast as she could down the deck. She saw Clint sit up and place the rifle to his shoulder. She stopped and raised her hands to her mouth.

Jason heard the sound of someone running toward him on the deck. Without thinking, he turned.

Ruby watched in disbelief as the man turned away from him. Ruby raised his gun and pulled the trigger.

"Bam! Crack"

Two shots echoed through the valley.

Jason fell to the floor.

Megan screamed.

Paula screamed.

Clint watched through the scope as the man flew against the side of his house. He quickly ejected the empty shell from the rifle and chambered another round. He continued to watch the man slumped against the building. Blood streamed from the hole in his chest. The man didn't move.

Chapter 36

Elk Run – Clint's House
Sunday September 30, 1979 11:15 AM

Clint lowered the rifle and switched on the safety. He pushed himself up off the ground and ran down the hill to his house.

Jason stood up, somewhat in shock, and checked his body for a wound. All he found was a second hole in his not-so-new jacket.

Paula walked slowly around the corner of the house and stared at Jason as he dropped the gun to the ground.

Megan came out of the front door and ran to meet Clint.

She crashed into his arms and hugged him as tight as she could.

"Oh Clint, I love you so much. I —"

"Honey! Stop. Shack's been shot. Can you help him?"

"Oh God, no. Yes. I'll get my bag."

Megan ran to her truck and retrieved the black bag from the back.

"Don't you go anywhere," Clint yelled at Jason.

Jason just stared back at the large man. Where was he going to go? He had failed Oscar, again. He slumped down on the porch floor, put his head in his hands and wept.

Paula watched as Clint and Megan ran back up the hill. Then, she turned to look at the man crying at her feet. She knelt down and put her arm around him.

Clint was gasping for breath and pain racked his body as they reached the dog lying where Clint had left him.

Clint watched as Megan pulled a syringe from the bag and filled it with some liquid. She cut off the bandage and clipped fur from around the wound.

* * *

Shack opened his eyes at the sound of something running toward him. It must be something big. Maybe it was a coyote. Maybe he was going to be eaten by him. He was so tired. He closed his eyes.

Shack jerked as the pointy needle was plunged into his rump. Oh no, now the porcupine was sticking him, then the coyote would eat him.

Shack jerked again as a warm liquid poured into a hole on his side. The burning sensation was almost as bad as the pain he felt when the bullet pounded into him. Finally, he decided to open his eyes to see what evil thing was attacking him.

"Hey boy," a soft woman's voice greeted him. "You're going to be okay."

Shack closed his eyes. Yes, this doctor was okay.

Chapter 37

Elk Run – Clint's House
Sunday September 30, 1979 7:30 PM

Clint pulled his truck behind the big black Suburban sitting in front of his house. He had forgotten that Paula had taken Jason to Stubs' to "get a few things". Clint didn't know what "things" Jason would have at Stubs' house, but it was time to put the final pieces of this puzzle together. Suddenly, he was very tired, and sore. His ribs, which had been aching all day, now jolted him with every move.

At the veterinary clinic, he was amazed at how fast and confidently Megan had worked alongside the doctor. Fortunately, the bullet had passed through Shack without hitting any bones or major arteries. Some rest and healing were all Shack needed. That sounded like something he needed himself. Megan's gentle touch and warm kiss she had given him as he was leaving made his heart flutter. He felt young and in love again. What a foolish old man.

He had called the sheriff while Megan and the doctor were getting Shack settled for the night. Stubs also was lucky. No broken bones. No major arteries hit. Stubs would be back to his normal grouchy, beer-drinking self in months. Knowing Stubs, he would be drinking something containing alcohol long before that. Clint hoped the hospital kept the rubbing alcohol locked up.

He took a deep breath and entered his house. It was eerily quiet. Jason was sitting at the kitchen table, his arms resting in front of him. He offered Clint no greeting and continued to stare at the solid tabletop.

Clint pulled out a chair opposite the man and sat down.

"It's been a long day. Talk to me, Jason. How did you know Ruby? How did you end up with that car they found in Rainbow Lake?"

Jason was tired. Tired of lying. Tired of hunting. Tired of treading down the path of death and destruction. Without lifting his head, Jason told Clint his story.

"When I came back from Nam, it was hell. I relived the agony of Vietnam in my nightmares and faced the hatred and humiliation of my own country during the day. Whether I was awake or asleep, I was in hell. Finally, I quit. I went to the streets and turned my back on everyone and everything."

Clint had heard the story many times. Different faces. Different names. Same story. He waited for Jason to continue.

One day, I met a man. In a way he was less of a man than most. He had one arm and one leg. Lost them in Nam. In other ways, in his heart, he was a bigger man than anyone I had ever met. His name was Oscar."

326

Clint jumped at the mention of the man's name. *Vasser.* Oscar. One arm. One leg. Clint said nothing.

"Oscar became my friend."

Tears now fell from the still man across the table, but he continued.

"He helped me. Helped me deal with my pain. Started to give me a dream. I helped him. He had a little apartment that needed fixing up. It was probably easier for me to help him than him me."

"One day, Oscar got a letter. His mother had died and left him over $ 300,000."

Clint began to squirm in the chair.

"Oscar made me an offer. He wanted to buy a little house with a little yard, a home. He offered me a place to stay. A chance to . . . choose a different path."

Clint watched the younger man struggle with his memories. He knew where it would lead. Still, Clint remained silent, afraid to speak.

"The night before we were to take the money . . ." something caught in Jason's throat.

"The stupid fool kept it in cash! Can you believe that! Said he wanted to see what that much money would look like."

After a moment, Jason shook his head and forced himself to continue.

"The night before we were to go look for a house, I went to a bar. First time in years. What a mistake! On the way back to my home . . . Home! Home was a cardboard box on the cement sidewalk."

"The night before . . . I got drunk. On the way home, I ran into Ruby and the little gang he ran with.

They beat me. Called me a loser. Called Oscar a cripple. I lost it and spilled my guts about Oscar's money and all of our plans."

Clint pushed himself off the chair and went to the refrigerator to get a beer. He pulled off the tab, took a big swallow and sat back down.

"The next day, Oscar was dead. Ruby killed him. Took his . . . our money. Took our dreams. Took our future. I vowed to kill him. For Oscar . . . and for me."

Clint couldn't move. The can in his hand felt like a heavy weight. Still, he couldn't speak.

"A few days ago, I heard Ruby and one of his side-kicks talking. Ruby had killed some guy and left his car on the street. Said he was going to go to some place called Elk Run to live with his uncle till the dust settled. I stole the car and drove it here. Ditched it in the lake. You know the rest."

Jason felt a heavy weight lift off his shoulder. He couldn't stop the tears from falling.

When he heard no response from Clint, he finally looked up. Tears were also streaming down Clint's cheeks. He hadn't known what to expect from the man, but he definitely hadn't expected tears. Jason stared curiously at the big man who suddenly seemed smaller.

Too many memories. Too much pain. Clint wiped his eyes with the back of his shirtsleeve. Finally, he spoke.

"Ruby didn't take Oscar's money."

Jason was stunned by the comment.

"How — How do you know who took Oscar's money? Did you know Oscar?"

Clint took a deep breath. It was time.

"I was a detective in *Vasser*. I handled Oscar's case. By myself. No one wanted to work with me anymore. I . . . wasn't the same person I was when I had first joined the force."

Now it was Jason's turn to remain silent. He couldn't believe the lives of all these people: Ruby, Oscar, Clint and himself, had all crossed paths. Twice. He waited for Clint to continue.

"I got the call around noon. I was the first person on the scene. Something didn't feel right. I was a good cop . . . at one time. Why would someone kill a crip . . . a handicapped person? From the look of the apartment, they were searching for something. I assumed they hadn't found it and kept looking for it. I didn't know what I was looking for. Then, I found some loose boards on the floor of a closet, which was covered with clothes. Under the boards, was a suitcase. In the suitcase was cash. Over $ 300,000."

Jason violently pushed his chair away from the table and stood up. He wanted to attack this man sitting across from him. Jason moved to the refrigerator instead and pulled out a beer. Sitting down, he gazed at the man across from him.

"Why?"

Clint looked down at his half empty can.

"I've asked myself that question many times. The truth is, I was at rock bottom. I was full of anger. I was . . . different. I . . . was greedy. This was my way out. My way of starting over."

"I put the suitcase in the trunk of my car before the coroner and anyone else arrived. I worked the case as hard as I could, which probably wasn't very hard. It was my last case. A few months later, I left. The precinct was glad to see me go and gave me six months severance pay. I invested most of Oscar's money and lived on my severance and savings. About five years ago, I moved here and bought this house. Every day, I've tried to give something back to the people around here, but it was never enough!"

The two men stared at each other. The ringing of the phone made them both jump. Clint finally stood to answer it.

"Hello?"

"Clint? It's sheriff—"

"What's wrong? Is Stubs—"

"No. No. Nothing's wrong. Stubs is still doing okay."

"Oh, God. Thank heavens. Then what's up?"

"Clint, I have a trooper Ollenberger from the New York state police here. He wants to question Jason in regards to the Mercedes and a murder in *Vasser*."

Clint looked at Jason.

"Clint? You there?"

"Ah, yeah. Rooster, Jason didn't kill that man in *Vasser*. The only thing he did was, kinda, borrow the car to get to Elk Run."

"Borrow? You mean steal. And then, he put it in the lake."

"Rooster, ask trooper Ollenberger what the cause of death was."

330

Clint waited while the sheriff spoke to the state police officer. Jason stood and went to the window. The night outside was dark. Darker than he had ever seen it. As dark as his soul felt.

"Clint? He was killed by several blows from a blunt instrument. Probably some kind of pistol."

"Rooster, tell the officer that if he compares Ruby's guns to the wounds, he'll probably get a match. He'll probably even find the man's blood on one of the pistols. Jason didn't kill that man, Ruby did. You've known me a long time. I know I'm right about this. As for the stolen car, can you get Ollenberger to drop the charges? It'll cost a lot of taxpayers' money to take Jason back to New York, and it won't serve any good purpose. I'll pay the family for the car and whoever I need to for the cleanup of the lake. Can you do that?"

There was silence on the phone.

"Rooster, you there?"

"Yeah. Yeah, I think I can do that. I believe this guy just wants to get back to the big city and his family. I'll work it out. You're sure about this?"

"Yeah, I'm sure."

"Okay, then. You get some rest. I'll be over tomorrow to see ya."

"Thanks Rooster."

Jason continued to stare out the window. He flipped a switch on the wall, and the darkness turned to a bright white glow. Standing next to the lake was the biggest animal he had ever seen. The large buck had antlers almost three feet wide. The old, wise animal lifted his head slowly and stared back at Jason. A bullfrog on the opposite bank croaked a lonely song. Other creatures of the night added their sweet sounds. Finally, the big buck lowered his head and continued drinking, unconcerned with the interruption.

"Jason, I know what I did was wrong. Nothing I've done in the past five years will ever make up for it. Stay here. Let me get the money together and give it back to you. It will take awhile, but you can stay as long as it takes. Please."

Jason turned away from the window and looked at the man who had befriended him.

"No. That money wasn't mine in the first place. It wasn't the money that allowed me to dream of a new life, it was Oscar. You saved my life today. Not just because you shot Ruby, but also because you stopped me from continuing down that path of destruction. I don't know if I could have killed Ruby or not. In a way, I'm glad I didn't have to find out. You keep the money. You keep doing what your doing. You've changed paths too. Stay on the one you're on."

"Then stay here anyway. I could use a hand around here. Especially with the hunting season coming. You'd love it up here."

Jason smiled. "I'm sure I would. And maybe someday I'll come back and take you up on the offer. But, I won't take handouts. I work. You pay."

Now it was Clint's turn to smile. "Okay, you have a deal. But what'll you do?"

"Well, there is a certain someone I need to go back and find."

"Then let me give . . . loan you some money."

"Ah, that won't be necessary," Jason said with a smirk.

Clint followed Jason's gaze toward the black vehicle. He remembered Stubs saying something about a bag of money. Perhaps this was one of the "things" Jason had collected from Stubs' house with Paula.

"You know, the police are probably going to impound Ruby's truck."

"Yeah, I know. I was wondering. If it's not too much trouble, could you talk that trooper into letting me drive it back to *Vasser*? After all, I'm heading that way, and I would save the taxpayers even more money."

Clint smiled and nodded his head. "Yeah, I think I can do that."

"Thanks."

"Don't mention it. You know, there's a cabin up on the top of the hill that belongs to me. Hasn't been used in a long time. Probably needs a lot of work. But, with a little help from some friends, I'm sure it would make a nice starter home for someone."

Jason smiled. "I think you're right."

Epilogue

Vasser, New York
One month later

The large man sat quietly behind the counter reading the morning paper. It was almost closing time, but he had been busy most of the day waiting on customers. As the weather got colder, more and more people came to the Army surplus store looking for good deals on warm clothing and boots. He finally had a chance to relax and check out the paper before going home for the evening. He turned to the second page and began reading.

Local Gang Members Found Dead
By James Tiny, Vasser Times Reporter

Early this morning, police were called to the scene of a multiple homicide at what was thought to be an abandoned building on 13th Street. After receiving an anonymous call, police went to the address to investigate the report of multiple gunshots. Three young men: Albert Wenthall, Robert Oakman and Ernest

Oakman were pronounced dead at the scene by coroner Mable Fishburn. The three individuals were reportedly part of a local gang referred to as the Red Rats. Police officials believe that the killings were a result of some inner-gang dispute. Robert and Ernest Oakman were brothers. A fourth member of the gang, Jeremiah Fontaigne, has not been located, and is wanted for questioning. The gang, previously known as the "Rubies", was once led by Arthur (Ruby) Simmons. Mr. Simmons was killed last month in a small town in northern Pennsylvania.

The old man gazed briefly at the grainy pictures beneath the story. The sound of the bell over the door caused him to moan.

"We're closing soon," he yelled from behind the paper. He heard the footsteps approach on the wooden floor. Putting down the paper, he stared at the overweight man approaching. His stomach hung over belt-less baggy pants. His round face and pudgy nose were covered in grime. The thin hair around the large bald spot on his head hung over his ears. The holes in the toes of his well-worn sneakers revealed sock-less feet. Tattoos covered his left arm. The man stopped in front of the counter, which held the wide variety of knives under the glass enclosure.

The old man stood weakly and gazed into the stranger's eyes. Tears formed in both their eyes as the stranger spoke.

"Dad?"

About the Author

Robert Bull grew up in a small one-traffic-light town "nestled in the Blue Ridge Mountains" of eastern Pennsylvania. After attending college, and two graduate schools in the evening, in central Pennsylvania, his employer moved him to the north hills of Pittsburgh, in western Pennsylvania. That is where he currently resides along with his wife and a host of ducks, geese, groundhogs, raccoons, snakes, whitetail deer and turkeys that roam his backyard (his wife doesn't roam the yard, but she does work in her flower garden and take occasional strolls).

Robert's interest in writing began in a ninth grade English class when he chose to write a short story rather than to "contrast or compare two items of interest" for a class assignment. Since he couldn't grasp the difference between "contrasting" and "comparing", it seemed easier to write a fantasy story about how he and his best friend trounced the villains, rescued the pretty damsel in distress, and saved the day. Many, many years later, after his son was born and was old enough to talk and understand the English word, Robert would practice his storytelling on him to pass the time while riding in the car. In fact, Moose and Speedy, two characters from Robert's first book, made regular appearances in the fictitious yarns spun while traveling over the Pennsylvania highways.

Today, Robert enjoys the outdoors and experiencing all of God's wonderful creations. Whether in the expansive dense mountains of Potter County or in the sunny sparse woods behind a home in suburban Pittsburgh, one never knows what exciting and new surprises lurk behind the next tree, around the next bend, or over the next knoll.

May God bless you and your family and bring you sunshine and happiness all the days of your life.

Printed in the United States
41786LVS00001B/27

9 781420 878943